# Dead Old

**Maureen Carter**

CREME DE LA CRIME

08-1300

First published in 2005
by Crème de la Crime.
Crème de la Crime Ltd, PO Box 523, Chesterfield,
Derbyshire S40 9AT

Typesetting by Yvette Warren
Cover design by Yvette Warren
Front cover illustration by Peter Roman

Printed and bound in England by Biddles Ltd, www.biddles.co.uk

ISBN  0-9547634-6-7

A CIP catalogue reference for this book is available from the
British Library

www.cremedelacrime.com

## Author's note

The idea for *Dead Old* was planted more than twenty years ago when as a television news reporter I covered the vicious murder of an old woman in Birmingham. The elderly victim had been picking flowers when she was attacked and robbed of just a few pounds. The image of a bunch of daffodils discarded at the scene has been with me ever since. My revulsion at the nature and pointlessness of the killing was exacerbated when I learned later that day that I'd known – albeit briefly – the victim. Before her retirement, she'd been a doctor. And for a few minutes one afternoon I'd been her patient.

*Dead Old* is of course a work of fiction, as are all its characters. But the daffodil image – like, perhaps, half-a-dozen others from my long career in journalism – is as moving and potent for me now as it was on the morning I first saw it.

## Acknowledgements

Huge thanks to Douglas Hill, Lynne Patrick and Iain Pattison.

For endless support and encouragement, thanks also to: Suzanne Lee, Corby and Stephen Young, Frances Lally, Paula and Charles Morris, Christine Green, Sophie Shannon.

For Beryl and Fran
and Peter Shannon

Sophia Carrington was becoming invisible. People passed her without a glance. Days went by when she didn't speak to another soul. She knew it happened to old people. She'd heard it often enough from her patients. Women over a certain age with eyes as empty as their days had told her so. Back then she hadn't believed it. Strictly speaking, she hadn't believed it would happen to her.

And now it had.

Not that Sophia felt old. The problem was, no one knew how she felt.

She reached for her hat from the hallstand and moved nearer to the mirror. No wonder everyone ignored her, she barely recognised herself. An old person peered back; an old woman with white hair and beige skin that didn't quite fit. She pursed her lips, hating the result. "God, Sophie, you've got a mouth like a mince pie."

*And that's another thing, girl, stop talking to yourself.*

People said it was the first sign of madness but Sophia knew better. It was loneliness.

She sighed and pulled the hat firmly down over her ears. It was a rather fetching cornflower-blue beret, bought by an admirer in the days when it matched her eyes. He was long dead and now the hat was worn to hide thinning hair. She shook her head, sighed again and tightened the belt on her coat. Like Sophia, the coat had seen better days, but it was fine for a spot of gardening. The pockets held scissors and twine. She added a few pounds and took her keys from the hook on the wall.

Then she remembered the note to Maude. She'd scribbled down the train times to Birmingham for Maude's visit next week. Sophia smiled. Maude was her oldest and dearest friend but she fussed and fretted over the slightest thing. Having the journey times in black and white would help a little. The envelope too went in her pocket. She must remember to pop it in the post box.

The entrance to the allotments was at the brow of Princes Rise. It was a stiff climb but Sophia told herself it was good exercise. She shared the plot with a neighbour. It would have been too much for just one of them and the arrangement worked well. Sophia grew flowers; Ernie preferred to grow vegetables. Come to think of it, Ernie usually had more to say to his greens than he did to her. Not that he'd be there. As he'd mentioned several times, Ernie was staying with his daughter and her family in Kidderminster. It was an all-too-rare weekend visit and the old man had been as excited as Sophia had ever seen him. She smiled as she recalled him dusting down an ancient battered suitcase before packing it with almost certainly unsuitable presents for grandchildren he rarely saw.

Her smile was tinged now with a hint of sadness. She suspected that Ernie, like herself, felt a touch lonely from time to time. He'd popped in that morning to ask her to keep an eye on the place. It wasn't a problem. She wasn't going anywhere; she rarely did. She'd be spending the night in with Trollope: Anthony, not Joanna.

But first things first. Earlier in the day, she'd had an inkling that the daffodils would be ready. They'd always been her favourite flower. She loved the way their golden brashness banished the greys of winter. Cutting them was like picking sunlight. Sophia smiled at the thought and made an effort to put a spring in her step. She was determined to slough off the uncharacteristic depression and enjoy what remained of the day, the warmest of the year so far.

Across the park, over the treetops, the city skyscape was

discernible on the horizon: a sprawling greyness of jutting concrete towers, dwarfed in every way by the nature around it. The sky was beautiful. She wanted to paint it, preserve it. Impossible, of course. The backcloth of colours changed every time she lifted her glance. Now the brightest of blues was streaked with tapering fingers of gold; smudges of mauves and lilacs lay like bruises on the tenderest of flesh.

It made her glad to be alive. Again she chided herself for her previous dark mood. She must try not to let real – or imagined – snubs and slights get her down. Life was good, her health was fine and she had no money worries. Sometimes she wondered what difference a family would make, but what was the point? There was nothing she could do about that now. She'd opted for a career in the days when most women saw marriage and motherhood as a job for life. She'd loved her work as a doctor, enjoyed the respect her position commanded and relished her independence. If an old age lonelier than she'd have liked was the price, it was a cost she could live with.

She was almost level with the gates. She usually crossed on the corner near the general store but a woman she vaguely recognised was waving from the other side of the road. How nice, Sophia thought, maybe we could take a stroll together. She lifted a hand to return the greeting before realising the woman was hailing a bus. Mortified, Sophia glanced round, hoping no one had seen her make an idiot of herself. There was only one man nearby and he was engrossed in a newspaper. She knew her embarrassment was out of all proportion to the simple mistake. Why couldn't she just laugh it off like anyone else?

Momentarily flustered, she decided to pop into the

shop. Mr Vaz usually had a kindly word, always asked how she felt, even though she had the good sense not to tell him. Maybe his old-fashioned courtesy would restore a little of her fragile self-esteem.

Emerging a few minutes later, Sophia held a flimsy plastic carrier containing a bar of dark chocolate and a half-bottle of brandy. She paused, dithering, in the middle of the pavement. Maybe she should go home, forget the flowers? Two youths were approaching, clad in black, with rings through their lips. It was clear from their body language they had no intention of making way for her. Nervous of making eye contact, Sophia glanced down and moved out of their path. They strutted past with nothing more wounding than a muffled "Shove it, grandma."

Sophia breathed a sigh of relief. She knew the days were long gone when a person's advanced age might be accorded a level of respect, but many youths nowadays showed a staggering contempt. They either saw the elderly as a waste of space or failed to notice them at all. It wasn't just the boys, either. Last week a schoolgirl had actually spat at her in the street. Sophia's eyes welled with tears at the memory. For a second or two she was tempted just to give up and go home, but she tightened the belt on her old coat and simultaneously stiffened her resolve. She wouldn't let unpleasant encounters deflect her. She'd come out for daffodils and she wouldn't return without them.

It was a busy road and she waited patiently for a gap in the traffic. As she stepped out, a gleaming red car with music blaring from dark-tinted windows appeared from nowhere. The driver beeped his horn as Sophia scuttled back to the kerb. She couldn't read his lips, didn't need to. His face was screwed into an ugly look that said it all. Why were people so aggressive, so impatient with the elderly? Even those who weren't rude were chillingly indifferent. They just didn't care. No one listened any more. No one had time.

Whereas Sophia had all the time in the world.

# 1

As wide boys go, Marty Skelton warranted a police escort. The grubby little man spent more time at Highgate nick than some of the officers. Marty's crimes, though minor, were myriad; his record only just fitted on to a floppy. Dodgy gear and hot goods didn't fall from lorries, they flew into his outstretched arms.

Those scrawny limbs, covered with cheap tattoos of loose women, were currently drawing back the remnants of a pair of bedroom curtains – Marty 's take on interior design being as tenuous as his grasp on the market economy. Early-morning exercise almost complete, Marty rounded off with a little weightlifting by raising the window as high as the frayed sash would allow. Eyes closed, he inhaled deep breaths of fresh air before lighting the first of the day's skinny roll-ups.

Still framed in the window, Marty surveyed his thief-dom and spotted an additional subject. A woman was sprawled on top of a rotting mattress at the bottom of the garden. Marty would have executed a double-take but for the fact his features were frozen in shocked disbelief. He rubbed a clammy hand over post-binge bleary eyes and looked again. The troubling vision was still there.

The Dreamland wasn't giving him any grief. It had been dumped over the non-existent fence a couple of weeks before Christmas. The woman, on the other hand, was a problem. He hadn't a clue who she was or how she got there, but he was damn sure she wasn't auditioning for Sleeping Beauty.

Hauling fake Levis over counterfeit CKs, Marty grabbed a mobile and descended the stairs two at a time. Thoughts vied for pole position as he headed for the action: Who? Why? When? And what was with the flowers? Marty's backyard was a growth-free zone but he could've sworn he'd caught a flash of daffodils.

As the distance from the woman narrowed, Marty's eyes widened to take in the bigger picture. In painting terms, it was a still life. There was more movement in the flea-ridden mattress than in the body. Marty stopped and stared, hoped desperately it was an alcohol-induced hallucination or that the message from his eyes had somehow been scrambled on the way to his brain. Either option was preferable to this. He hadn't imagined the flowers but couldn't believe where they were. He put a hand over his mouth. The human body as vase was a challenging concept for any art lover, let alone a man who couldn't tell a Picasso from a Pollock.

As for the liberal splashes of crimson, even Marty could see they hadn't been applied with a brush.

The sight and smells tipped the little man's already shaky equilibrium. His fist proved ineffectual in stemming a rising nausea, and he made a mental note to chuck his trainers in the Hotpoint. First, revolting though the thought was, he'd have to take a closer look. Clearly the sooner he reported this the better, but he needed a few facts before making the call. Marty checked there was enough credit on his mobile. It was a pay-as-you-go. Not that he had.

Johnny Depp was on the line again. She'd told him a million times not to phone her at the nick.

"Bev! Shall I get him to call back, or what?"

Reluctantly an eye opened. It wasn't Johnny Depp; it wasn't even Johnny Vaughan. Detective Sergeant Beverley Morriss wasn't on the job. Fully awake now, if not entirely alert, she clocked the time: half-past-late. She shot up and immediately regretted it. "No," she yelled; regretted that as well. "Tell him to hang on a minute, mum. I'm on my way."

Bev clutched her head in both hands and tried focusing on a part of her anatomy that didn't throb. The acute pain as she stubbed a toe on the foot of the bed was almost a relief compared with the dull malady afflicting every other cell.

She grabbed a rainbow-striped dressing gown from a hook on the door and wrestled with the belt before deciding déshabillé would do. Why, oh why, had she had that last drink or four? She put a hand to her forehead. The girls' night out had been the latest in a series of sorrow-drowning sessions; with hindsight, it could have sunk a flotilla. It was a month since she'd heard, but even now phrases from the appointment board's letter still made her wince. *On this occasion… not successful…*

Not successful? As in loser? She'd wanted the Acting Detective Inspector post so badly she could taste it. The failure probably explained the sour taste in her mouth. That and a vestige of the vindaloo she vaguely recalled picking at several hours earlier.

The post had become available because DI Mike Powell, her erstwhile boss, was on suspension pending an internal inquiry. There was no love lost between them; there'd never been any to lose in the first place. Bev had fantasised about stepping into his fancy Italian footwear, then running professional rings around him. Verbally she already did. And he loathed it; didn't know how to handle it. In Powell's book, women were either decorative or domestic. Bev made no particular effort to be either. Way she saw it: if life's too short to stuff mushrooms, it's not long enough to mess around with lip-gloss.

Anyway, as far as she was concerned, Powell was a yes-man without a single original idea under his expensive blond highlights. Christ, if the man weren't so dense he'd be an airhead. Nah, the DI post had her name all over it. It was a shame the men-in-suits couldn't read. The girls had done their best to cheer her up last night. Her best mate, Frankie, had even raised a laugh of sorts when she suggested Bev get a sex change. Either way you looked at it, it was a slap in the face.

She avoided looking in the mirror as she took the phone from her mum, at the same time attempting what she hoped was a bright smile. Emmy Morriss's pained expression made plain the attempt had failed. Bev clearly looked as bad as she felt. She ran a hand through her hair, not that it did any good, and mouthed, "Who is it?" The way Emmy had been twittering on, she probably had the man's life history by now.

Her mum shrugged. "Didn't ask. He sounds awfully nice, though." She added, almost as an afterthought, "He's from work."

Bev would have rolled her eyes but feared an ensuing wave of pain. Emmy pursed her lips, turned on her fluffy pink slippers and headed for the kitchen. There was nothing in Emmy's world that a cup of tea couldn't fix. Her mum was one of Powell's domestics: Delia with a Dyson. Bev loved her to bits but if she had to live at home much longer it would drive her round the bend. She'd only been back three weeks after a deal on a house she'd been hoping to buy had fallen through.

At least Bev's gran wasn't down yet. Sadie, unlike her

mum, wouldn't hold back from asking about Bev's night out. She'd want the low-down. Sadie had the curiosity of a big cat and an interview technique that made Paxman look like Graham Norton. Bev usually had no problem indulging the old lady, but not this morning.

"Hello?" A frog with laryngitis appeared to be lodged in Bev's throat; then she remembered all the Silk Cuts and indifferent Soave she'd got through in the Prince of Wales.

"God. You sound rough. You should have phoned in." Vince Hanlon's voice veered from sympathy to censure in seconds.

"You what?"

"If you're that sick, you should have called in."

She cleared her throat a couple of times. Highgate's longest-serving sergeant would have heard every lame excuse in the library. She opted for the truth; well, part of it.

"Sorry, Vince. Bad night. I overslept."

She tried to read the silence. Vince was a good mate but he had no time for slackers.

"Not like you, Bev. Anything up?"

Life, the universe, everything. "Nothing serious."

"If you say so." He paused in case she wanted to elaborate. "Any road, we've had this call. Some punter reckons there's something going off down Cable Street."

Cable Street? That was Kings Heath. She pulled up a mental picture of redbrick terraces, boarded windows and a smattering of graffiti. "Go on."

"That's it. An incident. That's all he said."

"Nutter?"

"How should I know? He didn't give a name. Needs checking out, Bev."

The smell of bacon grilling wafted in from Emmy's empire. "Vincie, mate, can't you send a uniform?"

She heard the sound as he slapped his forehead. "Silly me. Now why didn't I think of that? Come on, lass, do us a favour." The uncharacteristic sarcasm continued. "It'll have escaped your awesome powers of detection so far this morning, but we've got a factory fire in West Brom, a fatal in the city centre and Spiderman and Batman doing stand-up on a bridge over the M6."

A fry-up was out of the question, then. "I'll be a little while, Vince. Sure there's no one else?"

"Lass, I've got a sick list here longer than the General's." She could picture him now: jowls a-quiver, grizzled head shaking, paunch straining at the buttons of his shirt. Big Vince was Yogi Bear on happy pills. "Anyway, Bev, far as the guv's concerned, you're already there. If you get my drift."

The guv. Detective Superintendent Bill Byford. It took a second or two, owing to the mother of all hangovers but yes, the message was clear. Byford had been asking for her and Vince had done the decent thing: covered her back. Good old Vincie. She couldn't afford to get on the wrong side of the guv. Byford was a member of a dying breed: a man-in-a-suit who had time for Bev. "Cheers, mate. I owe you."

"It's on the slate," Vince said. "And there's not a lot of room left."

She did a quick calculation, simultaneously registering the smile in the sergeant's voice: three-minute shower, forty-five seconds wardrobe, forego what little slap she occasionally bothered with. "Ready in five, Vince." Shame about the bacon bap.

"Don't fret about wheels," Vince said. "I've sent madam a carriage."

Detective Constable Ossama Khan was holding open the passenger door when madam emerged from the house, chin-length hair the colour of Guinness still damp from the shower. Seconds later, he spotted Bev's mum chasing after her clutching a Barbie lunchbox. He couldn't make out what was said during the handover but Bev's face was a similar shade of pink by the time she got to the motor. Oz had the nous not to comment.

The flush couldn't hide the fact that she was seriously hung over. Her eyes might still be the clearest blue this side of an Optrex ad, but the puffiness around them wasn't doing her any favours. And the charcoal smudges beneath were a giveaway; the delicate skin under her eyes always darkened when she was tired. And emotional. He knew that, like he knew about the tiny rose tattoo on the small of her back, how she cried at soppy films and hated the crumbs when they ate croissants in bed.

"Morning, Sarge. I take it I'm driving?" He caught a whiff of mint on her breath as she brushed past and plonked herself into the passenger seat. "I'll take that as a yes," he muttered.

Apart from flared nostrils, he kept his face straight. Oz was well aware she'd been out getting hammered with the girls. Lucky girls. He'd barely seen her apart from work for three weeks; living with her mum was a hell of an effective contraceptive.

They drove in silence for a while. Not surprising. Bev was slumped in the seat, hand pressed against her forehead, eyes closed. Oz gave a wry smile. He understood now why she always wore blue for work. She reckoned it saved time in the mornings if everything you grabbed matched… after a fashion.

Today's get-up was a bit pick-and-mix. He didn't think much of the long navy jacket. He knew she thought it was slimming. Personally, he couldn't see a problem. At five six and nine stone, she was hardly porky. At least she'd teamed the jacket with a skirt, which he watched ride up her thighs as she twisted and turned to reach for the lunchbox she'd slung on to the back seat.

"Breakfast," she muttered through a mouthful.

Oz raised an eyebrow. The explanation was superfluous, given the smell of bacon and brown sauce. He lowered the window a couple of inches but only succeeded in adding rush-hour exhaust fumes to the odours already circulating round the car's interior. He sighed, took a left and turned into Butler Street. It was a rat-run off Kings Heath High Street, although it was more like a gentle meander since the recent installation of traffic-calmers. Oz was keeping an eye peeled for the next turning and inadvertently shot over a sleeping policeman.

"Nice one, Oz. As if I'm not in danger of throwing up anyway."

Given the inroads she was making on the sarnie, the argument didn't hold a lot of weight, but at least the calorie intake had perked her up a touch.

"Feeling a bit brighter, are we, Sarge?"

"Is that another rhetorical question, officer?" Out of the corner of her eye, she caught a half-smile, or was it a smirk? "Is there something amusing, Osama? Do share. Do lighten the load of this dull and dreary Monday morning with one of your merry little jests."

He tapped an elegant index finger on the steering wheel. "You always do that when you feel guilty about something."

She turned her body to face him; the skirt rose at least another inch. "Do what?"

"Talk posh. It's classic Morriss distraction."

So was the expanse of thigh. She left the hem where it was. "I didn't realise you'd read psychology, Sigmund." She knew damn well he hadn't. He'd taken law, and though he didn't brag about it, he'd come away with a First. Bev sometimes thought his track was so fast he'd make DI before her. Not that he had it easy at Highgate. Some of the station's hard men gave him a hard time. The racism was less in-your-face than it used to be but it was still there. Oz ticked all the boxes: Asian, academic and in line for accelerated promotion.

He was also the tastiest bloke in the nick. Think Darcy without the pride and prickliness. "Go on," she prompted.

"What?"

"Why am I feeling guilty?"

"Search me."

She shook her head; not a wise move.

"Headache, Sarge?"

That was definitely a smirk. She ignored it. They were in an almost stationary line of traffic trying to get on to the High Street. Three or four youths had congregated near the junction, jostling passers-by, yelling obscenities. They were in uniform but not for school: hoodies, black denims and trainers the size of two-berth boats.

"Look at that," Bev snarled. "Little sods. What use is an ASBO round here? Give kids like that an anti-social order, they think it's an award, juvie equivalent of a knighthood."

Oz saw her glance at the clock. "Don't go there, Sarge. We haven't got time."

She cast a Morriss-glare at one of the youths as they drove past. It garnered a raised finger and a pierced tongue. Her mental note of dark hair, eyeliner and pasty skin was so vague it was barely worth making. And Cable

14

Street was top of the list at the moment.

Oz couldn't add much to what Vince had said: a punter had called with a tip-off. Said the place was crawling with cameras.

"They're probably shooting *Dalziel and Pascoe*," Bev said. "They do a lot of location stuff round Moseley."

"Hey," Oz grinned. "We could be extras."

Bev ran a hand through her hair Hollywood-style. "Sorry, darlink. I only strip for my art."

"Your what?" He lifted a hand to ward off attack. "That's more like it. You looked like death warmed up back there."

"Yeah, yeah."

"I worry about you," Oz persisted.

"So does my mum. Give it a rest." She flashed a smile to take the sting from the words. Her relationship with Oz had its downside. She'd probably already opened up too much. Everyone knew her strengths; only Oz was aware of her weaknesses. Some of them.

Like the knock her confidence took during the Lucas inquiry. Two girls, one a teenage prostitute, had been killed. Bev had doggedly pursued the wrong man. Oz knew how badly it had affected her but only Bev knew how close she'd come to a disciplinary. Bev and the guv.

"Cable Street," she said. "Doesn't Bony M live there?"

"Who?"

"Marty Skelton? Bony M?" The blank look revealed a gap in Oz's musical education. "He's a one-man scam factory. Surely you've come across him? Bow-legged? Sandy hair? Straggly moustache? Christ, Oz, he's got his own mug at Highgate. The custody sergeants are thinking of charging him B and B."

"Small bloke? Tattoos? Got a veg stall down the market?"

"Flowers, isn't it?" She gave a one-shoulder shrug.

"Whatever."

A fine drizzle, barely enough to occupy the wipers, was falling desultorily as they turned into Cable Street. It was trellis territory with a smattering of pebbledash. A few houses had obviously been done up; others looked as if they'd been done over.

"There's loads of places for sale down here," Oz said.

Bev knew more about the current Birmingham property market than a chain of estate agents. She was after a place of her own. It didn't have to be a dream house, just one that didn't give her nightmares. "Prone to subsidence. Roads in a bad way. And no garaging."

Oz was only half-listening; he was scanning a near-empty street. "No cameras, either. Reckon it was a duff call?"

A flash car was almost blocking the pavement a few houses down on the right. Bev nodded in its direction. "Let's take a look." A BBC logo came into sight as they drew alongside. Either the Beeb had an exclusive or everyone else had left. On the other hand, the anonymous caller may have been tight with the truth.

"It's hardly crawling, is it?" Oz sounded peeved. "Where is everyone?"

"One way to find out."

Knocking on number 12's door wasn't it. "Best try the back," Bev said. "Hold on." She laid a hand on his arm. "Did you hear that honk?"

"Honk?"

"Yeah, look." She pointed up. "Wild geese."

He managed half a smile. "Come on. Let's get it over with."

The rear of the property was accessed down a narrow side alley strewn with damp newspapers and dog shit. Mouldy vegetable peel and a rotting chicken carcass spilled from a black bin liner; even the air was rancid.

Mean little gardens backed on to a narrow strip of communal land, with lethal-looking iron railings beyond it, bordering council allotments.

Distinguishing which residence was attracting the attention wasn't difficult. Satellite dishes sprouted from just about every wall but only one back yard had a film crew. And it wasn't shooting *Gardener's World*; the meagre bit of scrubland belonging to number 12 didn't even boast weeds. Unless you counted the two-legged variety.

"I might have known." Bev held back, hand on hip. "What's he up to now?"

Marty Skelton was having his fifteen minutes all right. Bev couldn't begin to imagine what the interview was about. As far as she knew, Marty only had one area of expertise and it was the sort you didn't broadcast.

She talked as she walked. "Well, well, well. If it isn't Marty Skelton. As I live and breathe."

"Button it, sister. We're recording." The TV reporter didn't even turn round, just shot out a hand to underline his message. Bev almost cuffed it.

"You're not my brother. And you can be halfway through open-heart surgery. I don't give a monkey's. You're this close to getting arrested. Buddy."

Three heads turned. There was a finger and thumb and no discernible gap in between.

Bev glared at Marty. Was the sneaky little toe-rag going red under all those freckles? "What's going on, Marty?"

"Inspector Morriss –"

Talk about toadying. Marty Skelton knew her rank as well as she did; she'd booked him enough times. She silenced him with a Morriss-glare. "Don't call me –"

The reporter laid a smooth hand on her forearm; the nails were too long and not overly clean. She shook it off angrily but the newsman was more tenacious.

"You're the *police*?" His voice held pleasure beyond his wildest imagining. Anyone'd think she was offering a blowjob. "Would you mind awfully, Inspector, if I just finish with Mr Skelton? Then perhaps we can just change shot… I'm dead keen on the daffodil angle –"

She'd have probably bopped him at that point but a heartfelt "Fucking hell!" from Oz demanded everyone's attention. Oz had ventured further into the wasteland. Bev followed, compelled by the expression on his face as much as in his voice.

The sight was so unexpected, so surreal, she almost giggled. For a split second she was sure it was an early April Fool. But this was no joke, however sick. She tried to blank out everything else, concentrate only on what lay before her.

An old woman sprawled on a damp, foul-smelling mattress in a cruel parody of peaceful sleep. Bev put out a steadying hand. It was so still, so quiet she could hear the pulse whoosh in her ears. She concentrated again on the macabre tableau. The woman's baggy pink knickers were round her twig-like ankles; one of her eyes was partially obscured by a blue beret that had probably been rammed on after the attack. The victim was filthy and scruffy and stank of human waste and booze.

But this was no death by natural causes. What sort of sick bastard rammed flowers down a dead woman's throat? It was an indignity too far.

Bev clenched her fists, briefly closed her eyes. The daffodils were some sort of sick message; the killer hadn't used them to choke his victim. The old lady hadn't died from asphyxiation. There was too much blood for that, far too much. And anyway, the murder weapons were still in place.

# 2

Bev rose to her feet, brushing mud and bits of unidentified vegetation from her skirt. "You're in shit so deep, Marty, you could be a turd."

Marty shoved his hands in the pockets of his jeans, shuffled his feet, gazed at the ground. The reporter broke what was becoming an uneasy silence. "What's the problem, officer?"

Bev switched her glare to the tall twenty-something newsman. Either he'd had a perm or his hair had curled in the drizzle. It gave him a curiously old-fashioned look, as did the double-breasted suit. It was well-cut and probably expensive but far too big for him, like the air of authority that he assumed went with a loud voice and posh accent. Not that Bev was biased, of course. She just thought he was a dickhead.

"Where shall we start, *sonny*?" She made the points by ticking her fingers. "Tramping over a murder scene? Contaminating evidence? Obstructing an inquiry? Or perverting the course of justice?"

"That's ridiculous. We haven't touched a thing. Mr Skelton says –"

Bev flapped a hand, her glance now on Marty. "What does Mr Skelton say? Exactly?"

Marty was saying precisely nothing. This was rare coming from a man who could flog the fuzz off a bruised peach. While Marty stalled, Bev tried to work out a likely sequence of events. Her hangover was receding slightly but it was still like swimming in cobwebs. An old woman, a bag lady by the look of it, had been brutally murdered. That was non-negotiable. Plus the fact she'd ended up in Marty's back yard.

"It's down to you, Marty. You talk here or Highgate. I don't care where."

"Can I just grab a quick interview?" The newsman flashed a practised smile as he straightened his tie. "A few words from the police point of view? I'm sure you've done this sort of thing before."

Bev swirled round, eyes flashing. This was taking the piss. "You just don't get it, do you? A line's been crossed here, sonny –"

He took a step nearer to Bev. "I'm not your sonny. And I don't like being patronised."

Bev installed herself in the middle of his personal space. She dropped her voice but the menace was unmistakeable: a trick she'd picked up from the guv. "A woman's dead here, sonny."

She could see flecks of loose skin in his eyebrows and a crumb of something caught between his front teeth. For a split second, she sensed an inner fury and thought he was going to go for her. But then, as quickly, the public face was back in place.

"You're right. I'm sorry, officer." He held out a hand. "I'm Richard Peck. BBC."

Bev folded her arms, tapped a foot. "And you're here doing what?"

Peck shrugged. "I'm trying to do my job. Surely you see this is a matter of public interest? If the killing's linked to the other attacks people have a right to know –"

Oh, please. Not the right-to-know line. She glared at the man, enunciated each word slowly, precisely. "They have a right to the facts."

"Talking of which. What about the flowers? Have daffodils featured in the other attacks?"

That thought hadn't just crossed Bev's mind, it was taking up residence. As she and every other cop in the city were aware, over the last month, three old women had been attacked and robbed. Though badly beaten, none had died. In each case, cash and jewellery had been taken. Bev knew a bunch of daffodils had been found at the home of one of the victims. There'd been no reason before now to give it significance. The media had already speculated endlessly about the incidents being linked but it was a possibility the guv didn't go along with.

Peck went for another winning smile. "Look, if you won't do an interview will you at least give me a statement? I can stick it in a piece-to-camera."

"Is it just me or what?" She pinched the bridge of her nose. "How often do you need telling? You shouldn't be here and you certainly can't use any of this stuff."

Peck glanced at his watch. "The first piece went out on the eight o'clock. So I'd say you were wrong there. And the woman from Central was pushing the daffodil line a lot harder than me."

Could it get any worse? Scenes-of-crime were going to have a collective coronary when they eventually arrived. Central TV had been and gone. God knew how many other media people had been milling around. How the hell had the press got here first?

She felt a hand on her elbow. It was Oz, who'd been on the phone to Highgate, rounding up the troops. He'd even located a couple of paracetemol. She slipped them distractedly into her pocket, her thoughts still on the media.

"They're on the way, Sarge. The full works."

Of course. Oz had been tipping off the good guys. She'd bet a pound to a penny Marty had been on the blower to the baddies. She narrowed her eyes. "Who did you call first, Marty?"

"You what?" He pulled at a fleshy ear lobe, glance still on the ground.

"Eye. Main chance. Cash for questions." She moved towards him, jabbed a finger at his scrawny chest. "Did you toss a coin? Heads the Bill, tails the Beeb?"

"I didn't call no one."

Bev turned on the reporter. "How much are you paying him?"

Peck shrugged, studied his nails.

"I asked you a question."

"A facility fee isn't payment. As such."

"Facility fee?" The snarl was almost audible. "Is that what decent people call a bung?" She sighed, shook her head. "I don't believe it. A woman's dead and all you're bothered about is a few quid and a bit of airtime. So did you tip off every news desk in the Midlands before calling Highgate?"

Marty sniffed; ran a nicotine-stained finger along his moustache. "I may have phoned a couple of contacts in the media."

"And the cops?" Bev pushed.

"Do me a favour."

There was a first for everything – even Marty telling it for real. Bev made a mental note. No. Better not risk it. She delved into her shoulder bag, brought out a notebook and pen. They might not find out, it might not be important, but if Marty hadn't made that call – who had?

Flecks of vomit clung to his sodden sweatshirt like porridge on canvas. Davy Roberts retched again and again but his belly was empty, the murky contents in a phone box on Keats Road. He'd give anything to get rid of the image in his head as easily. He leaned on the sink, stared in the mirror, surprised he couldn't see the revulsion on his face. He looked just the same. Blond hair, blue eyes. His mates called him baby-face. He hated it. He dipped his head in the sink; cold water splashed over the edges, showering the bathroom tiles and his filthy Nikes. Though his body felt on fire, sweat ran cold down the clammy skin on his spine.

"Davy! Is that you?"

His gran's voice, faint but high-pitched, drifted up from the bottom of the stairs. He pictured her standing with one podgy hand clutching the banister, the other clamped round a walking frame. If he didn't answer she'd drag herself up to find out what was going on. Automatically he clicked the lock on the door. Company was the last thing he needed.

He took a deep breath, forced his voice to sound normal. "Down in a min, gran."

"Where've you been? I been worried sick."

"Just nipped to the shop, gran. Shan't be a tick. I'll get you a bite of breakfast."

He hated lying to her, but sometimes there were things she really didn't need to know.

"A fry-up, Davy? A lion's breakfast?" Her voice sounded even more girlie than usual.

He groaned at the thought of bacon and eggs swilling in lard, but how could he disappoint her? He'd have been in a kids' home if she hadn't taken him in. Five years old he was when his ma snuffed it. As for his dad, he could be anywhere – or anyone, come to that. "You bet, gran."

Thank God he hadn't thrown up in here; she'd have been

fussing round, asking questions, demanding answers. He loved two people in this world and one was the fat cantankerous old woman downstairs, but she'd go apeshit if she knew the half of it. He glanced down ruefully at the sick, then carefully slipped the sweatshirt over his head. The stench hit his nostrils and he wrinkled his nose in disgust. He thrust the garment into a plastic carrier. He didn't want the damn thing anyway. He'd dump it later.

An hour or so on and Cable Street resembled *The Bill* with a live audience. Eager fans, mostly young mums and pensioners, were grouped opposite number 12; more spectators lined the railings at the back. In the absence of the governor, Bev had directed operations; the show was almost on the road.

Marty's place was cordoned off, uniforms were posted at strategic points, house-to-house teams were on the knock; SOCOs, search teams and a police photographer were chomping at the bit waiting for the path man to do his.

"I'm starving, Oz." Bev was ferreting in the bottom of her capacious shoulder bag.

"Again?"

She pursed her lips. "I was going to offer you my last Polo. But sod you." She popped the mint in her mouth.

Oz rolled his eyes. "There's a shop on the corner. What do you want?"

As Oz took off in search of sustenance, Bev ran through a mental checklist. Thank God the headache had gone. So had Marty Skelton. He was at Highgate now and any interviews there wouldn't be making the news. The Beeb crew had departed too, after giving statements and leaving contact numbers. Christ knew what the guv would have to say about the cock-up.

"Morning, morning. Not late, am I?"

Bev looked up with a smile, genuinely pleased as well as relieved to see the pathologist, Harry Gough. She always reckoned Harry had the look of Richard Burton about him. The old boy was a real smoothie in an Armani; a ladies' man through and through. It was difficult to believe he was retiring at the end of the year. Bev'd miss him like hell.

"Mr Gough. How you doing?"

He gave her a quick once-over. "By the look of it, a damn sight better than you, Beverley. Been burning the candle at both ends again, have we?" The resemblance to Burton was shattered the second Harry opened his mouth. His voice was pure Hackney gravel.

"New look, Mr Gough. Keeps the crime figures down."

"Oh?"

"Yeah. Scares the villains to death."

The mischievous grin on her face faded as she caught a glimpse of someone out of the corner of her eye. A woman was hovering just beyond the crime scene tape. Harry must have brought one of his lady friends along. It wouldn't be the first time.

The old goat reckoned his line of business turned them on. Bev sneaked a glance. Yes, definitely Harry's type. How did the song go? Tall and tanned and lean and lovely.

"Glad to see you've still got a sense of humour, Beverley."

She studied his face. It wasn't giving anything away but the voice had an edge.

"Oh?"

"You'll not have seen the telly this morning?" he asked.

"Enough to do here, Mr Gough."

"Locking stables?"

She had an idea where he was going now. "Stables?"

"As in bolting horses. Surprised you need me at all."

He was making no effort to keep his voice down. Bev glanced round. She didn't care if Harry brought along a harem but it was bad form to entertain it at her expense.

"Must admit," he continued, "I've never had a spotty youth on the news give me a cause of death before I've even laid eyes on the body."

Unable to find anything to say, Bev led Harry to the corpse and moved the screen to one side, struck again by how tiny the victim was. They'd found no ID, hadn't a clue where she came from. "Looks like she might've been living rough, Mr Gough. You can see the state she's in and she stinks of booze. She could have been dossing in the allotments."

He shrugged; that wasn't his territory. Bev took notes from Harry's running commentary. The most striking discovery was time of death. It was rarely possible to be accurate but Harry estimated she'd been killed the evening before, maybe as long ago as fifteen hours. Bev glanced at her watch. It was just coming up to ten a m now, so they were looking at Sunday evening, some time after seven.

It was also obvious the murder couldn't have been committed here. There wasn't enough blood, for one thing, and there was no way the body could have lain undiscovered for that long. She'd been killed elsewhere, and the body concealed. That meant there had to be another crime scene, maybe two.

Harry rose to his feet, voice tight with emotion. "There was no need for all this, you know, Bev. A single stab to the heart would almost certainly have killed her. There's a dozen here, possibly more. I can't be definite till she's been cleaned up. The bruising and abrasions to her face mean she was still alive when he gave her a beating. Savage bastard. Probably got a kick out of it. As for the flowers – sick beyond belief." He snapped off the surgical gloves and shoved them in a plastic bag. "I've done here. I'll pencil in the pm for late afternoon. Bill not about?"

It was pretty obvious that Detective Superintendent Byford was still to put in an appearance. Harry's query was a tad casual. Bev shook her head, well aware of the point the pathologist wasn't making. He put a hand under her elbow, steered her away from the body and lowered his voice. "When's the blond bombshell back?"

She rolled her eyes. Goughie knew as well as anyone about DI Powell's suspension. There was even a sweep-stake doing the rounds and the smart money was on the scenario that he'd be back but busted down a rank. Harry was on a fishing trip in search of the best odds.

"No idea," Bev said. "They've got some bloke coming over from Coventry. Danny Shields? Sergeant at Little Park Street?" Harry worked all over the region for the police; he might well have come across the guy.

He turned his mouth down, shook his head. "I'd have thought you were more than capable of standing in for Mike Powell."

Harry Gough didn't do meaningless platitudes. The unexpected praise caught her unawares. Even so, she was surprised to feel tears pricking her eyes. She turned away sharply. "Wrong sex, Mr Gough. You need balls." *Not go round breaking them.*

Harry laughed out loud. "Beverley!" He tapped her on the shoulder. "You've got more balls than Wimbledon, Sergeant. Don't play the little woman with me."

He was right. Maybe she just wasn't up to it on the day. Or maybe she'd put too many noses out of joint. Sod it.

She didn't know anymore. She turned and gave him her best smile. "Sorry, Mr Gough. Bad day."

"As well as night?" He tipped an imaginary hat. "Catch you later." He started to walk away then stopped, turned back. "And Beverley?" he winked, "If the worst comes to the worst, you can always borrow my scalpel."

She shook her head as she watched him disappear, then made her way to the front of the property where the lads were still waiting for a green light. Passing on the gist of Harry's findings didn't take long. The next stage was mostly down to scenes-of-crime. A single fibre could secure a conviction; forensics would be bagging and tagging for hours. It was painstaking and painfully slow. And given how the scene had been contaminated by every Tom, Dick and Jeremy, the job would be infinitely harder.

There were a few thoughts she needed to work on. She was making her way back to the car when the mobile rang.

"Sergeant. Highgate. Now." The governor obviously thought he needed no introduction. The line went dead.

"Guv. How kind of you to call," she simpered. "Thank you so much, Sergeant," she attempted Byford's basso profundo before reverting to the simper. "No, please, sir, don't even mention it." She gave the phone the finger and curled a lip. "Miserable old sod."

She clapped a hand over her mouth as she heard a click on the line. Shit. The guv had hung up. Hadn't he?

# 3

Behind a desk at Highgate, Detective Superintendent Bill Byford held the phone at arm's length, his lips tight, eyes narrowed. Miserable old sod, huh? Nice one, Bev. He placed the receiver back on its rest and gave a deep, almost resigned, sigh. He supposed he could have bawled her out, but maybe she had a point. She was only doing her job, but a pat on the back wouldn't have done any harm. Assuming there was any space among the knives. OK, that was an exaggeration, but Bev – witness that little performance – could be her own worst enemy.

He shook his head, aware of a tightening across his eyes that could signal the start of a headache. The tension had nothing to with Bev's latest charm offensive. Byford had more pressing concerns on his plate. Less than an hour before, he'd been sitting ill at ease in his GP's surgery. For weeks now – actually, he conceded, more like months – he'd been suffering stomach pains, nausea and, more recently, weight loss. At a well-covered six-two, he knew it wasn't obvious, but it would be if it continued. Byford had looked up the symptoms, finding they could be caused by a number of conditions. His big fear was that it was the big C. Not many people called it that nowadays, but when Byford was growing up everyone did. This morning he'd been pinning his hopes on an all-clear, but the grey area dished out by a doctor half his age felt like a no-man's-land. A solitary signpost indicated *more tests*, when Byford desperately wanted a result.

The fear and frustration partly explained his peremptory summons to Bev Morriss. That and the tetchy call he'd taken from Danny Shields even before he'd taken off his hat and coat. Recalling it now, he had to admit the new DI's criticism had been skilfully veiled. Byford was surprised it had been made at all. He sighed, ran both hands through thick black hair greying only at the temples and wondered idly if it was too late to start doing the lottery.

He glanced up as his admin assistant, Helen, breezed in without knocking. Again. He toyed with the idea of asking if she'd hurt her hand, but it seemed churlish, given she was bearing coffee and a Danish.

"Cheer up," she said. "It might never happen."

Byford considered the remark rich coming from a woman who habitually dressed like a funeral director. What was it with women in black? He searched her face for subtle signs of concern on his behalf. He'd had to tell her he was popping out but not where. No one knew about the medical appointment, not even his sons, Rich and Chris. They had families of their own to worry about. Hopefully there'd be nothing to burden them with anyway. Byford saw sickness as a sign of weakness; he'd admit to it only if forced.

"What've we got?" He took a bite of pastry as Helen ran through calls he'd missed during the time away from his desk. There was nothing earth-shattering, at least no more than usual. He pointed to the wodge of paperwork jammed under her elbow. "I'll sort that –"

"I know," she smiled. "Later."

He waited till she'd left the office, then adopted his usual pose: chair tipped back, feet on the desk. There was a stack of printouts from Kings Heath to wade through. What was left of the Danish was halfway to his mouth again before he remembered the doctor's words on diet and exercise.

Pulling a face, he lobbed the pastry into the bin and hastily covered it with an old *Private Eye*.

The reports made uneasy reading. Byford regarded Marty Skelton as a time-wasting distraction. The man was a scrote. If the price were right he'd sell his grandmother. But would he murder someone else's? Byford doubted it. Either way Marty had to be eliminated from the inquiry – or not – quickly. And that left a scenario that had been preying on the detective's mind since the minute he'd heard about the murder.

He took his feet down and stretched across the desk for a bulging file. Operation Streetwise had been ongoing for nearly a month. A gang of youths was targeting elderly women. They were getting away with paltry amounts of cash and bits of jewellery but the attacks were becoming increasingly violent.

Byford took out the police stills of the victims and studied each at length. If it turned out there was a link between these incidents and the killing of the old woman, he'd made a bad call. Worse, much worse, was the possibility that the death might have been avoided. If he'd issued more warnings, increased public awareness – would it have made a difference? It was impossible to say but he was still finding it difficult to forgive himself.

He glanced at his watch; the briefing was in an hour. It would be the first opportunity for the whole team to see the new DI in action. Had that played a part in his decision to assign Marty Skelton's initial interview to Bev? Possibly. She'd not been best pleased; she'd probably seen enough of Marty for one lifetime. But hopefully she'd get enough out of the little creep to give the briefing a steer. A few public brownie points in his sergeant's direction wouldn't go amiss.

He sat back, briefly closed his eyes. He was concerned about Bev. The qualities he admired in her were those that some of his senior colleagues couldn't abide. An original who spoke her mind wasn't a million miles from being a loner with a big mouth. Policing was teamwork, taking orders; it was tough if you had no time for the manager. He hoped for everyone's sake she'd get along better with Danny Shields than she had with Mike Powell.

One thing was certain: he couldn't allow concerns about his health to impinge on the inquiry. If that meant delegating more than he liked, so be it. He carried his coffee over to the window, pressed his forehead against the cool glass. The answers were out there somewhere.

So was the killer.

Jake loved the view from Starbucks in Borders. He could look at it all day. The Selfridges building was like some alien starship or a giant bouncy castle. Lots of people hated it but Jake thought it was ace. Though why the hell the planners had left the old church slap bang in the middle of all the cool stuff, he'd never know. It hadn't got a prayer. Retail therapy was the current religion round the Bullring. Jake sipped espresso, taking in the sights. The massive windows looked across bits of the city you'd otherwise miss. Jake liked that idea: a different perspective, a new way of seeing things.

The reflection was useful, too. He lifted a hand to touch up his hair. It'd taken a while to get used to the spikes but he loved them now, loved the way everyone avoided him, never made eye contact, just darted shifty glances when they thought he wasn't looking. It was like carrying round a placard that said Hard Bastard. People were so dim, really, when your average psychopath looked like

Mr Normal. He shrugged. Made no difference either way. Jake never dropped his guard.

He winked at the blonde showing her thong a few stools down but she blanked him: silly bitch. He sniffed and curled his lip, then turned his stool to survey the surroundings. Yep, he liked the Bullie. It was definitely good for business: full of rich pickings. He looked down at the wallet in his hand: classy Italian leather, still warm from the fat bloke's bum. There'd been such a crush on the escalator when Jake brushed up against him, the lard-arse had actually said sorry. Jake shook his head. What was that all about? People apologising when it wasn't down to them. Not Jake. He'd had his hand down the bloke's back pocket at the time and he sure as hell wasn't sorry. Opening the wallet, he counted the notes: nearly £200. Not bad. The others were still on the pick; they'd pool the lot later. Jake would get the biggest cut. Only fair. They'd be nothing without him.

Look at Kev and Robbie. If Jake hadn't fixed them up they'd still be getting buggered about in the kids' home. Now they had a place of their own. OK, it was a tatty flat in an empty tower block, but sod it: if the council couldn't be arsed to knock the friggin' thing down, whose lookout was that? Kev and Robbie were happy enough. Jake wanted young Davy in there as well. Davy was his star pupil: made the Artful Dodger look like a sore thumb. And with a face like that he could get away with murder. Anyway, Jake liked to keep an eye on his boys. He'd given them a good trade, had Jake. They made a decent enough living.

He laughed out loud, ignoring the uneasy glances in his direction. Oh, Jay, my son. That was good. That was very good.

An hour in a windowless room with Marty Skelton was bad. Chuck in a pair of cheesy, vomit-sodden trainers and the man's intermittent flatulence, and terminal traffic duty had its attractions. Whichever way you looked at it, Bev reckoned Interview Room One was going to need more than a dose of Jeyes and a squirt of polish before it was back to normal. As for Oz, he'd pushed his chair as far from the olfactory action as it would go.

"Run it past me one more time," Bev sighed, and raked a hand through hair she was itching to wash. Marty was rolling yet another fag: liquorice paper and a parsimonious pinch of shag. The tin ashtray in the middle of the metal table already held six damp butts that looked like the droppings of a constipated rodent. A corresponding number of empty coffee cups was scattered across the tabletop. What with the nicotine and the caffeine, Marty couldn't keep his skinny frame still. His feet were bouncing on the sludge-coloured lino and a tic fluttered in his right eyelid. He was either on something or up to something. As for his movements during the relevant hours of the inquiry, he hadn't budged an inch.

"You can have it as often as you like, darlin'." Either the tic was getting worse or he'd just winked. Bev pursed her lips and tapped her fingers on the table; Marty eventually got the picture. "I've told you what happened," he added. "It ain't gonna change."

The fact that Marty had eschewed a brief suggested there were enough witnesses to back him up. Normally, he wouldn't open his mouth without a tame lawyer checking every syllable. According to Marty, while the old woman was getting killed he'd been at the Red Lion getting rat-arsed. He'd stopped off for curry and chips on the way home, and taken both food and a bottle of Johnnie Walker to bed. Partway through the fourth telling, Bev's gaze drifted to the big-breasted women tattooed on Marty's arms. Her eyes widened as naked female flesh appeared to undulate in time to the flexing of what remained of Marty's muscles. She raised an eyebrow; the artwork made quite a change from eagles or anchors, and it was a damn sight more riveting than his alibi.

"What about when you were in bed?" Oz asked. "Did you hear anything suspicious?"

Bev almost jumped at the sound of Oz's voice, switching her attention back to the proceedings. But Marty in bed surrounded by greasy foil containers was not a thought she wanted to hold. "Did you get up in the night?" She knew as soon as the words were out they'd been a mistake.

"Sure did." He gave a lewd hand gesture just in case the double entendre had passed them by.

"Don't fuck with me, Marty." Again, it wasn't the aptest turn of phrase.

"Don't flatter yourself, darlin'." He sucked smoke through ill-fitting dentures and gently lifted a buttock. "I'll tell you one more time. I went to bed, I went to sleep and I was out of it. Nothing short of nook-lear would have woke me."

Bev curled a lip. Oz was surreptitiously sniffing his new Hugo Boss jacket. Eau de low-life. Great. She scraped her chair back. They wouldn't get any more. Not yet. Marty could sweat. Actually Marty didn't need permission. He was sweating like a pig on a spit.

Davy was dreading it. Jake would go ballistic. Davy was watching him now, drinking coffee over by the window. Starbucks was where they always met after working the Bullring. Davy hadn't got the bottle to join him yet. He didn't know how he was going to tell Jake he wanted out. Thing was, Jake had been dead good to him, a bit like Davy imagined a dad would be. Except that was stupid. Davy might not look it but he was seventeen and he reckoned Jake was only a few years older. He couldn't really explain but right from the word go, Jake had made him feel good: made him feel he was *somebody*.

Before Jake, Davy's mates had all been losers. Christ, they were either banged up in Feltham or dodging bullets in Basra. Then a few months back Jake had come up to Davy in Kings Heath High Street. He was tall and weird-looking, what with the spikes and the leathers, but he was smart. Jake was the smartest guy Davy had ever known. So Davy couldn't believe it when Jake said he could join the gang. Had to prove himself, of course, pick a pocket or three, that sort of thing. But Jake had shown him the ropes and Davy had been on the payroll ever since. Davy had never been so minted. But it wasn't just the cash. It was being with Jake. Jake was cool. And he used his head. They never took unnecessary risks. Took everything else, though.

Davy's smile faded. They'd been targeting coffin-dodgers recently. Like everything else, it was Jake's call. It was good practice, he reckoned, and easy money. But Davy hadn't liked it; specially not the knocking them about. Now Davy wanted out. Jake wouldn't like it. And there were times you didn't question Jake.

"What the–?" Bev was lost for a fitting expletive. It'd be a pisser to be late for the guv's briefing but it wasn't every day you saw Spiderman emerging from the gents at Highgate. A young PC with a cheeky grin waited outside, leaning casually against the wall. "It's OK, Sarge. He's with me."

She rolled her eyes. "Yeah, don't tell me: the Incredible Hulk's in the canteen."

"Batman, actually. And he's in Interview Two."

Of course: the early shout at Spaghetti Junction. Fathers 4 Justice making another big show. Ironic, really; a lot of women Bev came across couldn't trace their kids' dads for love nor money. F4J on the other hand had a higher profile than Father Christmas.

Spiderman almost lost a limb when he lunged at Bev, but he was only pointing out a few crumbs on her jacket. She'd just wolfed down a pasty at her desk, an attack of the munchies being the only legacy of the morning's hangover. Her rushed break had turned into a working lunch, owing to the fact the phone never stopped ringing. Though come to think of it, apart from the feedback from the Red Lion, the calls had been more domestic than detective duties. Her offer on a house in Highbury Road had been slung out. And her mum wondered if she could pop into Sainsbury's on the way home. *Home?* Why the hell she'd moved out of her last place before securing the next she'd never know. She brushed at the crumbs, reckoning if the pasty had been within a hundred miles of Cornwall, she was Kylie Minogue.

Bev watched as Spiderman and his police escort entered the lift, then glanced round with a frown. The clack of high heels echoing along the corridor was another thing you didn't often come across at Highgate. A woman came into sight, looking lost. Bev had seen her before but had to think for a second before placing her. Of course. Harry Gough's ladyfriend from this morning. The pathologist had probably left her at reception while he had a word with the coroner's officer.

"If you're after the ladies, you've just passed it," Bev

called. "Turn round, keep going and it's last door on the right."

"I beg your pardon?"

"The loo." Bev was alongside the woman now. She pointed the way and gave her a friendly smile before opening the conference room door. "This is a briefing, sweetheart. The public's not allowed in."

The room wasn't big and the twenty-strong squad made it appear even smaller. There was tension in the air, along with the sort of frisson that only came with a murder inquiry. As every man and woman in the room knew, a killer was out there. And if they didn't catch him, they could be looking at another victim.

Bev was about to perch on a desk at the back but the guv pointed out a seat next to him up front. She hadn't seen Byford since Friday. By the look of him, he'd had a couple of late nights. His complexion was sallow at the best of times but today the skin around his eyes looked bruised and the lines on his face appeared deeper than normal. What was he now? Fifty-two? Fifty-three? Bev reckoned he was beginning to look it.

She gave Bernie Flowers a quick nod as she sat down, which he returned with a "Wotcha, Bev." Bernie was chief of the police news bureau. He looked like a junior cabinet minister with his grey suits, grey ties and silver-rimmed specs, but in fact he was one of the sharpest operators around. Word had it he'd edited a national mass-circulation tabloid till a drink problem forced him out. Not long after his arrival at Highgate, one of the station clowns had made some crack about the sun never setting over the yardarm. No one knew exactly what Bernie said in response but the joke was never repeated.

Bev was still smiling at the recollection as Byford rose

and prepared to address the troops. Her smile was still there seconds later as the door at the back of the room swung open and almost every head turned to catch the late arrival. The smile froze.

The guv was welcoming the new DI – and Bev wanted to die.


Davy Roberts reckoned it had to be a joke. Jake could not be serious. Davy glanced at the other members of the gang but either they weren't listening or didn't care. Kev was shovelling a chocolate brownie down his neck and Robbie was checking cinema times in the *Evening News*. Starbucks would be closing any time soon and Davy was desperate to get it sorted. He'd soon realised there was no way he could tell Jake he wanted out but they couldn't just carry on as if nothing had happened.

"Come on, man," he asked Jake again. "What we gonna do?"

Jake rested his hand on the younger boy's arm, though there was nothing relaxed about the touch. "I've told you once: zilch."

Davy was beginning to wish he'd kept his big mouth shut. Jake was scarier like this than when he was on the rant.

"But, Jake –" He hated pleading but he had to get through. "She's dead."

"So?" Jake increased the pressure.

"What if someone was watching?" Baiting an old biddy in the street and nicking a bar of chocolate was fair game but this morning's show had been gross.

"There was no one around." Jake's voice was soft and low, the Birmingham accent barely discernible. "And even if there was – so what?"

Davy said nothing, too scared to voice his suspicion. Jake picked up on it anyway. "I get it." He was still speaking softly. "You think we went back and finished the job after you'd gone? Is that it, Davy?" He tightened his grip on the boy's arm.

Tears pricked Davy's eyes. It wasn't just the pain; he was desperate not to lose Jake's friendship. But Jake's face was creased with contempt.

The other gang members were tuned in now. "You wanna watch what you say," Kev sneered. "Little tosser."

Robbie never said much; he had a line in threatening looks.

Davy thought his arm was about to snap.

"We know where *we* were, don't we, lads? " Jake didn't wait for a response. "You were the one buggered off on your own. How do we know where you went, what you were up to? Sitting there like butter wouldn't melt."

"You're joking, aren't you?" Davy tried a faltering smile but Jake was deadly serious. "Come on, Jake, you know I'd never –"

"Never what?" Jake ran a finger along Davy's cheek. "Smack an old girl round the face?"

Kev and Robbie sat back, brawny arms crossed. They were enjoying the master-class; it was the closest they'd come to school for years. With their shaven heads and acne scars they looked like the Brothers Grimm. With his blond hair and blue eyes, Davy was definitely not one of the family.

Jake wrenched Davy's arm one last time before finally releasing his grip. "Only joking. You wouldn't hurt a fly, would you, Davy?"

He smiled uncertainly. Was Jake winding him up? He could never tell. "I'm only saying that maybe we need to lie

40

low. Keep our heads down for a bit." Davy didn't just want to lie low; he never wanted to go near another wrinkly as long as he lived. Except his gran.

Jake appeared to give it deep thought, nodding slightly with a finger pressed on his pursed lips. "Maybe you're right, my old son." Then he leaned in so close Davy could smell the espresso on his breath. "Tell you what, though. For old times' sake – there's just one little job I'd like you to do."

# 4

Detective Inspector Danny Shields.

*Daniella.*

Bev wanted the floor to open. She needed to disappear for a while. A couple of light years might do the trick. No. A miracle would be better. Dear God, raise me from the dead embarrassed. The new DI wasn't just a woman, she was the woman Bev had casually dismissed as Harry's latest totty and – oh, shit – the woman she'd just blithely despatched to the toilet. Talk about cringe. Bev's toes were so curled they had cramp. She tried concentrating on the case – difficult with Danny Girl in the next seat.

Byford was still running through the introductions. Reactions from the floor were predictable, with most of the men casting covert glances at the new DI's legs. Bev pulled her skirt down as far it would go, covered her lap with a clipboard. With the social niceties out of the way, the guv was in business. He took up position alongside the murder board, started outlining the previous attacks and comparing them with the latest crime. The talk was illustrated; they'd all seen the police photographs on the board before. Three pairs of frightened eyes stared from faces battered purple; grossly swollen bumps and coarse black sutures exacerbated the horror.

Until today Bev had sensed that some of the team was growing inured to the sight, the shocking images losing their impact. She'd even caught a few sick granny jokes doing the rounds. But now a new picture had been added to the gallery of shame. This morning's still nameless victim was up there with Iris Collins, Joan Goddard and

Ena Bolton. Were they linked? Bev was unsure; there were glaring inconsistencies as well as apparent connections.

The first three victims were widows in their late seventies. Ena and Joan lived within a couple of streets of each other in Kings Heath. Iris had a three-storey redbrick in Moseley. *Had* being the operative word. She was too frightened now to live alone, let alone too frail. She'd moved in with her daughter.

Iris Collins had been attacked first. Initially her daughter Angela believed that Iris had fallen downstairs. She'd driven over from Harborne to take Iris to the hairdresser's. It was a regular weekly appointment, thank God. The old woman had lain on the hall floor for only one night. Already enfeebled by a heart condition and mild dementia, Iris could barely speak by the time her daughter arrived. It was three days before Angela discovered that Iris's wedding ring was missing and the life savings her mother kept under the mattress had disappeared, and alerted the police.

Bev had read the interview notes. According to DC Carol Mansfield, the old woman had been vague, incoherent, kept blathering on about a baby. A week later when the gang struck again, it appeared the allusion might have more significance than the ramblings of a confused pensioner.

Bev interviewed Joan Goddard in hospital within a couple of hours of the assault. There was no doubt what caused the injuries; fist and footmarks were still visible. The old woman's mind was sharp, as her eyesight had been until the first punch detached a retina. Joan blamed herself for that, she told Bev. The yobs had been waiting for her when she returned from the shops: three masked youths in the tiny sitting room, she may have heard a fourth upstairs. She'd snatched at the nearest one's balaclava, caught a glimpse of his face. It was a costly move that unleashed a rain of blows and a string of verbal abuse. They'd torn off her rings, stolen her purse. Joan kept her savings in the bank. She'd told them time and again but they still tore the place apart and pissed in her bed.

It was when Bev was leaving that Joan provided the first and slenderest of leads. It also added credence to Iris's so-called blathering. The youth Joan glimpsed had a baby face: blond hair, blue eyes, round cheeks. The E-fit was so vague, the guv had dithered about releasing it. Short of anything else, he'd authorised its issue to the media. There'd been no useful response.

The third victim, Ena Bolton, had no chance to snatch anything. Three, maybe four youths had been lying in wait when she returned home after an evening's bingo. The fact they weren't wearing masks hadn't mattered. They'd already smashed every light bulb in the house. Two gang members had bound, gagged and blindfolded her. The battering left her bruised, bleeding and struggling to recall the tiniest detail to help identify her attackers. She didn't care about the few pounds they'd stolen but they'd also taken her dog. Ena had shown Bev the spaniel's picture: head cocked to the side, one ear up, one down, an out-stretched paw. Humph was deaf and a little lame. Ena had doted on him for fifteen years.

Bev had dropped by Ena's place a few times now. The calls hadn't just been part of the inquiry; Ena was a sweet old dear. It was during the last visit that Ena had mentioned the daffodils. A neighbour or friend had apparently left flowers in the house while she'd been in hospital. "Such a kind thought, don't you agree, dear?" Bev had smiled and nodded, and until that morning never gave it another…

"Thoughts, Sergeant?"

Byford was clearly waiting for an answer. The keys jangling in his pocket were as good an indication as the mild impatience on his face.

Busk or bluster? Bugger it. "Sorry, guv, didn't catch what you said."

Byford's left eyebrow was in a mid-way arch, which according to Bev's interpretation meant growing exasperation. It was confirmed in his voice. "Marty Skelton? Is he in the frame?"

She wished she could say yes. It would certainly lift a bit of pressure off the guv's shoulders. She held out empty palms. "I'd say not. There's a couple of checks outstanding but the alibi looks sound. The barmaid at the Red Lion reckons Marty was so off his face he could barely focus."

"And how relevant is that? Exactly?" Danny Shields treated Bev to a thin smile. Her expression was one of polite interest, but the words, however softly spoken, were a challenge. A challenge picked up by the entire team; backs straightened, ears strained. Everyone knew Bev had applied for the acting DI post. Now they watched the woman appointed uncross her long legs and lean forward.

"The pathologist estimates that the victim died early on Sunday evening," Shields went on. "Skelton could easily have killed her, then gone to the pub to establish an alibi. The man's alcoholic intake could be entirely commensurate with his guilt."

The voice had class; must lecture a lot.

"Yeah," Bev drawled. "Except he got to the Lion at lunchtime and never set foot outside the place till gone eleven."

Bev's contempt was barely masked. Shields let the silence linger for a few more seconds, then snapped. "Why wasn't that in your report?"

Bev shrugged. "Only just had it confirmed. DC New called it in. He's at the pub with DS Kent."

A joker quipped, "Nothing new there then." No one laughed; everyone was waiting for Shields's response. A tuneless rendition of *The Archers* theme tune drifted in from the corridor, courtesy of a tone-deaf whistler.

Shields narrowed her eyes. "Information of that calibre should be passed upwards immediately." A raised hand forestalled any protest. "Time is of the essence. The first twenty-four hours in a murder inquiry are crucial."

"Pass the eggs," muttered Bev. Byford ran a hand over his face.

"I beg your pardon?" Shields asked.

"The legs." Bev pointed at Bernie's chair. The news chief had it tipped back at a precarious angle. "I thought it was about to go. Wouldn't want Bernie to take a dive."

The sniggers were audible. Shields glanced at Bev, then made a note on a lined pad on her lap.

"Obviously this later stuff will be in my report." Bev paused. "When I've had time to write it. For what it's worth, guv –" she turned pointedly to Byford – "I actually think Marty's a distraction. Maybe even a deliberate distraction. Let's assume for a min we're looking at the same gang that attacked Iris and the others?" She waited for his assenting nod. "I think we need to go back to the beginning, only this time ask the old dears different questions."

Another nod. "Go on."

"As it stands, the only link is the approximate age of the murder victim. The other attacks happened in the old women's homes, and none of them were life-threatening. It didn't look as if the woman this morning had anything worth nicking. On the face of it, there's not much there. But what if there's something else; something we've missed?"

"Like?" Byford asked.

She related Ena's story about the daffodils. "It may be nothing. But if the same thing happened at Iris and Joan's... We'll know the attacks are down to the same gang." *And now they've killed.* The thought went unspoken but was shared by everyone.

"Worth a look," Byford said. "I'm interested too in the timings. This theory of yours that the body was most likely concealed?"

"There's a load of sheds on the allotments. Reg and the lads are giving it priority."

"ID is priority at this stage, surely?" Shields turned her glance to Byford. "What about a news conference? Witness appeal? I don't mind doing the honours."

He silenced Bev with a look. "Thanks, Inspector, I may take you up on that. Although given the access the media's already had, I can't imagine they'll be falling over themselves for a talking head."

A few bongs à la *News at Ten* chimed from the ranks but a Byford eyebrow muffled further sound effects. He then assigned the clowns responsible to the team that was already ploughing through the paperwork generated by the early coverage.

Bev used the break to cast covert glances of her own at the new DI. The woman had to be in her mid-thirties; had a figure to diet for and unlined café latte skin. She was mixed race but Bev'd be hard pushed to give a breakdown. The almond eyes and chestnut hair co-ordinated like a colour chart. Yet somehow the whole was less than attractive. Her sharp features gave her an aloofness bordering on the chilly. Bev showed her emotions in her face; Shields had so far revealed nothing, though the smirk when Byford told Bev he wanted a word about the morning's media fiasco came close.

The ID issue was still unresolved. Bev waited for a gap and threw in a thought. "I have a hunch the old dear was sleeping rough. She was filthy, scruffy, been on the pop. Might be worth a check with the shelters. See if someone can shed a bit of light."

Byford nodded. "Good thought. We'll get on to social services as well."

"Actually –" Shields looked up from her pad. "I don't agree with Sergeant Morriss's hunch." The stress on Bev's rank was subtle; the stress on hunch wasn't. "I made a closer examination. The victim was well-nourished. The dirt was superficial. I don't think she'd been drinking. I think the alcohol was poured over her by the assailant, probably to show his contempt." She paused for even more effect. "In fact, I believe the woman was wearing old gardening clothes. There was twine and scissors in her pocket. I believe she may have been tending one of the allotments. She may even have picked the flowers herself. That, in my opinion, is where we should concentrate inquiries. I think you'll find the daffodils, if you'll pardon the expression, are a red herring."

There were a few polite smiles but not from Bev. She opened her mouth to speak but Shields hadn't finished. "I'd go further and say I can see no connection with the ongoing inquiry. There was nothing planned about this murder. It was vicious, frenzied almost. The killer or killers were probably stoned or drunk: blind drunk."

Shields was probably having a pop, but at the moment that wasn't important. Bev was more concerned about the DI's take on the case. She replayed the Cable Street scenario in her head. Had she read it wrong? Made unforgivable assumptions? Missed the pointers? And how and when had Shields picked them up?

"Did you hear me, Sergeant?" Shields asked.

Bev frowned. "Sorry. Say again."

"I said in my opinion it's premature to discard Marty Skelton. And it harms the investigation when people jump to conclusions."

Bev glimpsed Byford fold his arms. Like everyone else he was watching her. She knew they expected a full-blown Morriss strop. She nearly obliged. It was the glint of malice in Shields's eyes that stopped her. For some reason the woman was spoiling for a fight.

"You're absolutely right, ma'am." Bev flashed her warmest smile. "I'll aim to keep an open mind." The pause was perfectly timed. "Like you."

"OK." Byford had clearly had enough. "Let's get on with it. There's a mountain of stuff to get through."

Further actions were assigned: Carol Mansfield and Del Chambers would check out allotment holders. Ken Rose and Brian Latham would visit the shelters and contact social services. Daz and Gary were following up Marty's marathon in the Red Lion. Bev and Oz would re-interview Iris et al. Everyone else would be on the streets of Kings Heath.

Bev was almost out of the door when Shields called her back.

"A word, Sergeant." The woman hadn't moved from her chair.

Bev hesitated briefly. Oz was fetching the car round. On the other hand, it was worth mending fences with Shields. It was only sense; they had to work together. Bev offered a hand. "Bit late, but welcome to Highgate."

Shields pointed to the seat opposite. "I don't like your attitude."

"Oh?" Bev sat, tapped her fingers on her thigh. "About?"

"Where shall I start?" Shields rose and circled the table. It was a common tactic. Cops used it all the time to intimidate the poor sod still seated. "First, all that crap you came out with at Cable Street. 'Oh, Mr Gough, I didn't get the job because I don't have the balls. I'm only a little woman.'" The girlie voice was as inaccurate as the quote. But Shields had got the gist right.

Bev made an effort not to squirm. "I didn't – "

Shields stood in front of her and leaned down close. "It may have escaped your attention but *I'm* a senior female officer and *you* assumed I was some ditzy airhead after the loo, whom you addressed as 'sweetheart'. That makes you as culpable as the men you complain about."

Bev shrugged but felt far from indifferent.

Shields started circling again. "Get this clear, Sergeant. You didn't make DI because you lack the necessary skills. You're slack, you have no attention to detail and you're not a team player. You get an idea and that's it. Blinkered and stubborn."

"I'm not listening to this." Bev stood. "You don't even know me."

"I was warned before I arrived. Do you know what they call you behind your back?" She paused but Bev didn't rise to the bait. "No. I didn't think so." She jabbed a finger at the chair. "And I haven't finished yet."

Bev sat, arms folded, seething but at the same time shocked.

"You're good at making assumptions, aren't you? This morning, for example, you assumed the victim was a bag lady. You assumed she'd been drinking. It's not good enough. Anyway, from what I saw, the only person at Cable Street who'd been 'on the pop', as you so eloquently put it, was you."

Bev balled her fists. "That's it –"

"No. It isn't. Sergeant, I'm not accusing you of drinking on the job, not even you would be that dense, but in my view you were clearly suffering the effects of an appalling hangover."

Bev opened her mouth to remonstrate but Shields lifted her hand again. It was obviously a habit of hers. "I don't give a damn if *you* were suffering, Morriss." Shields gathered her papers, tucked them neatly under her arm. "But the second I think this investigation is suffering because of your incompetence, you'll be off the case. Do I make myself clear?"

The word crystal sprang to mind but so did its association with balls. Anyway, Bev would have been wasting her breath; when she looked up the DI had already gone.

Maude Taylor rang her friend's number again. Like all the other times, it went unanswered. The old woman stood gazing through the window into her garden. A scruffy magpie was teasing next-door's ginger tom. Normally Maude would have observed the antics with delight, but she was distracted, her thoughts elsewhere. She was wondering if it was too soon to contact the police.

It was so unlike Sophia not to be in touch. They rang

51

twice a day; an arrangement set in stone. Leaning on her stick, Maude crossed to the sideboard and poured a large sherry. Why, oh, why had Sophia moved from Guildford? Birmingham was miles away. What if she'd had a fall? What if she'd had a stroke? What if she'd been attacked?

Maude took several calming breaths and a sip of Bristol Cream. She really must stop this. Sophia would be aghast; she'd always been the clear thinker, always taken the lead. Odd, really. Maude was so much taller, more solid-looking – ample was the word – whereas a gentle breeze would blow Sophia away. Appearances were often deceptive.

She glanced across the room, a smile lighting up her face. The photograph, now in a silver frame, was on the piano. She'd come across it again just the other week, sorting through old boxes and cases in the spare room. Amazing to think it had been taken seventy years ago. Two little girls on a beach in Devon. Sophia stood behind, resting her hands on Maude's shoulders. Her hair streamed like ribbons in the wind, ink-black shiny ribbons. Maude with her mousy plait had always wanted hair like that. Maude was sure Sophia would remember why they were laughing.

She was still smiling when the phone rang.

"Mrs Taylor?"

"Who is this?" Disappointment sharpened her voice.

"Mrs Carrington asked me to call."

Her hand went to her throat. "What's happened?"

"She's gone away for a few days. Asked me to let you know."

Thank God.

"You still there, love?"

The initial relief was already slipping away. "When will she be back?" Maude was due to go up for a few days later in the week. The trip had been planned for ages.

"Sorry, love. I'm only a neighbour. She just asked me to give you a bell so you wouldn't worry, like."

She absently noted the Birmingham accent, but was more concerned with what he was saying, not how. "Why couldn't she call herself?"

"As I say, I'm just a neighbour."

"Of course." He sounded such a nice young man and it was good of him to call.

"Thank you, Mr...?"

"Just call me Simon."

There were so many questions she should be asking and her mind couldn't come up with a single one. "Could I take your number, dear? In case I need to get in touch?"

"Got a pen?"

Where was it? It should be here. She'd have to grab the felt tip off the notice board in the kitchen. "Could you hold on a moment, Simon?"

"Take your time."

Maude hurried but the pen wasn't in its place. By the time she'd found a pencil in the dresser drawer she was convinced he'd be gone.

"Hello? Sorry to..." It was her fault. If she hadn't taken so...

The voice rattled off an 0121 number.

"Thank you so –" He had gone this time. It was a shame; she had several questions now. Never mind. If she didn't hear soon she could always get back. Sophia was fine. That was the main thing.


"You OK, Bill?"

The pathologist's question startled Byford. The Detective Superintendent hated post mortems. Always had, always would. The sights, the sounds, the stench; images that returned to haunt years after you thought they'd gone. As far as possible, he tried to switch off. This time he'd turned over and fears of his own mortality had flashed on the screen.

Harry Gough – gowned, gloved and bloodied – was still waiting for a response.

"I'm fine," Byford said.

"Stop sighing, then. You're putting me off." The pathologist gently placed a liver on the shiny scales suspended above the slab. Byford averted his gaze and prayed to God that when the time came he'd escape all this. On the other hand, who'd want to die like his father and brother? He closed his eyes, pinched the bridge of his nose.

"And if you're fine, I'm Jamie Oliver." Harry studied Byford over half-moon glasses.

Byford could do without the visual examination, never mind the wisecracks. He didn't want Harry on his case and there was nothing funny here. A broken and battered old body: thirteen stab wounds, twice as many shattered bones. And they still couldn't even grace it with a name. He shook his head, wondered what sort of monster could inflict this violence on a little old woman.

The two straight-bladed black-handled knives removed from the body would reveal nothing. Byford would bet his pension on that. The killer might be mad; he wasn't stupid. But the knives weren't the only evidence. Harry's assistant had spent hours working the body, collecting samples, taking swabs, recording data. Every fibre, every speck, every loose hair was en route to forensics.

"She had a good few years ahead of her." Harry nodded at the slab. "Great nick for her age."

"So she wasn't a drunken old lush, then?" Shields's wide

54

smile seemed inappropriate. It was hardly a cause for celebration.

Byford had almost forgotten the DI's presence. Maybe she shared his aversion, was distancing herself from the indignities of dissection. On the other hand, the snide remark suggested she was developing an aversion of her own and the target, Bev Morriss, was very much alive and kicking.

Harry ignored the interruption. "Non-smoker. Didn't drink much, heart sound as a bell. I'd say this was one old lady who took good care of herself." He pushed his glasses into a thatch of suspiciously dark hair and winked at Byford. "Definitely not one of Bev's old bag ladies."

What was going on here? Byford frowned. "Easy enough call, given what she had to go on."

Harry grinned. "She'd certainly had a bit to go on."

"What do you mean?" Byford's voice was calm, the challenge was in his slate-grey eyes. Harry was reminded of storm clouds.

The pathologist raised his hands; he'd only meant it as a joke. "Not a thing."

"Oh, come on, Mr Gough," Shields coaxed. "Morriss said herself she'd had a late night."

"So? Who doesn't?" Byford said.

"Absolutely, sir." Shields studied her nails. "And hang-overs."

Byford narrowed his eyes. "And you're saying...?" He knew Bev liked a drink. Knew, too, she'd been under pressure in the last few months. He'd been there himself a couple of years back. If it didn't affect her work, who cared?

"No one would mind ordinarily," Shields murmured. "But who knows? If she'd been there a little earlier?"

He frowned, recalled the conversation with Vince

Hanlon about Bev being on the scene first thing. There was no way Bev could have arrived any earlier. Unless Vince had been covering up for her. "Are you making this official, Inspector?"

"No, sir."

Byford didn't know the mortuary had a tannoy until a call went out for Danny Shields. The DI headed for the door, pausing briefly to add, "I've already had a word with her."

Harry blew out his cheeks. "Quite a handful."

"Her or Bev?" Byford asked.

Harry nodded at the door.

"Has she got a point, though?" Byford asked.

"I reckon she's got a sewing kit."

Apparently Shields had called Harry to sound him out on the theory that the old woman had been sleeping rough. "I told her it was a non-starter. She was no more bag lady than me. Thing is, Bill, I knew it was Bev's idea 'cause she floated it at Cable Street."

"What did you say to Shields exactly?" Byford asked.

"I told her the old girl was well-nourished. The dirt was superficial. I even reckoned she might have been doing a bit of gardening. She had some twine and a pair of scissors in a pocket. The soil under her nails was consistent with that."

"You told Shields all this on the phone?"

"Yeah. Funny thing, though, she'd been there herself and not said a bloody word. I only realised who I'd been talking to when she turned up here with you."

"She didn't introduce herself?"

"I thought she was with the media, at the time. Keeping a distance, you know? So why'd she take a pop like that?"

Byford rubbed a hand over his face. No doubt he'd be

finding out.

"Anyway, Bill. As I say." Harry was removing the gown. "The old lady would have been good for a few years yet. She died from the stab wounds, loss of blood, shock. Hopefully she was already out of it; she took a hell of a beating. And I know what I'd do to the bastard who killed her." The voice held venom. Byford had noticed before how Harry hated violence against old people. For most police officers, crimes involving children were worse. The guv knew that maintaining motivation would become a factor if the case dragged on.

"Tell you what, Bill." Harry rubbed his eyes with the heels of his hands. "I'll be glad to get out of this bloody game."

The pathologist's plans were an open secret. He was bowing out just before Christmas, hitting the Caribbean with a laptop. Harry Gough fancied himself as another Ian Rankin. He'd done the time, now he was going to write the crime.

Byford was toying with the idea of early retirement himself. He was aware that if his wife Margaret were alive he'd probably have packed it in already. It was three years now but he missed her, missed being married, loathed going back to an empty house. Work gave the illusion of a full life. But it was an illusion; he knew that. Knew, too, that worry over his health was making him question the future.

"Penny for them?"

For a second or two he considered confiding in Harry. They weren't close but they sank the occasional pint at the Jug of Ale. Harry was a medico; he'd have valid input. It didn't have to be cancer. It was just that, somehow, voicing his fear gave it more substance. He kept quiet about the tests but mentioned his thoughts on quitting the force.

Harry gave Byford's shoulder a gentle punch. "Go for it, Bill. I tell you, I'm counting the days. No more early shouts, no more late calls, no more freezing your bollocks off in all weathers, picking up the pieces of another bleeding murder or motorway pile up, Nah, mate, sun, sea, sand and sex. Lots of. For ever and ever."

"Amen," Byford provided. "I'll drink to that." Both men turned as DI Shields popped her head round the door.

"That was Highgate on the phone," she said. "Iris Collins won't be helping our inquiries into daffodils. Or anything else come to that. Sergeant Morriss appears to have finished the old girl off."

# 5

It was a bad joke in worse taste. Iris Collins's weak heart had given out an hour or more before Bev even set foot on the doorstep of the house in Harborne. It hadn't stopped the sick humour doing the rounds at Highgate. Vince hummed the opening bars of the *Funeral March* whenever he saw her, and some clown had stuck a bunch of daffs on her desk.

It was OK for that lot. They hadn't been there, hadn't seen the wasted limbs, the wizened features, witnessed the daughter's pain and fury over her mother's death. The general thinking on the team was that Iris Collins was just an old woman who'd had her time. Bev had even heard the old 'she'd had a good innings' line trotted out. What the hell was that supposed to mean? Iris would probably still be batting out on the pitch if a bunch of mindless thugs hadn't scared her witless.

Bev leaned back in the chair, blew out her cheeks, idly registered her fringe needed a trim. Iris's death had impacted on the direction of the investigation as well. Short of a ouija board, the daffodil line was going nowhere. She doubted whether Angela, Iris's daughter, had even taken their gentle questioning on board: questions they'd not yet had a chance to put to the second victim, Joan Goddard. Neighbours didn't know where Mrs Goddard had gone, never mind when she'd be back.

Bev sighed. Maybe Shields was right. Maybe the daffodils had sod all to do with anything. Not so much red as yellow herrings. She groaned. *Not funny, Bev.* Boy, it had been a long day. And it wasn't over yet. There was a flat in Balsall Heath to view at eight o'clock. Though she didn't really want a flat and didn't really want to live in Balsall Heath.

A quick glance at her watch confirmed it'd be cutting it fine if she nipped home to change. Anyway, although the office was small, grey and purely functional apart from her brown suede beanbag and a *Pirates of the Caribbean* poster, it also happened to be empty. And time alone was luxury enough these days. It wasn't that she didn't love her mum and Sadie but...

Stifling a yawn, she scrolled through the latest from Cable Street: scores of interviews, not a single lead; nothing earth-shattering from the search teams, either. They'd be out again at first light. Bev closed her eyes, pictured the old woman's body. What a shit way to die. They had to get an ID. Knowing who she was might give them a steer on why she'd been murdered.

"Haven't you got a home to go to?"

She shot up. How come the guv always made her feel guilty? She was a police officer, for Christ's sake. "Guv. How's it going?"

Byford perched on the edge of her desk. "I've released Marty Skelton."

"Oh?" Only surprise was how long he'd been detained.

Byford's lips twitched. "Quite the star, Marty. He's in shot on virtually every frame from the pub."

"Thank God for CCTV?"

"Thank God it wasn't karaoke night."

She grinned but noticed Byford's smile didn't reach his eyes. "It was unfortunate, Bev. That cock-up with the media."

And that was why. He'd come to give her a bollocking. Sod that. The unofficial news briefing at Cable Street was a pisser but it wasn't down to her. "Not for Marty, guv. Talk about chequebook journalism. Bloke must've made a mint out there."

She was avoiding the issue. Byford forced it. "What time did you get there?"

*Why are you asking?* She'd mull that one over later. Right now it was a tough call. The truth and Vince Hanlon would be in the dog poo. A lie and her unscheduled lie-in would be on the agenda.

"Soon as, guv. Marty made sure his media pals got first shout." That was obfuscation covered in fudge, and by the look on the guv's face he'd seen through it. She held her breath, waiting for the explosion. But he dropped a different bombshell.

"The BBC reports, first thing, quoted an *Inspector* Morriss, did you know that?"

She felt her colour rise, neck to hairline. "Christ, guv, I didn't give him the time of day."

"I've watched the tapes, Bev."

Hold on. It was coming back to her now. Marty had been arse-licking. The reporter had picked up on it. Her heart sank. She'd tried to put him right, but then Oz had discovered the body. She'd not given it another thought after that.

"Well?"

"A misunderstanding, guv." Technically it was her sin of omission, but an old woman had been murdered. Who gave a fuck about rank? Bev did. She sat back, arms folded. "Anyway, there's only one female DI round here. Everyone knows that."

Byford shook his head. It was tough but she was making it worse. "Do you have a problem with that?"

"Nope."

The wail of a police siren from outside broke the silence.

"I'm told she's a sharp operator, Bev. She comes highly commended."

From Crufts? "I'll take your word on that, guv." She was uneasy with this conversation, still reeling from the post-briefing confrontation with Shields. She couldn't talk about it, hadn't even mentioned it to Oz.

Byford sighed. "Don't take my word, Bev. Get to know her. Make her welcome."

There was a message in there somewhere. If she could read it.

"Cuts both ways, guv."

She thought he was about to add something but he just shook his head. She watched as he rose and stretched his arms. "I'm out of here. Early shout in the morning."

Thank God. The worst was probably over. "You joined a gym, guv?"

"What?"

"You've lost weight. Looking a bit trim." If anyone said the same to her she'd be looking a lot happier than he did. "That's a compliment, guv."

"Sorry. I was miles away." He put on his trademark fedora and tapped the brow. "See you first thing."

"Sure." She was thinking of getting into the exercise thing herself. "The gym, guv. You didn't answer the question."

He turned at the door. "Neither did you." She looked puzzled. "The time you got to Cable Street."

### KILLER DAFFODILS
### WHY NO POLICE WARNING?

*Killer daffodils?* The billboard creased you up – if you hadn't laid eyes on the corpse. Bev had only bought the evening rag because it was on her mum's list. It was in the back of the motor with the rest of the stuff. Thank God for late-night shopping. But her mum had better not get used to home deliveries. Bev sighed. Shame it wasn't so easy to buy a house.

The flat in Balsall Heath was the pits. The seller was a cheesy bloke in a sad wig and a surplus of saliva. Bev had to wipe white flecks off her jacket every time he parted his rubbery lips. She'd made no excuses and left.

Oz was sulking because she'd viewed the place on her own, so now an early night beckoned. She chewed her lip, picturing Oz. He'd been well put out, but what was the point in him trailing round property with her when he was never going to live in it? Maybe she could have put it better. Telling him he had more chance of shacking up with Kate Moss was a tad harsh. She loved Oz to bits, fancied him like mad but not even Mr Depp would be allowed that close to home.

A red light flashed on the dash. Shit. Not to worry. There was a Texaco on the Moseley Road. She'd get baccy and Polos at the same time. She hadn't had a smoke all day, unless you counted Marty's roll-ups. Mind, she and the girls had been billowing it out last night. Emmy wouldn't let her light up in the house so it'd probably be a crafty fag outside.

"Twenty Silk Cut please, love," Bev said.

There was something familiar about the skinny kid behind the counter. She'd been texting, thumbs furiously tapping the pads on a flash-looking mobile. Every bony finger was covered in rings but it was the silver scars criss-crossing the knuckles that clinched it for Bev. "Jules?"

She waited till the girl looked up and added another

stunningly incisive question. "What you doing here?"

"Auditioning for *Star Wars*. What's it look like?" The girl blew the biggest pinkest glob of gum Bev had ever seen. Shame it burst. Neither of them could keep a straight face.

"You haven't changed a bit, kid," Bev laughed.

But she had. Jules was one of the teenage prostitutes Bev had got close to last year. So where was the slap? The skirt that doubled as a waistband? As for the hair, it was more Bev's Guinness than the aubergine of old. The girl currently perched on the stool behind the glass was fresh-faced and fine-featured, her gear more H&M than S&M.

"You can talk. You still look like a friggin' social worker. Never seen you in anything but blue." She winked. "'Cept when you was on the game."

Bev rolled her eyes. "How are the girls?"

Jules didn't see them much; she'd jacked it in.

"Great," Bev said. She meant it; she still had nightmares about kids on the streets.

Unwittingly, perhaps, the girl ran a finger along a scar on her right hand. She was lucky. Flogging petrol was a damn sight safer than turning tricks.

"Yeah, well, it's early yet. Have to see how it goes."

"How long have you been here?"

"Two days." As long as that? "Mind, I only do nights. I'm at college. GCSEs."

"Good on you, girl." Bev shouldered her bag. "You still got my number?"

"Why, you still looking for work?"

Bev was still smiling when she pulled up outside her mum's house. She hoped it'd pan out for Jules. She'd keep in touch, take her out for a meal from time to time. Social worker indeed. Bev reached behind for the bags, wavering between a supper of scrambled eggs or Emmy's steak and kidney pie. Home cooking was fine until you started looking like the back of a house. Her favourite skirt pinched and she'd only been back three weeks.

The *Evening News* fell into her lap and she did a double-take. Not at the main picture but at the double-column in the bottom left of the front page. The photograph had been taken from the end of the garden at 12 Cable Street, a moody shot of a ludicrously mournful Marty Skelton gazing down from an upstairs window. Her first thought was that NIMBY should snap up the copyright for a poster campaign. Her second was serious. The horrible little man was holding a more than a melodramatic pose.

Marty looked like a fox who'd been to cunning college.

"Inspector –" Uriah Heep, eat your heart out, this was a hand-wringing masterclass.

"Cut the crap, Marty." Bev was halfway down the hall before he'd even turned round. She didn't think what she was looking for was down here. "Upstairs. Now."

A wave of wolf-whistles and catcalls cascaded from the kitchen. She poked her head in. Marty had a few lads round. Four middle-aged fat boys crammed round a formica-topped table. The place stank of booze, balti and body odour. Recycle the empty cans and you could scaffold a small town.

Judging by the pile of grimy tenners at the empty place, Marty was a dab hand at poker as well as press relations. It was doubtful if the other players could make out anything through the shroud of smoke but she flashed her ID anyway. "Mr Skelton's helping me with inquiries."

"Takin' down 'is particulars, are you, darlin'?" Baldy was a couple of jokers short of a deck.

"How original," she smiled. "Come on, Marty. Now."

"Can I just finish this hand?"

A tapped foot suggested not. He led the way, not a word of protest. Lots of others, though. Shame she couldn't see his face. She always associated verbal diarrhoea with nerves, and nerves with guilt. Threadbare carpet ran out halfway up the stairs. There were bare floorboards on the landing and posters of naked women on the walls. The air stank of piss, Brylcreem and sweaty socks. And something else.

"OK, where is it?"

"What?" Marty nervously stroked his mangy moustache. Bev half-expected it to come off in his hand.

"The dog. Where is it and where'd you get it?"

The snuffles and asthmatic panting coming from the back bedroom answered the first enquiry; Marty ignored the second. "That? It's an old stray. Took it in out the kindness of my heart." What did he want? A commendation?

"The animal was nicked, Marty. An old woman gets the shit beaten out of her. Then her dog goes walkies."

Bev studied Marty's face. Something was going on behind those shifty amber eyes. It didn't emerge from his mouth.

"Sick, isn't it, Marty?"

All of a sudden the floorboards were fascinating. "Wasn't down to me."

"Says you."

"I had nothing to do with it."

"Who, then?"

He must know something, surely? Maybe he was consulting his conscience. *Stupid girl.*

"Told you: I found it on the streets."

"Where?"

"Can't remember."

"I don't believe you."

"You have to," he pleaded.

"Where does it say that, Marty? What book is that in?"

He knew something. She was sure of it now. Silence is a powerful tool in a police interview. It didn't always work.

"OK. Break the party up downstairs."

"What?"

"I'm taking you to the station."

"You can't do that."

"Watch me."

Marty rubbed the back of his neck with a hand, scuffed a trainer across the bare boards. "He said he was gonna drown it."

She kept her voice flat, knew her pulse was rising. "Who did?"

"This bloke."

"What bloke?"

" In the pub."

"What pub?" Stone. Blood. For fuck's sake.

"I don't know."

"Are you taking the piss?"

"No. Honest. I'd had a drink or two…"

"That's not like you, Marty. So?"

"I can't remember."

"Right. I've had enough. Get your coat. And Marty." She jabbed a finger in the middle of his scrawny chest. "I'll not tell you again: don't call me Inspector."

# 6

It was the early brief at Highgate; the inquiry was entering its second day. The body language from the floor spoke volumes. Bev had never seen so many slouches and sprawls. Not surprising. They'd been working their metaphorical balls off and come up without so much as a sniff: no ID, no motive, no lead. Bev had just outlined last night's development but Marty Skelton's contribution was not proving as crucial as she'd hoped.

She resumed her seat at the front and only then noticed a clump of dog hairs on the sleeve of her jacket. Shit. Thanks, Humph. With Marty banged up for questioning, Bev had given the dog a bed for the night before reuniting him with Ena Bolton on her way in. Breakfast had gone by the board again but it was worth it. Bev reckoned the old dear had lost ten years in as many seconds. Even Emmy and Sadie had been smitten. They'd been talking about getting a dog when she last saw them. Bev smiled as she surreptitiously brushed off-white hair from midnight-blue polyester.

"So let's recap." DI Shields unfolded her lean frame from the chair and paced the floor. Even Bev had to admit she looked immaculate: classy taupe skirt suit, matching heels, hair in a neat ponytail, subtle make-up. The fingers she ticked to underline her points ended in perfect nails painted scarlet. "We have an old lag, an old dog and a mystery man in a pub with no name." Shields paused, glanced at the audience. "So what's the punch-line? I mean, this is a joke, isn't it?"

No one was laughing. Bev seethed. She wasn't looking

for a medal but cheap cracks she could do without. She tried to keep her voice calm. "The toe-rag who snatched that dog smacked an old woman in the mouth. He could be the same bastard who stabbed the next one to death."

Shields slipped a hand into the pocket of her linen jacket. "There's no way of knowing he's the same man Marty met in the pub. As for him being the killer, that assumes a link with the ongoing operation that – pardon me if I've missed something – has yet to be established."

Bev shrugged a grudging acceptance. She wasn't going to get into a slanging match. Anyway, the bloody woman was right. A connection between the cases wasn't a given. And a gut instinct wasn't hard fact. But Marty Skelton was no Francis of Assisi. Bev couldn't see him taking pity on an old dog unless he thought it was about to be killed. He'd been spooked by something. Or someone. Marty's problem was the booze. A goldfish had more memory. Tallish darkish youngish was the best-ish he could come up with. As for the name of the pub? Forget it. Marty had.

"I should get a bit more out of Marty this morning," Bev said. "At least he'll be sober after a night in the cells."

Shields was running a pen down the notes on her clipboard. "I want you and DC Khan in Cable Street. House-to-house. You've interviewed Marty Skelton twice with no joy. I'll see him next." She looked up and smiled. "I'll let you know what I get."

Bev glanced at the guv, hoping he'd intervene. Byford was staring into the middle distance. Maybe he hadn't heard.

In her office, Bev angrily shoved a mobile phone and a few papers into her shoulder bag. Oz perched on the edge of the desk, crossed leg swinging, watching every move.

"Don't say a word," she muttered through clenched teeth.

"You could take that up, you know."

"What?"

"Ventriloquism."

"It's not the voice I'd like to throw." What was Danny Shields's game? "I was so close to getting something out of him, Oz." OK, that was an exaggeration, but Shields would stand even less chance. "She'll get right up Marty's nose. He'll stay so quiet he might as well have taken a vow of silence."

"He might like a bit of posh," Oz said.

Unlike Oz, she wasn't smiling. It wasn't funny. Marty was all they had.

"Come on, Sarge. What is it you always say to me? Don't let the bastards grind you down."

She slung an empty Diet Coke can into the bin. "Sanctimonious bullshit."

He laughed and it struck her again how attractive he was. He'd teamed the charcoal leather with the black denims today, but it wasn't the gear. He seemed easier in his skin nowadays, more confident. It must be a year now since they'd teamed up professionally. Not much less since they'd got it together personally. He was definitely coming out of his shell. That was good. Wasn't it? She might have explored the thought but he'd peeled a post-it note off her keyboard and was passing it across. Another message from her mum. Christ, had Emmy lost the use of her legs? The note went into the bin as well, then Bev sighed and shook her head. "I wouldn't care, Oz, but Marty could come up with a real gem."

"So? That's great. We need a break."

She bit her lip. Of course it'd be great if Marty came up with the goods. But who'd get the glory? Ordinarily, she wouldn't care; she was a team player whatever the suits upstairs thought. But she resented like shit the fact that Shields stood to clean up. It was childish and churlish and she knew it. She wasn't about to tell Oz, though. On the other hand he wasn't stupid; he was giving her one of his looks. He opened his mouth to add a few words just as the phone rang. Oz was nearest but she got there first.

The call was brief. Oz could tell by her voice it was a goer, not some time-wasting loony tune. She took a few notes, clarified the quickest route from Highgate, then replaced the receiver. You didn't need to have heard the conversation. It was all but written on her face. And it was looking good.

"This isn't the way to Cable Street," Oz said.

"Well spotted, Sherlock." Bev was in the driving seat. They were on the Highgate Road heading towards Moseley, passing a hodgepodge of fast-food joints, late-till-eights, video stores and takeaways. Someone had told her once how many languages were spoken round here. Fifty? Sixty? She couldn't recall but wasn't surprised.

"I hate that Sherlock stuff. You know that." The tight jaw confirmed it but Bev wasn't focused on Oz's anatomical lexicon, and she was barely listening. The voice in her head belonged to a Mr Tom Marlow and if he looked even a touch the way he'd sounded on the phone, the encounter would be a pleasure. More than that, she saw a case with cracks.

"We're taking the scenic route," Bev said. "Via Belmont Way." She knew he was staring at her.

"That's Moseley Village, Sarge."

"Think it's going to rain? Looks pretty grey out there."

"I think you're changing the subject."

She let the silence ride. They both knew what it said. The lights at the crossroads in the middle of Moseley were on red. She pulled up, tapped a finger on the wheel. She'd viewed a couple of houses round here. Moseley Village: that was a laugh. It couldn't be less rustic. On the other hand, it was more upmarket than most Birmingham suburbs. It had a buzz about it, with lively wine bars, decent restaurants, and loads of arty, ethnic shops. She made a mental note to give the local estate agents a prod.

"What about the house-to-house in Kings Heath?" Oz eventually asked.

"What about it?"

"She won't like it."

"And I should care, why?"

"Look, Bev." The first name was a rare slip at work. "I don't know what's going on with you and –"

"No. You don't. So button it." She pulled away from the lights, sneaked a glance at his profile, his jaw was going to ache with all that clenching. "Look, I'm sorry, mate. Nothing's going on. Let's drop it. Right?"

"Sure. And water's not wet."

She sighed.

"I'm here if you need to talk. That's all I'm saying."

It took five minutes to get there. The silence made it seem longer.

Belmont Way shouted money and class. Bev locked the motor, looked round and gave a low whistle. "Christ, Oz, they could charge admission to get in to some of these pads. Look at that one over there. It's got turrets and a bell tower."

He didn't respond. Maybe architecture wasn't his forte.

Warwick House, their destination, was turret-free and bell-less but it still had a huge amount going for it.

The property appeared to be divided into a number of apartments but Bev wasn't studying its construction. She was concentrating on the bone structure of its owner, Tom Marlow. The cheekbones were chiselled, almost as defined as Oz's. The eyes were almost as blue as hers and the brown collar-length hair so dark that in some light it probably looked black.

She stopped herself running a hand through her own, held it out instead. "Mr Marlow. Detective Sergeant Morriss. And this is DC Khan. It was good of you to call."

"My pleasure. I only hope I can be of help. Do come in and, please, call me Tom."

If voices were cars, Tom Marlow's was a Silver Ghost. She wasn't brilliant with ages but guessed he was older than he looked. A natural ease and confidence suggested more than mid-twenties. He was smaller than Oz, around five-nine or -ten, but no one would be kicking sand in Marlow's face. They followed him into a large light-filled room; half-a-dozen cream rugs broke up an expanse of polished wooden flooring that probably cost more than every carpet she owned. Marlow indicated a couple of chesterfields. Their depth was deceptive and the ivory leather smooth; she'd never clenched buttocks so fast.

"Can I get you a drink? Tea? Coffee?"

"Coffee would be super. Thank you."

"Latte, cappuccino, espresso?" What was this? Starbucks? Chez Morriss it was either filter or Fine Blend. "Latte. Super."

Super? Oz's face was a picture.

"DC Khan?" The man's smile was lopsided. Bev rather liked it.

"Sorry?"

"Anything to drink?"

Oz glanced at his watch. "Nothing. Thanks."

Normally she'd have a nose round but hauling herself up from the depths of the leather seat was going to require muscles she had yet to locate. She sank back.

"Did you have to do that?" she asked.

"What?"

"The time check. It wasn't exactly subtle."

He took out a notebook and pen.

Suit yourself, she thought, and gave the room a visual once-over. As clues to character went, it didn't. She wasn't expecting knick-knacks and lava lamps but most people were into photographs and books. The only reading matter was an *Independent* and an *Evening News* overlapping on a heavy glass-topped table. A pre-Raphaelite hung over an Adam fireplace. She squinted but even close up wouldn't be able to tell if either was genuine.

Coffee was easier.

"Super. Thanks." It was the best latte she'd ever tasted. "Perhaps you could take us through Sunday evening, Mr Marlow."

"Please, Sergeant, call me Tom." Oz's pen tapped a beat on virginal paper. "As I said on the phone, I was driving through Kings Heath early evening."

"About what time?" Bev asked.

He laid a finger on pursed lips. "It must have been around 5, 5.30."

Bev glanced at Oz. The timing was about right. Oz nodded; he'd already made a note.

"As I say," Marlow continued, "a little old lady suddenly stepped into the road. I had to brake sharply to avoid her. To be honest, I was quite shaken. I pulled over just for a minute or so. Anyway, she went into that shop on the corner of Princes Rise."

"Jimmy Vaz's?" Oz asked.

"Yes, that's right." Tom agreed without looking over. He'd kept almost constant eye contact with Bev. She usually found it a turn-off but not this time.

"Did you see her come out of the shop?" she asked.

"Unfortunately not. I had an appointment. I didn't want to be late. And of course there was no reason then to think –"

She nodded. "Can you be any tighter with the timing?"

He leaned back, linked hands behind his head. "It was probably nearer 5.30, come to think of it." She was thinking slightly more about the effect on his physique; the tight granddad shirt suggested a taut six-pack.

"Yes," he said. "It was definitely five o'clock when I left here. And I had to stop for petrol and to use the hole-in-the-wall."

"And you think it might be the woman we're trying to identify?"

"She certainly fits the description on the local news: old grey coat, blue hat."

"Was she carrying anything?"

"No. I'm sure she wasn't."

Bev nodded. "And you'd never seen her before?"

"'Fraid not."

They wouldn't be cracking open the champagne but at least it appeared to be a genuine sighting. It could prompt other witnesses to come forward. Jimmy Vaz was the obvious next stop.

"Is there anything, anything at all, that you think might help further?"

He did that thing with his finger on his lips again. "I really wish there were. It makes my blood boil to read what's going on." He reached for the *Evening News*. "Have you seen this?"

You couldn't miss it. The paper was going big on Iris Collins's death. Her bewildered and battered face dominated the front page. The fact that the old woman had died from a heart attack was buried in the story. The headline screamed MURDER, toned down only by judicious use of question and quotation marks. According to the reporter, the attack was so vicious it led to her death. In other words, they killed her. Bev shook her head in disbelief and slung the paper back on the table.

"Is it true what they're saying?" Tom Marlow asked. "That the same people killed the woman I saw?"

*You tell me.* "We're at the early stages of the inquiry, Mr Marlow. It's impossible to say."

"Of course. I understand. And that sort of stuff can't be helping."

"We're used to it by now." Bev attempted a nonchalance she didn't feel. It wasn't just the sensational reporting; the paper was after a police scalp. Byford's was first in line.

"If anything comes back to me, I'll definitely be in touch. I know it sounds naff but I think you people do a wonderful job." He came across and took the cup from her. She was convinced the touch of fingers was accidental. Not quite so sure when she handed him her card.

"The switchboard can get busy. Use this if you need to."

"Thanks, Sergeant Morriss. I will." He read it, then slipped it into a breast pocket.

Oz was already at the door.

She felt a light touch on her shoulder and turned her head. His eyes had tiny flecks of amber.

"There's one other thing…" He paused, as if weighing up whether to continue.

"Go on," Bev urged.

"It's probably nothing, but I did see a group of kids hanging round the park gates."

Their departure was delayed by about twenty minutes. Marlow was reluctant to add to what little he'd said, in case it was irrelevant and pointed them in the wrong direction. Bev reckoned any direction was better than none. She kept the thought to herself, assuring Marlow that most of the steers they were given didn't lead anywhere. It went with the territory. They still checked everything: elimination was as important as confirmation.

The standard line had the desired effect. The descriptions Marlow furnished weren't brilliant but the hairs rose on Bev's nape when he mentioned a youth with a baby face. They'd have to re-issue the earlier E-fit. And Marlow would be going into the station to help compile another: a tall youth with a pale complexion, black spiky hair and face studs.

"Smarmy git." Oz tore the wrapper from a KitKat and passed Bev a finger. It was slightly stale but they were in Kings Heath, only a couple of streets from the shop on Princes Rise, and if Jimmy Vaz came up with the goods they'd be sharing more than a bit of soggy chocolate.

She lowered the window a touch; it was getting warm in the car. "What you going on about, Oz?"

"Latte, cappuccino, espresso?" The impersonation was spot on. He even had the lopsided smile to a T.

"You liked him, then?" She licked her lips to remove any chocolate.

"Not as much as he liked you."

"Don't be ridiculous." She turned to hide a smile. Flattered and a tad flustered. She thought she'd imagined the attention Marlow had been sending her way, but Oz had clearly picked up on it as well.

"A man who dresses to match his soft furnishings has got to be a poof," Oz added knowledgeably.

"Yeah, yeah. Whatever. We got quality stuff. That's all that matters."

"Super."

She burst out laughing. "Daft sod."

Oz couldn't let it go. "He was coming on to you."

She didn't really think so, but even if he was, so what? No harm in a bit of casual flirting. Oz didn't normally get jealous. He was so damn tasty he didn't need to. Marlow gave him a run for his money and that was why Oz was throwing his toys out of the pram.

"Make your mind up. A minute ago you had him down as a poof." She flashed him a smile.

The sun was so bright now she pulled down the visor. It was mild for March and people seemed to be making the most of it: young mums with pushchairs heading for the park, a couple of blokes washing their motors, a woman cleaning her windows.

"Best call Highgate, Oz. Let them know where we are."

As she looked for a spot to park the motor, she gathered from his voice and the odd phrase there was something amiss.

"News conference?" Oz was saying. "Now?" He put his hand over the phone and mouthed, "DI Shields wants a word."

Bev rolled her eyes. "Tell her to hang on while I pull in." She'd clocked a slot a few places down the road from the shop. The call was one-sided; mostly Shields. Bev's knuckles turned whiter the longer it went on. She put the phone down and sat motionless for a short time. The deep breathing helped; she eventually turned to Oz. "We're not doing the Vaz interview."

"I picked up on that. Who is?"

She started the car. The three-point-turn was perfect. "Take a guess."

Maude Taylor could have taken the train; that was the original idea. But Sophia had been part of that plan, and where was she now? Maude checked the mirror and pulled into the middle lane; the traffic wasn't as bad as she'd feared. The Fiesta was functional even though her sports-car days had been more fun. The fact was that now she was getting on in years, she found driving an ordeal. She had to steel herself for long journeys, determined not to lose her nerve completely. She sighed. It was a trial but even the M40 was better than another sleepless night of not knowing.

Sophia still wasn't answering the phone and the neighbour, Simon, had been no help. Maude had called but a recorded voice said the number had not been recognised. Recalling the frantic search for a pen and her rising panic, she wasn't entirely surprised. She knew one thing for sure: if the situation were reversed Sophia wouldn't sit around dithering.

If she was home by the time Maude arrived, all well and good. They'd laugh off the premature trip and make the most of the extra time together. If not, Maude would let herself in and work out where to go from there.

# 7

Back at Highgate, an increasingly hostile news conference was underway in the press briefing room. Matt Snow, crime correspondent of the *Evening News*, was centre stage. He fancied himself as leader of the pack and was clearly on the scent of a steaming trail. Separated by only a few feet, and the highly polished surface of a mahogany desk, were Bev, Byford and news bureau chief Bernie Flowers, their nonchalant pose and air of authority slipping perceptibly. DI Shields, presumably pissed off at getting zilch on the Marty Skelton front, was even now interviewing Jimmy Vaz over at his corner shop in Kings Heath. Which left the three Bs to take the flak. Bev shifted uneasily in her chair as the audience of bored-looking hacks sat up and sharpened their collective wits.

"I need more than this to go on, Superintendent." Matt Snow held his reporter's spiral notebook ostentatiously aloft, displaying an empty page to anyone who cared to look.

Bev stifled a snort. Snow was the author of the report on Iris Collins's 'murder'. He'd gone a hell of a long way then without appreciable police input. She sat back, folded her arms tightly across her chest. Snow wasn't so much a thorn as a rose bush in the flank of the police. Everyone knew he was desperate to break into telly. No one dared tell him his face was made for radio. As for the voice: pure Birmingham barrow boy.

Byford was struggling to stay cool. "I can't give you what I don't have, Mr Snow."

It wasn't working. Bev was close enough to count the beads of sweat on the guv's top lip. He was in the full glare of more than a few TV lights. A bog-standard appeal for witnesses and par-for-the-course call for help in identifying the victim wasn't going to cut any ice with bolshie journalists after blood.

Bev checked the line-up: the Beeb, Central, local radio and three or four rags. It wasn't a bad turnout but she'd expected more: old dears obviously weren't as sexy as young kids. Talking of sex, there was one face she'd not seen before, and not one you'd easily forget: imagine Catherine Zeta Jones on a tighter budget. The dark-haired lovely looked about Bev's age, twenty-six, twenty-seven. The comparison stopped there. The woman exuded radiance and poise. Classy was the word, Bev thought, as she watched the reporter take copious notes, apparently oblivious of her effect on the men in the room.

Snow was showing off, obviously desperate to make an impression. Even though he had Byford in his sights, he kept glancing round to see if the new hack on the block was watching. "It strikes me, Superintendent, you didn't release what you did have."

"Sorry, I don't do riddles." The guv reached for a glass of water. Bev wondered if anyone else had noticed the tremor in his hand.

"There's nothing enigmatic about a gang of teenagers terrorising old women. Why didn't you issue a warning? At least the old dears would have been on their guard."

Bev knew Byford had agonised over it. The balance was difficult: weighing up what might or might not be a genuine threat against panicking more than half the elderly population of Birmingham. Details of the attacks had been released as separate incidents. The media had been desperate to forge a link that the guv had consistently refused to go along with. It hadn't stopped the coverage getting more lurid by the day.

"Now look here." Byford dropped his pen on the table. Bev didn't think it was deliberate. "I'm not —"

"Our viewers are asking for answers as well. We're getting loads of calls on this."

Bev knew that voice. It was Marty Skelton's mate, Richard Peck, the man from the Beeb. Both reporters got to their feet, perhaps hoping the extra height would add weight to their argument. Peck towered over Matt Snow but the *Evening News* man was like a dog with a bag of bones. Bev wondered if he got the cheap brown suits as a job lot. She'd never seen him in anything else. Not that she could talk. She watched as he brushed a dull blond fringe out of caramel-coloured eyes already filled with contempt.

"You didn't issue a police warning and you tried to prevent the media issuing one."

"Rubbish," Byford snapped. "And since when has anything ever stopped the media speculating?"

Snow jabbed a stubby finger. "I'm only sorry we didn't push harder. It's obvious elderly women in this city are at risk. I tried to warn them. I wish I'd done more."

Perhaps he was waiting for a round of applause. No. He wanted a wider audience for the corollary. "How do you feel about it, Superintendent? The police are supposed to protect the vulnerable in our society. Do you regret letting them down?"

Bev flinched. That one was below the belt. *Come on, guv.*

Byford leaned forward, hands pressed on the desk. "I deal with evidence, not emotion, Mr Snow."

You wouldn't think so looking at his face, nor the imprint left by his moist palms on the wood. She wondered if she should pass him a note with the gist of the Marlow interview. She'd not had time to brief him since the hasty summons back to base. A couple of E-fits wouldn't get him out of the hole but they might prevent further digging. She scribbled a few words but Snow was still on the attack.

"Try telling that to the victims and their families, Superintendent."

She should probably hang fire but the guv looked in desperate need of a break. She cleared her throat. "We should be in a position to release new information before the end of the day." The confident tone even surprised Bev. It worked briefly. The pack sniffed a new scent. "We can't say any more at the moment but it could be a significant development." Sweat was pooling and cooling in the small of her back. She glanced at the guv. His face was a blank. Not surprising, really.

Snow scratched his ear, head cocked to one side. "What sort of 'significant development' are we talking about?"

Bev swallowed hard. "It's too early to say but you'll get a release soon as."

Peck sat down but Snow held his ground. "'Scuse me if I don't hold my breath."

A print journalist used the standoff to throw in a query about the daffodils. There was nothing new to report. The guv glossed over it. Radio WM asked for a one-to-one which seemed to signal the session was winding down. Chairs were scraped back and pens pocketed. Bev blew out her cheeks. Thank God it was over.

Byford gathered a few papers. "Thanks, ladies and –"

No one had told Snow. "How many more old women are going to die before the killers are caught?"

Byford's hands stilled momentarily. "We're doing every-thing in our power to arrest those responsible but there's still no firm evidence the Cable Street murder is linked to the other attacks. We don't even have proof that the first three assaults were carried out by the same assailants."

Bev noticed Snow cast another glance in the direction of the lovely Miss Jones. The reporter had her head down, writing furiously. "Even now," the reporter carped, "after three assaults and two deaths, you still can't admit it, can you?"

Byford jammed his hands in his pockets. Bev heard a jangle of keys. "I'm not ruling it out. There's always the possibility."

"I put it to you again," said Snow. "How many more deaths will there be before you admit you're wrong?"

She opened her mouth to remonstrate but Byford silenced her with a hand. No one was going to grace that with a response.

"I've said it before, I'll say it again. It's vital we establish the identity of the woman whose body was found yesterday. No one who fits the description has been reported missing. Maybe she lives alone? Has an elderly neighbour failed to return? If anyone can help –"

Snow had heard it all before. "What about a warning?"

"An old woman's been murdered. The killer or killers are still at large. I don't think it needs spelling out."

"I do. And tonight we'll be asking our readers what they think." Snow stowed his notebook in the back pocket of his trousers, the journalistic equivalent of a V-sign. "We'll be asking them if they feel safe on the streets. Asking them what they think of the police operation. I wonder if they'll share your confidence in the way you're running this inquiry."

Trial by redtop; it wouldn't be a first. Byford shrugged. "I'll look forward to that, Mr Snow."

Whatever riposte Snow may have fired was lost in the sound of a door slamming against the back wall.

One way to make an entrance, thought Bev. Everyone turned and watched as DI Shields strode to the front, headed straight for the guv. She knelt in close, whispered in his ear. Byford nodded a couple of times, jotted down a few words. Byford's face didn't change, though his voice had a softer edge when he addressed the gathering again.

"As a result of information received, there are a number of significant developments you need to know. We're anxious to trace anyone who was in the vicinity of Princes Rise at around 5.30 on Sunday evening. A woman we believe to be the victim was seen entering the shop on the corner there with Keats Road. We particularly want to speak to a middle-aged man wearing an England football shirt and blue mud-stained jeans. A key witness is working on a detailed description of a youth also seen in the area at the relevant time. We'll have an E-fit for you in a few hours."

Bev heard a few moans about deadlines and news desks but Byford stilled the buzz with a hand. He was saving the best until last.

"One more thing. We now know the identity of the murder victim. We can confirm she's a Birmingham woman in her late seventies. We'll be releasing her name as soon as relatives have been informed."

"Thanks, Danny. Good work, Danny. Three bags full, Danny."

Bev's Byford impersonation was rubbish. Oz got it in one.

"Sarge." His lips were pursed. "We've got an ID, I don't see the problem."

Shields had ordered them back to Kings Heath to mop

up the Cable Street house-to-house calls they'd failed to complete earlier. Not that they needed a bucket. People were either at work or so keen to crack *Countdown* they barely opened the door. Bev shrugged. Oz was right. But twice now, Shields had muscled in on interviews that Bev felt should have been hers. It still rankled. Not content with stealing Bev's thunder, she'd then pissed on her parade.

"Go on, say it. It's pathetic." She glanced at Oz out of the corner of her eye.

"You want it straight?"

"Sure."

"It's pathetic."

He wasn't even looking at her. She hoisted her shoulder bag higher, shoved her hands in her pockets.

"Look, Sarge. We've got a job to do and it doesn't help if you're at each other's throats. Maybe you need to back off a bit."

"When I want your advice I'll ask for it."

Oz shrugged. "Suit yourself."

Numbers 15, 19, 27 and 30 were as much help as a paper raincoat. The proverbial three monkeys had seen, heard and said more. The silences between the door-knocking were stretching. Bev was no good at the tight-lipped stuff.

"Fancy going out tonight?" Apart from the odd drink and a curry, they'd barely seen each other outside work since she'd moved back to her mum's. Maybe they needed a bit of duvet time. She hated feeling like a nun. God knew what the enforced celibacy was doing to Oz.

"Sorry, I've made arrangements."

"No sweat." There was no rancour in her voice but she had to turn her head. She'd reached the stage where she'd decided to open up with Oz. Maybe she was making too much of it but that felt like a rejection.

The seven o'clock news bulletin on Radio WM led with the old woman's ID: Veronica Amery, aged seventy-eight. Bev heard it in the motor on the way home, a bottle of Pinot Grigio on the passenger seat and a wet umbrella on the floor. The sudden downpour back in Cable Street had said it all: the door-to-doors had been a washout.

She was about to switch off the engine when she heard a voice she knew: female and fruity, as in ripe plums. DI Danny Shields was appealing for relatives of the dead woman to come forward. Bev frowned. Who'd made the ID, then? Presumably Jimmy Vaz. Not that it mattered. The next stage was more important: piecing together the victim's life. As jigsaws go, a name was just one of the corners.

Bev was flat out on the sofa watching some flaky celebrity of whom she'd never heard eat insects and animal parts she'd never imagined. Maybe she should try something similar; it was one way to lose weight. The top button of her trousers was already undone and she was contemplating easing down the zip an inch. It was her mum's fault. Comfort food? It wasn't doing anything for Bev's peace of mind.

Her mum and Sadie had nipped out to a neighbour's for their monthly dose of culture. The Crime Lovers' Book Club had been meeting for nearly two years now. Forget Austen and Amis: this was Morse and Miss Marple, with the occasional dash of mean streets. Bev smiled at the thought of the half-dozen or so genteel women gathered over the road discussing the finer points of murder and mutilation. Sadie was always on at Bev to join, but the way Bev saw it she barely had time to read books, let alone talk bollocks about them afterwards.

She heard the key in the door and the sort of raucous

giggling that usually followed a book club night. Bev suspected the group only met to get tiddly and swap gossip.

"Hello, love." Emmy popped her head round the door. "Fancy a cup of something?"

Bev joined the other Morriss women in the kitchen. The room was warm and cosy, lots of polished pine and pink gingham. The soft lighting meant Emmy wasn't in action at the Aga. All three perched on stools at the breakfast bar, enjoying a little time together. Bev skimmed the blurb on the back of the book chosen for next month's read, listened with a smile as her mum and gran talked her through the night's highlights. Their eyes sparkled as they finished each other's sentences or interrupted with a vital point. They were like a couple of kids. By the time they'd finished, Bev felt she'd been there anyway.

Bev had been studying Emmy closely. Everyone said they were like peas in a pod, but apart from their build, Bev had never really registered it before. Now she saw herself in her mum's features, or how she'd look in a few years. Maybe she'd best stop frowning straightaway. And laughing. Sod that for a game of soldiers. At least if she inherited the grey, it might add a touch of gravitas to the Guinness.

Her mum shoved the biscuits across and Bev had dunked two digestives in her tea before recalling her former belt-tightening resolve.

"Is my bike still in the shed, mum?"

Emmy looked sceptical. "Why? Who needs it?"

Bev curled a lip. "Very droll."

Sadie snorted, sounding not unlike her only grand-daughter. Sadie was a star: a skinny little thing with a lovely face. She was late seventies but had twinkly blue eyes and a Hollywood bone structure. The thick sable hair was usually pinned up but she could sit on it when she let it down. Bev loved brushing it for her.

"You haven't been on that bike since you were in pigtails, our Bev." Fifty years in Birmingham and Sadie still sounded as if she'd just stepped off the coach from Blackburn.

"So?" Bev said. "You never forget how to ride a bike."

Sadie chortled. "I remember every time you fell off as well." She pointed to the dresser. "Pass us my specs, lovie."

Sadie had more glasses than an optician. She was always losing them, but she also co-ordinated the frames with a not inconsiderable wardrobe that frequently included Bev's T-shirts and trainers. The pair she handed over looked like a cast-off from Dame Edna.

"I'm serious about the bike," Bev said. Cycling had to be better than a gym full of testosterone and tight lycra. She frowned; the guv never had answered her query about the gym. Come to think of it, post-news conference he'd hardly spoken to her at all. There'd been a time when they'd get together at the end of a day, toss ideas around less formally than at the briefings. She missed those little chats. Ditto Oz. Where was he? He'd said he'd made arrangements, she doubted he was talking flowers. She closed her eyes, tried to banish niggling thoughts.

"What's up, lovie?"

Her gran's emotional radar was sharper than NASA's.

"I'm fine, bit tired." She faked a yawn and overdid a stretch. "I need more exercise."

Sadie winked at her daughter. "Best stock up on the Germolene, Em."

While the kettle boiled, Maude Taylor searched the house in Kings Heath. It was exactly as she expected to find it:

89

clean, tidy and comfortable. There was just one problem. Where was its owner? There was no sign of Sophia, no clue to her whereabouts.

Maude was almost sure her friend hadn't gone away. Her toothbrush and other toiletries were in the bathroom. Suitcases were under the bed. She tried hard to come up with a convincing scenario. Sophia could conceivably have left in such a rush that there'd been no time to pack. But Sophia had no family and few remaining friends. Who could have made such an urgent claim on her?

Maude returned to the kitchen. It was spotless, un-cluttered, a place for everything and everything in its place. Except for the vases. Sophia would never have left them lined up on the windowsill like that. Where could she be? Maude barely felt up to the task of trying to find out. She was exhausted. The hold-up on the M42 had been interminable. It was eight o'clock now. She was too tired even to contemplate eating. She'd have an early night; recoup her energy for tomorrow. First thing, she'd try to find that nice young man, Simon. He was a neighbour. He couldn't be that hard to track down. If she had no joy, she'd have to call in the police. Who knew? Sophia might be back by then.

Having made a decision, Maude felt slightly better. She poured tea into a china cup, took the drink into the sitting room and was asleep before it had cooled.

# 8

Apart from a colony of rust and a cape of cobwebs, the purple Raleigh was in better shape than its rider. It had taken Bev fifteen minutes to cycle to Highgate, mostly downhill. She'd almost booked a woman for applying mascara while she was driving but the lights turned green. Bev didn't have the horsepower to keep up with a 4x4. At the nick, it was a tough call which was worse: the numb bum on dismounting or the chorus of *Daisy, Daisy* from the station clowns.

There wasn't much else to laugh about. The only upside to the early brief was its brevity. It didn't take long to hear there'd been no significant developments overnight and no one wanted to dwell on the *Evening News*. Its early edition was flagging full 'explosive' results of its police poll later in the day.

Bev glanced at the guv: another sleepless night. He looked drawn. No doubt the media hanging and quartering would come later.

"We'll give it forty-eight hours," Byford said. "Then I'm thinking we'll go for a reconstruction."

She turned her mouth down, registered similar expressions on other faces. Most of the squad considered it premature.

"Problem with that, Sergeant?" The query came from Shields. The DI certainly wouldn't be riding a bike in that get-up. The dogtooth two-piece looked like Chanel.

Bev brushed her fringe out of her eyes, wondering why Shields had singled her out. She wasn't in the mood. "Nope."

"I know it's a bit early…" Byford's hand stroked his jaw-line. Was he wavering? That wasn't like the guv.

"I'm with you, sir," Shields said. "We need a break in this case. I'm happy to take on the organisation."

"Thanks, Danny. I'll let you know."

Shields returned his smile, made notes on her pad. Bev gave a sotto snort. *Bet it's a sodding shopping list.*


"I got everything, gran."

Davy Roberts took the KwikSave bags straight through to the kitchen. The air was stale and once-yellow walls were slick with grease, the residue of countless fry-ups in second-hand fat. He bunged the shopping on the table and shook his fingers to restore circulation restricted by a ton of tinned veg and canned mince. As usual, Gert was hunched over a Mills and Boon. She dog-eared a page before laying it aside.

"You're a good lad, Davy. Don't know what I'd do without you."

Neither did he and it worried him to death. How would the old girl manage on her own? The walking frame wasn't much cop; even getting out of a chair was a struggle these days. Less she went out, worse it got. Said she was agoraphobic. Sounded better if it had a name. But Davy reckoned names were the problem; she got a load of lip every time she set a foot out the door. Kids were dead cruel. Mind, Gert was probably the fattest woman they'd seen in the flesh.

"What you got in there?" Davy followed her glance, moved the Boots bag out of reach.

"It's mine, gran." Her face fell. "It's a surprise. I'll show you later."

Most people only saw as far as the mounds of mottled

flab but Davy reckoned his gran had beautiful eyes, pale green with tiny darker flecks. He smiled back. "Cuppa tea? I got the doughnuts."

"Smashing."

He was filling the kettle when Gert asked if he'd remembered the newspaper.

The water went everywhere. The pictures had been splashed across the front page. They weren't brilliant, not like proper photographs, but they still put the wind up Davy. He dabbed ineffectually at his sodden sweatshirt with a tea towel. "Sorry, gran. It was too early. They hadn't come in."

She sighed. The paper was a ritual, like *EastEnders* and *Corrie*. A life prescribed by tabloids and telly; and a daily injection of pap fiction.

"Don't worry." He was half out of his top, voice muffled. "I'll pick one up later. You've not forgot I'm out tonight, have you?" He smiled but she wasn't looking at his face.

"Whatever's that?" She was pointing to his arm, squinting, eyes sunk in the dough of her face. The bruise was livid, shades from plum to purple. "It's not one of them tattoos, is it, Davy?"

He picked a lie. "Nah. It's a bruise, gran. I walked into a lamp-post."

"Are them Ryan kids at it again?" The Ryan twins had got identical ASBOs banning them from Kings Heath High Street. They lived round the corner in Princes Rise and had been in Davy's year at school. They'd hadn't laid a fingernail on him since Jake introduced Stanley. The knife had made a permanent impression on the boys.

Gert tutted, shook her head, jowls flapping. "I can't abide bullies. Nasty pieces of work. Should be locked up, if you ask me. You'd tell me, son, wouldn't you? I'd sort the little sods out."

Davy handed her a family bag of doughnuts. He nodded, said nothing.

DI Shields held the phone at arm's length. "It's for you, Sergeant." The sneer was audible. "Your mother."

Bev's hand was on the door. Thank God she had her back to the incident room. She knew her face would be as red as the DI's lippie. She muttered a thanks, and huddled into the receiver. "What is it? I'm on my way out."

The estate agents had called: a two-bedroom terrace, just on the market, completely refurbished, an absolute snip. Bev listened, tried to keep the impatience out of her voice, then wound up the conversation. Shields was doing the same with her watch.

"What's Highgate's policy?" The DI was perched on the edge of a desk, swinging a leg that clearly knew its way round a workout.

"Sorry?" Bev said.

"Personal calls. Is there a policy here? We discouraged them at Little Park Street."

Bev bit her lip. "I'm not –"

"Good."

The DI was already on her way out. A ladder ran the length of her tights. It pleased Bev no end, but the waste bin still took the brunt of her Doc Marten. This thing with Shields was getting to her. The aggro was pretty much constant. She'd never experienced anything like it, didn't know how to handle it.

Maybe Frankie'd have a few thoughts. Bev and Francesca Perlagio went back to day one at Springfield Primary in Stirchley. They were closer than sisters. Frankie cut to the chase better than a scythe and never minced her words. Bev decided to give her a bell. On her own time, of course.

"Shouldn't you be in Kings Heath?" DI Shields had returned and was now framed in the doorway.

Bev grabbed her bag, car keys in hand. "On my way."

"Good. Look in here, will you?" A name and address was scribbled on a scrap of paper: Maude Taylor, Park View, Princes Rise. "It was a bad line and the old dear sounded gaga to me. Still. As you're passing –"

Bev recognised the address. It was an outstanding on the house-to-house. There was one other in the same street. She might kill two birds… First she had an old bird to calm down.

"I'm not an idiot, Sergeant Morriss."

"Of course not, Mrs Taylor." Bev was politeness personified. She had to be. According to the old woman, DI Shields had bad-mouthed her before slamming the phone down.

"She was very rude. I'm not accustomed to being spoken to like that." Maude Taylor was deeply distressed and it couldn't all be down to Shields's way with words.

"I apologise for any misunderstanding. Can we talk inside?"

The woman looked ill. She was trembling and none too steady on her feet. Bev offered a willing arm and what she hoped was a winning smile. There was a second's hesitation, then Maude allowed herself to be gently escorted back into the house.

She was a big woman, a head taller than Bev and solid, with big hair that resembled an off-white meringue. The beige ensemble was a bit old-lady-bland but not the purple pashmina effortlessly draped across Maude's ample bosom. Her heavy wooden stick was the only indication of physical infirmity. Mentally she was well there but her emotions were all over the shop.

Bev made for the scent of basil and lemons. A quick glance registered a seriously cool kitchen: all moody blues and terracotta bowls. She loved the old wicker baskets someone had hung from the ceiling. She helped Maude settle in a wheel-back chair, spotted tears gliding down the old woman's face. New Men might cry these days but not old women. Not in front of an audience. Bev bustled round, keeping a solicitous eye on Maude, while rustling up tea and making small talk, anything to give the old lady a few minutes' grace. Maude's dignity was in place at about the same time as the Earl Grey and Rich Tea. She blew her nose, then tucked the handkerchief into the sleeve of a hand-knitted cardigan.

"Thank you, Sergeant. You can stop now."

Bev widened her eyes; so much for subtle diplomacy. "Sorry, I –"

Maude flapped a hand. "I know. You were trying to be kind. And I thank you for that. Now why don't you sit down so we can talk?"

Bev smiled. She could see Maude in a Merchant Ivory production, cast as great-aunt to someone like Helena Bonham Carter. "You don't miss much, do you, Mrs Taylor?" The remark wasn't calculated but it scored points.

Maude inclined her head and took a genteel sip of tea.

"Anyway, I'm really glad you called," Bev said. "We've tried the house a couple of times in connection with one of our inquiries. I guess you've been away?"

Maude looked puzzled, then shook her head, impatient. "No, no, dear. This isn't my house. It's my friend's, Sophia Carrington's. That's why I rang the police. Sophia is missing. I'm afraid something awful's happened to her."

Bev frowned, thoughts racing. "Start from the beginning, Mrs Taylor."

Maude explained about the twice-daily phone calls. "I've heard nothing from her, you see. It's so unlike Sophia. I'd have come sooner. But the young man was so reassuring."

This did not sound good. "Young man?"

"He said he was a neighbour. He told me she'd been called away. He was so convincing. But I've knocked on every door in the street. No one's even heard of a Simon living round here."

"How old's your friend, Mrs Taylor?"

"Why, my age. Seventy-six."

Bev's heart was heading for her Doc Martens. "Can you describe her for me?"

It had reached the soles by the time Maude finished. The mention of an allotment and a blue beret clinched it. Bev was ninety-nine point nine per cent sure that the murder victim was Sophia Carrington, not Veronica Amery. It was a police cock-up. Big time.

She took a deep breath, and reached for Maude's surprisingly small smooth hand. She hated this part of the job.


"Kick it in. We ain't got time to piss about." Sergeant Reg Layton, a chubby little charmer with a pencil moustache and a mouth like a main sewer, was in charge of the search team on the council allotments in Kings Heath.

The flimsy shed door looked as if it would succumb to the slightest puff from an asthmatic wolf. It caved in completely with the sudden pressure of a size ten police boot.

Neither Reg nor his sidekick, the enthusiastic Constable

Del Chambers, ventured into the ramshackle structure. The officers' job was to find evidence, not trample it, and the stench emanating from the dark damp interior screamed crime scene.

Reg called it in; Chambers cordoned it off. SOCOs were on site in twenty minutes. A growing gaggle of mawkish onlookers, mainly women wearing headscarves and old men in flat caps and mufflers, was kept at bay by blue and white police tape flapping in a gentle breeze.

The interior was cramped and crammed. Auxiliary lighting cast vaguely menacing shadows over an array of gardening tools, seed packets, plastic pots and wire netting. There was room inside for only one crime officer and the process took several hours, bagged more than thirty items. Blood type would be determined by forensics. There was no shortage for testing. A huge dark blot stained the already filthy wooden floor.

Along with the usual finds of bus tickets, cigarette butts and sweet wrappers, the search came up with a number of hairs and fibres that might or might not prove significant. And it was clear that if anyone had been careless enough to leave fingerprints, the most likely surface was on the empty half-bottle of brandy tossed into the back corner.

"So who the fuck's Veronica Amery?"

It was a first. Byford didn't do the F-word. Well, Bev'd never heard him. It was nearing the end of a day she'd be glad to see the back of. She'd popped her head round the guv's door on her way out, surprised to see him still at his desk. Even more surprised he wasn't entirely up to speed.

"No idea yet," she said. "But she's not the victim."

Where had he been all afternoon? Surely DI Shields had filled him in on all this?

Byford rose, paced the floor. "I don't believe it."

Bev had found it difficult at first, but she'd had longer to take it in. The last few hours had been a nightmare. After alerting Highgate to the question mark over the ID, she'd escorted Maude to view the body. It was the only way to be a hundred per cent sure. The devastation on Maude's face was an image Bev wouldn't forget. Reluctantly she'd had to leave the old woman in the care of a FLO. Although sorting the fall-out was going to take more than family liaison.

"It's a complete cock-up," Byford said. It could be worse; probably would be when the Amery woman showed. A neighbour reckoned she was abroad. Byford snatched Bev's report from his desk. "This Maude Taylor. I take it she's on the level? She's not some sort of nutter?"

Bev pursed her lips. "The woman's straight as a die. There's absolutely no doubt. The victim's Sophia Carrington. She's seventy-six and she's lived in the city two years."

The dodgy ID, Bev had discovered, was down to Jimmy Vaz. Not deliberately or maliciously, just an old bloke who'd made a mistake. Loads of old ladies came into the shop, he knew them all by sight, obviously wasn't so hot on names. She could see how it had happened. Jimmy had been under pressure to come up with the goods. It wouldn't be right to make him a scapegoat.

The guv nodded. He was perched on the sill now, next to the cactus she'd given him for Christmas. By the look of it, it wouldn't see Easter. "With hindsight, we'd have been better off hanging fire. We should've waited for confirmation before releasing it." He was so quiet he might have been talking to himself.

"You must have had a good steer, guv."

He waited till she made eye contact. "What's that

99

supposed to mean?"

"Whoever held Jimmy's hand must have done the checks?"

He narrowed his eyes. "Where are you going with this, Bev?"

The woman had asked for it. "DI —"

"DI Shields wanted another twenty-four hours."

"Right." She closed her mouth before inserting another foot in it.

"I authorised the release, not Danny. It was a bad call."

No wonder he was looking so rough.

"Where is she, anyway?" Bev asked.

"A community liaison meeting. I asked her to sit in for me."

Given recent events, that could be a hot seat. Bev glanced at her watch. It was time to call it a day.

"Fancy a pint, guv?" A drink might do him good; she hated seeing him like this. He wasn't even listening. She paused at the door. "At least things'll start moving now."

They'd be interviewing Maude again in the morning, assuming she was in a fit state. They'd need every bit of history they could get. As for the present, there were still loads of calls off the back of the media coverage. Although a dozen or more youths had been traced, questioned and eliminated, it hadn't even scratched the surface.

But the shed on the allotment could turn out to be the forensic equivalent of striking oil. The owner had finally been traced and immediately eliminated as a suspect. Ernie Fellingham lived a couple of doors up from Sophia, and had just returned from a few days at his daughter's. He was an old man with dodgy knees and he'd been gutted to hear about the murder. They might get some useful background from him when he'd got over the shock.

Bev looked at Byford, wished she knew what he was thinking. He was still staring listlessly into the middle distance. And if there was writing on the wall, it wasn't anything good.

## COP OUT

The sub must've liked the headline; it covered most of the front page. The head and shoulders didn't do Byford any favours. Neither did the vituperative piece of bile from Matt Snow. Just in case the double meaning was lost on readers, the reporter's copy milked the pun inside as well. The bottom line was that Byford should bow out. An exclusive poll on page five seemed to agree.

Bev flung the tabloid on the ring-scarred table. The Prince of Wales was the only watering-hole within walking distance of Highgate. It wasn't exactly busy. The nicotine-and-racing-green décor didn't attract much casual trade these days. So why was Oz taking forever with the drinks?

"Have you seen that crap?" She started before he'd even sat down. She nodded at the *Evening News*, now spattered with fall-out from the ashtray. Making the guv look as if he had a nasty case of the pox.

Oz handed her a glass of Pinot and a packet of dry roasted, then picked up the paper and gave it a shake.

"A bloody good cop and that runt's crucifying him." Half the wine had already disappeared down her throat.

He finished reading, folded the paper and placed it on the table.

"Well?" she demanded.

"You know him better than me." Oz was on orange juice.

She saw red. "What's that supposed to mean?"

"I don't want a row, Bev." He helped himself to a nut.

She lit a cigarette, practised smoke rings.

Oz flapped a hand. "I thought you'd given up. Again."

She was still seething. "Come on, Oz. You work with the guv. What are you saying?"

The words were lost in a crude guffaw from the far corner. Bev glanced across. If they were eighteen, she was Chief Constable. Under-age drinking wasn't exactly big league. She'd been there, done that. Anyway, Oz still hadn't answered.

"I think he's under a lot of pressure." His words were weighed, the tone measured.

"'Course he is. We all are. Your point being?"

Oz hesitated. "Look, Bev, maybe he can't take it like he used to."

"That's ridiculous." It was an automatic response; maybe she didn't want to give it careful consideration. Byford was The Man. He was the age her dad would have been if he hadn't died from cancer, and though she probably wouldn't admit it, she regarded the guv in the same paternal light. She recalled the last time she'd seen Byford, perched on the sill in his office. He'd looked shit. She put the image to one side; maybe she'd take it out later.

"You haven't heard, have you, Bev?"

There was something in his voice she didn't like. "Heard what?"

He was tracing the rim of his glass with a finger. "The rumours going round Highgate."

She sniffed. "There's always rumours going round Highgate."

"Suit yourself." He sipped the juice.

Oz was better at silences.

"For Christ's sake. Are you going to tell me or what?"

"Byford's thinking of leaving. Early retirement."

She felt the colour drain from her face. She didn't believe it. Couldn't believe it. "Right, yeah. Says who?"

"Vince told me. It's all over the place."

It couldn't be. The guv would have said something, surely? She reached for her glass; it was empty. She snatched it and stood. "Want another?"

Her mobile rang while she was at the bar. Tom Marlow. She smiled, genuinely delighted to hear a friendly voice. It was even more attractive now she had a face to go with it. It wasn't urgent and he was away on business until tomorrow evening but could they meet for a drink? There was something he wanted to discuss. Of course she could.

Oz smiled as she returned with the refills. "You look as if you've won the lottery."

"Frankie. Seeing her tomorrow." She couldn't meet his eyes, didn't know why she'd lied. "Anyway, I'm gonna ask him. First thing."

"You've lost me."

Bev sighed. "The guv. If he's calling it a day, I'm a child bride."

"Who's the lucky man?"

"The pope's dad."

# 9

"Didn't last long, did it, Sarge?"

Bev glanced round as she locked her trusty MG Midget. Darren New, who'd arrived on shift at the same time, nodded at the bike railings; the rusty steed languished in a row of gleaming peers. She gave a Morriss-snort.

"Tell me about it." She'd had to walk home last night, as deflated as the Raleigh's front tyre. She'd have bummed a lift but Oz had already headed off.

"It's only a puncture. I'll fix it if you want."

"Thanks, Daz. I'll let you know." She was having second thoughts on the cycling lark. Loved the theory; not too keen on the practical. Anyway, she'd enjoyed the walk last night.

They were both heading for the incident room. "Much on today?" Daz asked.

She smiled. "Loads." There was even a change of clothes in the boot if she couldn't get away on time. She could swap the French navy two-piece for a sexy but subtle ell-bee-dee. Not that the meet with Tom Marlow wasn't work, of course. As for the rest of the day, Maude Taylor would take up the lion's share. Once the briefing was out of the way.

There was the customary banter and joshing as people turned up, found a place to perch. She ran her fingers through her hair, calculating the likelihood of fitting in a quick trim. Her fingers were still in her fringe when DI Shields sashayed into view. The DI waited for the buzz to die down. The sage coatdress looked good, although there was a button missing. It wasn't the only absentee.

"Superintendent Byford won't be in today," the DI announced. "He could be out for the rest of the week."

Shit and double-shit. "What's the problem?" Bev asked.

"Nothing to do with the inquiry, Sergeant."

"That's not what I asked."

"I'm not here to answer pointless questions." She turned her back. Bev's fists were balled. Again. They had a mind of their own when it came to the DI. "We have an unsolved murder on our hands. The Superintendent's concerned about focus," she said. "We don't need another cock-up."

Bev could barely keep a lid on it. The guv may have defended Shields but it was the DI who'd driven Jimmy Vaz to identify the body, and not just in the bloody car. Bev opened her mouth to remonstrate but Shields was in full flow, spouting about teamwork and tight ships.

Bev tuned out, her thoughts on the governor. They'd worked together four years and she'd never known him take so much as a half-day. Was it pressure from outside or above? Only one way to find out, and it wasn't via Shields.

"... it goes without saying I'll do the interview." The DI slipped a slim gold pen into a breast pocket. "Any questions?"

Bev frowned; she'd missed the first bit. "Sorry. What was that?"

"I asked if there are any questions?"

"No. The interview. What did you say?"

"Maude Taylor. She's a key player. Obviously as senior officer I'll lead."

Bev's eyes flashed. Playing second fiddle to Shields wasn't how she'd read the score.

"Carol, I want you there as well. Women of Taylor's age aren't always happy with male officers."

DC Mansfield looked slightly uncomfortable. She

nodded, then dropped her head, curtains of red hair masking a pale face that showed the slightest blush. Bev's flush was down to fury.

"Sergeant Morriss," Shields smiled. "There's a woman waiting at reception. Have a word, will you?"

"No." Bev was on her feet, arms folded. Shields had muscled in on the Marty Skelton interview, the Jimmy Vaz interview; she'd not move in on Maude Taylor.

"I beg your pardon?"

"Maude Taylor's mine."

"I don't think so."

"Maude Taylor's an old woman, dead emotional right now. You really pissed her off yesterday. She won't give you the time of day."

Shields's eyes narrowed. "Ready, Carol?"

The DI turned at the door. "And Sergeant, careful what you say to the woman at the desk. I believe she's a reporter. A simple 'no comment' should do it."

Gert Roberts's gaping mouth was a black hole, a state not entirely due to the orthodontic challenge of her few remaining teeth. Her chubby hand went to her chest and she blinked furiously; she wasn't imagining things. "Whatever have you done to your hair?"

Davy, hands on narrow hips, turned his head from side to side with a grin. "Don't you like it, gran?"

Ebony, it said on the pack; he'd used the lot. Done it when he got back last night. Just as well he'd had a jar or two.

"It'll take a bit of getting used to."

She was right there. Her blue-eyed blond-haired baby-faced grandson now looked like something out of the Addams family. He should have bought proper scissors while he was at it.

"It'll grow on you, gran." He winked. "And on me." It was easy to make her laugh.

Jake hadn't even cracked a smile. Davy'd slipped out first thing, hooked up at the Subway sandwich bar in Kings Heath High Street for what you might call a working breakfast. Jake hadn't clocked him at first, walked straight past the table. Had a face like a cat's bum when he cottoned on. Told Davy it was an effing waste of time, the police weren't even close. Easy to say.

"You OK, Davy?" Gert asked.

Davy smiled; no sense upsetting the old girl. "Sure am. Just thinking 'bout making a bacon sarnie."

That brightened her up. He strolled to the fridge, pulled out lard and a pack of smoked streaky. He wished that was all he had on his mind. Jake had dumped a load of grief on him. He chewed his lip absently as he slung half a dozen rashers into the pan. It didn't seem fair. He'd done exactly what Jake wanted, delivered the goods this morning. The cop didn't even know he'd been tailing her. It was supposed to have been his last job, 'for old times' sake'.

Davy shoved his hands in his pockets, ambled to the window and gazed through the grime. His mind's eye wasn't on the garden. It was re-running the action with Jake. He couldn't believe what he'd got to do now. Jake had moved the goalposts to another pitch.

Gert's bulk was reflected in the glass. Given what Jake threatened to do to her, Davy had no option. He glanced round, shot back to the cooker; caught the bacon in the nick of time.

"I can see I'm wasting your time. I'll get out of your hair." The reporter slid her notebook into a black leather case.

Bev had recognised the face immediately. She was the looker from the news conference and she was as welcome as a cold sore. DI Shields was en route to Maude Taylor's and Bev was stuck with Lois Lane. It wasn't the woman's fault: she was engaging and impeccably polite. She wanted to pull together a series of articles on crime and the elderly, was looking to develop it into a book. Could an officer involved in the inquiry help?

"I'm sorry," Bev said. "We're really up against it at the mo." They were still in reception, not that Big Vince was complaining; Lois was easy on the eye. He was on the phone but still in full ogle mode.

"That's OK," the reporter said. "I understand. I know how busy you must be."

Up close she was even more stunning: blue-black hair halfway down her back, and eyes so green Bev almost asked if she wore lenses. She thought about the request again; it was fair enough. "Maybe later," Bev offered. "When the dust's settled?" Dummy. What journo wants a story covered in dead skin?

"That's a thought. Thanks, Sergeant Morriss." Name check. Nice touch. Bev had been so pre-occupied with the Shields thing she hadn't even registered the reporter's name. She asked for a business card. It was better than admitting a memory lapse. Italic script against expensive ivory: Grace Kane, journalist and author. There were a couple of numbers as well.

"I didn't think you'd speak to me at all. Not after that news conference." Grace was looking at the floor, her face obscured by glossy hair.

"How d'you mean?"

"I felt ashamed to call myself a journalist. The way that little man in the brown suit tore into your boss was appalling."

Bev couldn't agree more. She glanced round at the desk. Darren New was handing Vince a mug. He mouthed something but she didn't catch it.

"I read the article. It was so over the top." Grace shook her head. "How does he live with himself?"

Bev cocked an eyebrow. She was a journo, wasn't she? It was a bit pot and kettle.

Grace smiled, pushed hair behind an ear. "I can see what you're thinking. I don't blame you."

Bev narrowed her eyes: am I a cynical old tart or is this for real?

"Can I tell you something?" Grace asked. "This isn't just another job to me. I'm kind of personally involved." She hesitated, studied Bev's face before continuing. "A few years back, my grandmother was attacked. We were asleep when a man broke in. He beat her, raped her then used a pillow to smother her. It might have been better if she'd died."

What could Bev say? Her face showed her feelings.

"No one could ever tell me why. I guess I'm still trying to find out." She cleared her throat; the voice became brisker, more business-like. "These days I specialise in writing about the elderly. I've had pieces in *The Guardian*, *The Independent*, most of the quality supplements. I could let you have some of my stuff if you like."

"Call for you, Bev." She glanced round. Vince.

"I'd better let you go." Grace smiled. "Can I just say I'm not into sound bites? If we do get to talk, it'll be a series of taped interviews. I'd really like to speak to your boss as well. He struck me as a decent man. I'll leave it with you." She reached out a hand. "Thanks for your time."

Bev took the phone from Vince, rolled her eyes at his nice-girls-places-like-this remark. He sure wasn't referring to her. "Hello?" The line was dead. "Who was it, Vince?"

"Some kid. Wouldn't give a name."

She turned her mouth down. Didn't know many kids. Mind, Vince reckoned anyone under thirty was a pimply youth.

"Talking of names," Daz said. "Who was the chick you were talking to?"

Chick? Daz could be a right airhead. He still dined out on the time he was in the States and some woman mistook him for Tom Cruise.

"For your information, she's called Grace."

"Amazing."

Another eye-roll.

"Put a word in for us, Sarge."

"Scrotum?"

"Jealous?"

"Not my type."

"Come on, you pair," Vince said. "Some of us have got work to do."

Bev and Daz walked out, still sparring. Vince called her back, phone in outstretched arm. "It's about time you got a secretary."

She blew him a kiss as she took the receiver.

"Bev? It's Carol." DC Mansfield, second violinist. "Maude Taylor won't play."

The Morriss fist was in the air. "Oh?"

"DI Shields is hopping."

"Old lady give her a kicking, did she?"

"Kick her? She won't even talk to her. Shields wants you here. Like now."

The call came as a hell of a shock. They had a cancellation – could he get in? One minute Byford was at home picking

110

at a bowl of bran flakes, the next he was being prepped for tests at the General. In a way it was a relief. It was the not knowing that was hardest to bear. Given the waiting lists, he'd seriously considered private treatment. Depending on what they discovered, he still might.

"It's a routine procedure. Nothing to worry about. You should be OK to leave this afternoon."

Byford couldn't speak; his mouth was too dry. The consultant's smile grated. And how seriously could anyone take a man with red braces and Simpsons socks? But he knew his irritation stemmed from fear. No, more than fear; he felt isolated. He'd confided in no one; had no one he wanted to confide in. The cover story for work was so lame it had crutches. He hoped it wasn't tempting fate to conjure up a family emergency.

He half-listened as the consultant ran through what was involved. He winced at words like *tube* and *camera*. Truth was, he almost didn't want to know. How did Bev put it when she'd heard enough on a subject? *Too much information, mate.* Now he knew what she meant. What mattered was that once it was over he'd have a name for whatever it was that was scaring him half to death.

The consultant perched a buttock on the edge of the bed. "Thing to bear in mind, Mr Byford, is that the weight loss, the cramps, the fatigue – they can be due to a number of conditions. I'm aware of your family history but it doesn't have to mean cancer."

Byford knew that. He'd been on any number of medical websites.

"The beauty of this technique is that if everything looks good, we'll be able to tell you straight away."

Byford nodded. "And if it doesn't?"

# 10

It did not look good. Shields was in full seethe-mode, leaning against the side of an unmarked police car parked outside Maude Taylor's place in Princes Rise. The DI's arms were clamped tightly round her body, legs crossed at the ankle. The old woman was standing in the front window looking defiant. Not surprisingly, Carol Mansfield was keeping her head down in the car. Bev took it all in with a swift glance as she parked a few doors down.

"I'd stop that if I were you, Sarge," Oz cautioned.

"Oh?"

"The humming," he said. "*Who's Sorry Now*. Not subtle."

She sniffed. "True, though. Look at the face on her." She noticed the briefest tightening of his lips. It wasn't the first time he'd failed to hide his impatience.

Shields made no attempt. Bev was locking the car when the DI materialised an inch from her face. "What did you say to the old woman?"

Bev felt her colour rise, struggled to keep her hands down. "How –"

"Did you instruct her not to talk to anyone?"

Bev hesitated. She'd certainly asked Maude not to talk to the press. Could the old woman have mistaken the request?

Shields took the pause as an admission of guilt. "You told her you'd be back to continue the interview today?"

Bev nodded. There'd been no reason not to.

"For a woman with a reputation for having a mouth on her, you're not saying a lot."

"Know why?" Bev pocketed the keys and pointed Oz towards the house. "There's not a single word I can say I won't regret."

For a second she thought the DI was about to grab her arm. It was Shields's words that stopped her.

"I don't approve of my officers cherry-picking witnesses."

Cherry-picking? Bev turned. "I beg your pardon?"

"Maude Taylor's an important witness. You got at her. She won't talk to anyone else."

Bev narrowed her eyes. "Bullshit. It's you she won't talk to. You can't badmouth someone and then expect them to play ball."

Shields hesitated but not for long. "Don't foul this up, Morriss. If anything goes wrong, it'll be down to you." Bev shifted under the weight of the DI's contempt. "It's true what they say, isn't it?" The question was rhetorical. "You'll never be a team player. Though no one actually puts it quite like that."

There was an old bag in the house. Jake wasn't expecting that. He checked the address again. It was definitely the cop's place. Davy had seen her go in, even waited till she went upstairs, pulled the curtains. The old woman was looking through the nets at the front. She'd clocked him. The bus shelter was a gift; Jake made out he was reading the timetable. Nosy cow'd think twice before phoning Neighbourhood Watch or the cops. He grinned. That'd be a laugh, considering.

Next time he looked, the piss-dribbler was out of sight. Jake adjusted his shades, glad he'd worn them even though it looked as if it was going to piss down. Davy'd done good to come up with the address. Good and stupid. Following the cop home was one thing – slashing the tyre on her bike something else. It was a hell of a risk. Still. It wasn't Jake's neck on the block. He took a last drag on his spliff. Best not push his luck. He'd take a look round the back, then hit the road. The cop's granny was a real bonus. All he had to do now was work out when.

"It was the Sunday, Sergeant. Sophia should have phoned in the evening. I think I knew immediately something was wrong." There was something different about Maude Taylor. Bev was still trying to put her finger on it. She looked a bit knackered, maybe, but it wasn't just that. "It had never happened before, you see. Never. We spoke twice a day, every day."

"How did she seem the last time you spoke?" Bev asked. "That'd be the Sunday morning? Anything out of the ordinary?"

Maude shook her head vigorously; the regal meringue was unmoved. "Absolutely not. We were looking forward to spending time together, planning where'd we go, what we'd do –"

Bev paused; this was too much for an old woman. "I'm sorry, Mrs Taylor. Would you like a break?"

"No." She rapped the floor with her stick. "The man who killed her is out there. Nothing will give me greater pleasure than to see him brought to justice."

Bingo! That was it. Maude wasn't a frail old dear anymore. She was all girded loins and stiffened sinews. Or maybe yesterday had been a one-off. Maybe this was the real Maude Taylor. She'd certainly sent Shields packing. The DI was probably still picking fleas from her ear.

"This neighbour – the man who called himself Simon –" Bev began.

"Balderdash. I see that now. I should have trusted my instinct. If I'd alerted the police immediately, maybe –"

Bev pressed the old woman's hand. It was stone cold. "It wouldn't have made any difference, Mrs Taylor. Sophia was already dead by then."

They still wanted to talk to the mysterious Simon, though. Oz was out there knocking on doors, retracing Maude's steps. Tracking down a young man with a Birmingham accent. In Birmingham. Easy-peasy.

"Did you notice anything odd when you arrived?" Bev asked.

"I've thought about that a lot, Sergeant. I checked everywhere. My greatest fear was that Sophia would be lying dead in the house."

Bev nodded. She'd seen the stats: twelve thousand oldies died alone at home every year in the UK. Sad or what?

"My relief was short-lived," Maude continued. "I couldn't imagine where she'd go without this." Maude reached for an expensive-looking brown leather bag at her feet.

That was a turn-up. Bev eyes widened.

"I looked through it," Maude said. "I thought her address book might be in there. I'd have called every number if need be."

There wasn't much: a purse, a comb with a strand of white hair, a powder compact. Bev looked up. "The book's missing?"

"I can't say for sure. She used to keep a little black one by the side of the phone but it was very old: pages coming out, the cover was torn and rather tatty."

"Would she have replaced it?"

Maude looked down. "I'm not entirely sure she'd have needed to. You get to a certain age, Sergeant, and many of your friends are no longer at the end of a telephone."

Bev added a line to her notes. "Anything else out of the ordinary, Mrs Taylor?"

Maude hesitated briefly. "There was one thing: a line of vases on the windowsill in the kitchen. Sophia hates clutter. She never leaves things out like that."

Bev couldn't put it off any longer. "We found daffodils… near Sophia's body, Mrs Taylor. Could that be significant?"

Maude's fingers went to the cross round her neck. "Sophia loved flowers, Sergeant Morriss. She had green fingers. Adored gardening. As to daffodils, I don't really know."

Was there something else? The old woman appeared to have something on her mind. Bev let the silence lengthen. Then wished she hadn't.

"When you say 'near the body' what do you mean exactly, Sergeant?"

"Thought you might like a cuppa." Thank God for family liaison. Bev smiled at Jude Eastwood as she popped a tray with two mugs on the table, weak tea by the look of it. The fifty-something Jude patted Maude on the shoulder and bestowed an industrial-strength smile. "You all right, Mrs T? Can I get you a blanket or anything?"

Oh boy. Did the woman come with a volume control? Bev raised an eyebrow but Maude was studying the ceiling.

"I'll get on, then, shall I?" Jude waggled her fingers on the way out.

"She'll have to go," Maude muttered. "She's driving me mad."

Bev grinned. "I'm sure she means well."

"I'm not in the final stages of Alzheimer's, Sergeant."

"Who's the prime minister?"

Maude laughed.

The distraction worked. Bev looked at her notes. She had some of Sophia's back-story now. Seventy-six years compressed into a few lines. It didn't seem a lot.

Sophia Carrington was born in Guildford in 1930. Her father was a doctor, which probably explained her career choice. She studied medicine in London in the early fifties. Trained in Birmingham before moving back to Surrey. She'd done a stint at the Guildford Royal Infirmary, then joined a group practice as a GP. She remained single. Had no children. No siblings. Talk about being married to the job. Sounded damn lonely to Bev.

"When did Sophia retire, Mrs Taylor?"

Maude took a sip of tea, pulled a face. "It was ten years back. But she still helped out if they were short-staffed: holidays, sick leave that sort of thing." Bev wondered what was on Maude's mind. "She was a very good doctor, Sergeant. It meant everything to her. She used to say her patients were her family. I felt a little like that about the children in my classes. I wonder now whether it was worth it…" She was twisting a diamond ring on the third finger of her right hand.

"And Sophia? Would she have wondered that, too?"

Maude laughed. "I wouldn't think so. And even if she had, she wouldn't have admitted it in a million years."

You wouldn't, would you? Acknowledge the biggest part of your life had been a waste. Bev bit her lip. "Did she want to get married? Have kids?"

"She had her career, Sergeant." You can't cuddle up to that at the end of the day. "And is it entirely relevant?"

Bev smiled. "Just curious."

"Sophia made her choice. She lived with it. She was happy with it. She wouldn't thank you for your pity."

The tea was beyond tepid. Bev put the mug down. "Do

you have any pictures of her, Mrs Taylor?"

Maude smiled. "I came across whole boxes of the things last night. They're upstairs."

Bev moved to lend a hand until she saw The Look on Maude's face. Forty-odd years in the classroom had bestowed the capitals. She waited a minute, then shot out of the chair, prowled over to the bookshelves. There were hefty medical tomes and a stack of classics, impressive but not a bunch of fun. A scout round netted no games or CDs; no sewing or painting; no photographs. Apart from a couple of framed certificates, the walls were empty. It felt sparse and lonely to Bev. What must it have felt like to Sophia? Maybe that's why she spent so much time gardening, growing things. Bev rolled her eyes. *Bit simplistic, Doctor Morriss.*

Miles away, she jumped several inches when the door flew open.

"Oz! Don't do that to me."

"Why? What are you up to?"

They were both seated when Maude returned. She handed an A4 envelope to Bev. "You can hold on to them for a while if you like. I have my own copies at home."

"Thanks, Mrs Taylor. Just one more question before we go. Did Sophia have any enemies? Is there anyone you know who'd want to harm her?"

"No." The response was swift and sure. "I had a sleepless night, Sergeant. I gave it a good deal of thought. There were no aggrieved patients, no malpractice suits. Nothing like that."

At the door, Bev gave Maude numbers where she could be reached. "Thanks for your time, Mrs Taylor. We'll be in touch."

The old woman laid a hand on Bev's arm. "Everyone

liked Sophia, Sergeant Morriss. She was a doctor. She saved lives. She healed the sick. She didn't have an enemy in the world."

Bev nodded. They both knew that wasn't entirely true.

"Oz, are you gonna get married, have kids?" Bev asked.

"You what?"

"Keep your eyes on the road." They were on the way back to Highgate: another day over, another dead end. She gave it a few seconds. "Seriously. Are you?"

His smile was a little wobbly. "What's brought this on?"

"Answer the question."

"Suppose so. Most people do."

She was staring through the passenger window. A year ago, a month ago, even a day ago, she'd have said no. Cracked the old line about her maternal instincts being in line with a promiscuous cuckoo's. Now? She shook her head. Best not to think about it. "Wonder what's up with the guv."

Oz sighed. "Where did that come from? I can't keep up with you."

"I'd noticed." She tapped his arm playfully. "Joke, Genghis."

"As to the guv, no one knows a thing. I've asked round."

So had Bev. She'd have to do a bit of extra-curricular. She was desperate to find out something else as well. "Oz?" That was a definite wheedle.

Oz's response was a suspicious "Yeah?"

"You can tell me. I definitely won't hit you."

"That's a shame." He winked. "Tell you what?"

"What the others call me behind my back. Is there a new nickname?" Shields's spiteful barbs were rankling. Bev would rather know than be in the dark.

119

Oz shook his head. "Not that I've heard."

Either he was protecting her or Shields was lying through her pearly-whites. She'd not forgotten how the DI had called her Morriss during their last spat. Only one other person regularly used her surname, and that was Mike Powell. She turned her mouth down. Another thought not to pursue.

Oz hadn't dropped an earlier musing. "Are you gonna, then?" Oz said.

"What?"

"Marry me? Have my babies?"

She cocked an eyebrow. "Are you still on the medication?"

Byford was nursing a tumbler of Laphroaig. It was a large measure, and not the first. It had been a long day. And the evening could be longer. The remains of a TV dinner were congealing on a tray beside him. Even without his loss of appetite, he reckoned the packaging would be tastier than the pasta bake.

He rested his head on the back of the sofa and closed his eyes. He could still see the consultant's smile when he'd brought the news. The man probably thought he'd be grateful. To Byford's current way of thinking, it was almost the worst of all possible worlds. Almost. It was neither death sentence nor all-clear. The colonoscopy had been inconclusive. It happened. They'd had to take tissue samples as well. They'd have the analysis in a few days. Then they'd know. For sure.

The glass was empty. Byford poured a generous double. It was probably unwise, given the anti-inflammatories. But what was the point? He knew already. In his heart, he knew. He'd never missed Margaret so much. She'd have chivvied him out of this maudlin pit of self-pity.

He must have drifted off again. The doorbell woke him with a start. He rubbed his eyes. If it was anyone selling anything...

"There was a run on grapes, guv." Bev handed over the biggest bunch of bananas he'd ever seen. "The elephant's parking the motor."

He shook his head, lips twitching. "You'd best come in."

"Nice place, guv." She'd never seen it before, was pushing her luck being there. She'd had real doubts driving over. The guv's private life was a closed book with the pages stuck together.

"I'll get you a glass." He halted in the doorway. "Try not to break anything."

He'd winked. Just joking, then. She had a little wander; he hadn't said she couldn't look. The dark woods and warm reds worked well; bet he had a cleaner. Sinatra, Stones, Mahler, Madonna. Madonna? She moved on. She'd never met the guv's sons. They were even taller than their old man in the picture. The one on the right was rather tasty.

"I thought I told you not to touch." He was smiling.

"Sorry, guv. It's the detective in me."

"Clouseau?"

"I'll have the bananas back if you're not careful."

He gestured to a seat. "It's good to see you, Bev. But to what do I owe the pleasure?"

"Cheers." She took a sip. No point messing round. "I was worried about you."

The left eyebrow was going. "Worried?"

"Yeah. You never have time off. No one'd say anything. I just want to make sure you're OK."

"I'm touched." She could see that.

In for a penny. "Not doing a dry run, are you, guv?"

"You've lost me there, Bev."

"For the early retirement." There was a joke in the voice but her eyes were boring into his. "That's what the clowns at Highgate reckon."

"You're joking." No one could fake that look: pure shock.

She beamed. "I knew it was a pile of doo. You're not going anywhere, are you, guv?"

He wouldn't lie to her. "I might. I haven't decided yet. I'm amazed anyone knows I'm even considering it." He'd only hinted at it to one person, and Harry Gough was discretion itself. He pictured the scene at the morgue again, then recalled one other player: DI Shields hovering at the door.

"What is it, guv?"

"Nothing." He had no proof.

She swirled the dregs of the malt. "You can tell me to back off, guv, but is it a health thing?" She couldn't think of any other reason why he'd throw it all in, and it could explain why he looked so knackered. The pause was so long, she doubted he'd come out with the truth, certainly not the whole truth.

"I'm having tests, Bev."

Shit. Must be serious.

"It's nothing serious." The smile didn't convince her.

"When will you know?"

"A few days." The shrug didn't, either.

"Look, guv, if you want to talk about it –"

He wanted to confide in her. But he couldn't. Not yet. "Thanks. I might just do that."

"Any time, guv."

"Bev. Keep it to yourself, right?"

"You don't need to ask."

Howls of laughter from next-door's telly broke the silence.

"Come on." Byford wasn't good at enforced joviality. "Let's have another."

"Just a small one, ta, guv." She had to be on her way soon. She'd leave the MG at home and call a cab. It didn't take long to fill him in on the latest. After the discovery in the shed they were re-interviewing all the allotment holders; the immediate area was now plastered with police posters appealing for information; they were still hauling in local likely lads for questioning and they were following up a load of info from Maude Taylor. It was solid plod-work. Essential but dull.

"It's all well and good. Bev, but we're no nearer a collar. Tell you what worries me?"

It was bugging the hell out of her as well. "Another attack?"

"Exactly."

And if there was another victim, pray to God the villain got careless.


There couldn't be any cock-ups. Not this time. No one had seen him and no one was watching. He was dead certain of that. He was all in black, just another dark shadow. For the umpteenth time he checked his pocket. The mask would go on last, just as he went in. It was all in the timing. He had to get that right. He couldn't believe it was only six minutes since he'd looked. He broke off a couple of squares of dark chocolate, counted the seconds as they slowly melted in his mouth. How long now?

The soft glow of his watch showed 10.37.

# 11

"The night is young and lovely. Like the senorita."

Luigi's moustache-twirl was a figment of Bev's imagination. The elderly waiter was no Lothario. He had the build of a jockey and a face that took in squatters.

"You're an old smoothie, Luigi. And I still don't want the tiramisu." The dress was tight enough as it was.

"I know." A gold filling flashed in his smile. "The little lady's sweet already."

She rolled her eyes. Luigi left with an order for coffee. Tom Marlow leaned conspiratorially across the table and beckoned her forward, asked in all seriousness, "Do you come here often?"

"Never set foot in the place in my life."

Their laughter turned heads at the next table. It had been like that all evening, starting with a couple of glasses of Pinot in a bar off New Street. It rarely happened that she clicked so easily with a guy, certainly not a potential witness. But Tom was more than just a pretty face. It might have been her suggestion they move on to San Carlo's. The restaurant was only across the road and though it was packed, Luigi could always find a table for Bev. Apart from needing to soak up the alcohol, it meant more time with a man she wanted to know better.

The half-smile was incredibly sexy. He was interested in her as a woman, didn't continually take the piss or treat her like one of the lads. He was attentive and amusing. And he laughed at her jokes.

"Luigi's in love with you, you know that?" he asked.

"He's my sugar daddy. Didn't I tell you?"

He studied her face, took his time. "You're very good with people, Bev. They like you, trust you. I wish I had that gift."

"When's your birthday?"

He smiled again. "Will you excuse me one moment?"

She watched him head towards the gents, noticed a few female heads turn as he strode past. The white T-shirt under the black Armani made him look a bit like a trendy vicar. Thank God she'd made an effort. Not socialite, perhaps, but definitely not social worker. She knew it wasn't going anywhere but was grateful for the distraction. She was worried sick about the guv; the Shields thing was getting to her; her domestic set-up was driving her doo-lally. Tonight had been the first in a while she'd really enjoyed.

She smiled as Luigi served coffee, then left her to her thoughts. She had to admit the first couple of minutes in the bar had been a tad awkward. Then Tom confessed he hadn't a thing to add to the inquiry; he'd used it as an excuse to ask her out. He'd understand if she wanted him to leave. She didn't. He was a twenty-six-year-old property developer who played piano and loved to ski, though not necessarily at the same time. The more she learned, the keener she was to find out more.

He was in the house. How did he get in? She'd checked every door, every window, twice, three times. But he was in the hallway, just standing there, listening. Surely he could hear her heart? It was beating, thrashing against her ribs. She had a sudden terrifying thought. Supposing he wasn't alone? She strained to hear anything over the pulse in her ears. What if she collapsed? She put a hand to her chest. No. She wouldn't make it easy. What was that? Oh God. He was on the stairs. Was he one of the men terrorising old women? She'd seen their faces on the news. Knew the terrible things they'd done. What was he going to do? What did he want? Would he kill her? Was it possible to die of fright?

"Do you ever get scared?" Marlow said.

How many times had Bev been asked that? Most people envisaged policing as wall-to-wall murder and mayhem, ignored the fact that it was mainly plodding and slogging followed by rainforests of paperwork. It had its moments, sure, when a life could be on the line, but they were a blue-moon event. Usually she deflected further queries but there was something in Marlow's voice.

"You can't afford to get scared," she said. "After, maybe." When it sinks in and the flashbacks start and the night-mares continue.

He nodded. "It's a hell of a job –"

"For a woman?" The smile didn't disguise the challenge in her eyes.

"I didn't mean that. I just wondered what attracted you."

"I fancied the uniform."

He raised a hand. "You don't like talking about it. Sorry. Let's change the subject."

It was too late. The scene was in her head again. The police tape cordoning off the back of the sports hall at her comprehensive school, a classmate in a body bag. The lead detective had gently coaxed a fifteen-year-old Bev through several interview sessions. She'd been closer to Donna than the other girls and he needed her help, he said. She'd forgotten his name now but he'd been kind and calm and he'd made her feel she was doing something for Donna. The killer was caught within days, a paedophile released early on licence.

Bev was stirring the espresso though she hadn't added sugar. "I guess I feel I can make a difference."

Tom cocked his head slightly.

"Most people live by the rules, yeah?" she said. "They may not like them, they may not want to, but they do. They're pretty decent. They play the game. Then there are others who don't give a flying fart. They see something they want? They take it. They see something they don't like? They destroy it. Have you any idea how shit it is to tell a mother her daughter's never coming home again, or a wife that her husband's on life support because some smack-head's beaten him to a pulp?"

She glanced round, aware that Tom wasn't the only listener, and lowered her voice. "Sorry. I get fired up. I hate the bastards who make other people's lives a misery. The more we put away the better."

He nodded slowly. "Don't apologise. I can see how much it means to you."

She could count on the fingers of one finger how many people she'd shared that with. "Yeah, well."

"No, really. You have passion, commitment. You must be really good at what you do."

She was about to answer but noticed him glance at his watch. Slightly miffed, she pre-empted him. "We'd best get the bill."

"Only checking if there's time for more coffee before they throw us out."

That half-smile was a killer. "Sure," she nodded. "That'd be good."

She watched as he beckoned Luigi, wondered what she'd say if he asked her back to his place, wondered how good that would be. Not that she would, of course. Not with Oz in the picture. She couldn't. Could she?

The call on her mobile pushed all speculation out of her head. It took a few seconds before she recognised the voice. The message was instantly clear. There'd been another attack.

# 12

"There'll be a lot of bruising but I don't think I broke anything." Maude Taylor paused and added a rueful, "More's the pity."

Bev shook her head. The way things were going, the old woman was lucky not to have inflicted more damage. She'd probably have ended up in court on an assault charge. At the moment she was in the spare bedroom, propped up by several pillows. She'd been in bits until Bev dispensed a nightcap large enough to sedate a safari park. SOCOs, complete with goody bags, were just about ready to leave. Bev was still trying to get her head round the details.

"Where do you think you hit him, Mrs Taylor?"

"Difficult to say, dear. It was rather dark." The hint of satisfaction in the old woman's voice suggested the double Armagnac had kicked in.

"He'll have a sore head, that's for sure." They'd found a clump of short dark hairs inside the attacker's mask. So it didn't look as if this episode was down to blondie. Baby Face must've been tucked up in bed or having a night off. Just as well. Maude's sedation could have been terminal if there'd been two assailants.

"It's such a shame I didn't see his face. As soon as I grabbed the mask, he ran like the wind."

Shame was an understatement. They had a shedload of E-fits but none of them did. They needed finer detail. They were chasing shadows, trying to catch smoke. They hadn't even established how many were in the gang. Three? Maybe four? There was Iris and Joan's Baby Face,

Marty Skelton's Tall Dark Dog-loather and Tom Marlow's Pale Youth With Studs. That's assuming they were connected in the first place. And that they'd graduated to murder. Bev blew out her cheeks.

"Are you all right, dear?" Maude asked.

"Me? I'm fine." Miles away but fine. "What about you? You were very brave to go for him like that." *And stupid.*

"I was very stupid, as you well know." Maude laid a hand on her chest. "There was a moment or two, dear, when I thought I'd die of fright. Then I thought of what he'd done to Sophia. I was absolutely furious. I just hit out. The awful thing is –" she couldn't meet Bev's eyes – "I wanted to hurt him. I really wanted to hurt him."

Bev took the old lady's hand; it was the only way to stop the tremor. "We don't know for sure it's the same man, Mrs Taylor." Not that there was much doubt. The crime scene guys reckoned whoever it was had a key. Sophia Carrington's house keys were missing.

"I don't believe in coincidences," Maude said.

Neither did Bev. Hopefully the lab might come up with a few conclusions. "And you're sure nothing was taken?"

"I'm not sure of anything, to be honest." She was shivering now, delayed shock. Bev pulled up the duvet, tucked it in closer.

"Try and get some sleep. We'll talk again in the morning."

"Thank you for getting here, dear. You weren't in bed, were you?"

Close. Bev smiled, shook her head. Tom had been all concern, even offered a lift to Kings Heath. She'd made a joke about not mixing business with pleasure. She hadn't been sure what to make of his parting remark. She'd mulled it over in the cab. A man saying he'd 'better get used to this sort of thing' made assumptions which both tickled her pink and pissed her off.

"You'd been so kind and I desperately needed to see a familiar face."

Bev wagged a finger, softened the admonition with a wry smile. "You'd have had one if you hadn't sent Jude packing." The family liaison officer had become too familiar; Maude had told her to piss off, though not in so many words.

"You're right," the old woman managed a weak smile. "At least I didn't hit her with my stick."

Bev shook her head. "Mrs. T. What are you like?"

She shuddered. "Anything but that, Sergeant. You'd better start calling me Maude."

"Maude it is." Bev got to her feet. "I'll be off. And don't worry. As well as the uniformed officer at the door, there'll be patrols 24/7."

"Thank you, dear."

Bev was halfway down the stairs when the old woman called her back. She found Maude sitting up in bed, clutching the duvet to her neck. "You think he'll try again, don't you?"

If he hadn't found what he wanted, an old woman, even a feisty old woman with a stout stick, wouldn't deter him. Bev crossed her fingers behind her back. "He'd have to be mad to do that, wouldn't he?"

"The old bag went for me. She's fucking crazy." Davy was in a phone box round the corner from his home. It stank of vomit and piss and sweat, some of it his.

"Did you get the stuff?"

"You're not listening, Jake. I told you: she attacked me. She was lying in wait with a knife."

"She cut you?" Could be handy. Jake waited. The pause

131

was too long.

"No. I knocked it out of her hand."

"Liar."

"I'm not. I got whacked." Davy hated the whine in his voice.

"Christ, man. She's not in the fuckin' SAS. Get a grip."

"Fuck you. I'm going home." He didn't care anymore. He'd nearly pissed himself on that landing and his arms now had matching bruises. He braced himself for a load of verbal abuse but this time Jake's voice was soft and low.

"Sorry, Davy. Was that one or two?"

That was better. The old Jake was back. Davy breathed a sigh of relief. Lately he'd begun to feel he didn't know Jake any more. Or like him. "One or two what, Jake?"

"Apologies."

"Sorry?"

"You fucking will be if you don't get your arse round there and get what I want."

"I can't." He didn't know which was worse: the threats or the silence. "Jake?"

"I'm waiting."

"I can't go back." He wasn't going to tell Jake but he'd have to now. "The old cow saw my face. She grabbed the mask."

"She still got it?" Even better.

"Yeah."

"That's OK. Makes it easier."

"What for?"

"For you to go back."

Thank God there was a phone line between them. "I'm not going back, Jake."

"You will, Davy. You'll do anything I tell you. Or the old girl'll get it."

132

Davy pictured his gran back at home. Last time he'd seen her she'd been ploughing her way through a family pack of liquorice allsorts, reading another romance. Jake was right. He had no choice.

# 13

"What time did you get in last night?"

Bev almost choked on her cinammon toast. "I beg your pardon?"

Emmy Morriss licked a finger and turned a page of her tabloid, instantly taken with: *I stole my sister's husband. Why does she hate me?*

"I didn't hear you come home. I was worried."

Bev exchanged an eye-roll with her gran. Sadie's was quite scary, given the magnification from today's lime-green glasses. "I'm a big girl now, mum."

A drawled 'yes' meant Emmy wasn't listening properly.

Bev glanced at the headline. "Good, is it?"

Her mum blew a smattering of crumbs off the paper. "It helps the job." She did two days a week in Kings Heath library.

"Oh yeah?" Bev said. "How does that work?"

"Articles like this are about people, aren't they? What makes them tick."

"Sick, perhaps." Bev winked at Sadie but her gran had her head down in the book club's latest read. Bev screwed her eyes, tried to make out the title upside-down. *Beneath the Skin.* Sounded more top-shelf than middlebrow.

"That's not nice, dear," Emmy protested. "Lots of our callers are sick. Some are suicidal."

Shoot. She'd forgotten the Samaritans' stuff. "Sorry, mum. How's that going these days?"

Emmy put in a couple of nights a month, sometimes more. Bev reckoned she might as well stay home if all she needed was a bunch of problems to sort. Her mum laid the paper down and lowered her voice. "Well, obviously, I can't go into details –"

"Good," Sadie interjected without looking up. "Any chance of a boiled egg?"

Bev grinned. The old girl got away with murder. Bev'd miss her when she finally found another place to live. Not that a move was exactly imminent; it wasn't even vaguely imminent, though there were a couple of properties to view today.

"I'll eat out tonight, mum. Don't save me anything."

Emmy sniffed, turned a page. "I wasn't going to."

The smell hit Bev as soon as she entered the swing doors. Highgate reception looked like a branch of Interflora. A bouquet of red roses, all cellophane and scarlet ribbons, very nearly obscured Vince Hanlon. No mean feat, given the Sergeant's bulk.

"What's all this, Vincie?" Bev asked. "You trying to get round me?"

"Not me, mate." He beckoned her forward, handed over a small envelope. Her name had never looked so good: perfect copperplate. Vince had a Masters in deciphering the written word upside-down. She stepped back to a point where X-ray vision wouldn't have had a chance.

*Luigi sends his love,* she read. *As well.*

"You should smile like that more often," Vince said. "Better than a face-lift, that is."

She raised an eyebrow but gave him the benefit of the doubt.

"Who's madam's secret admirer, then? Anyone we know?"

Bev frowned. He certainly wouldn't be the only one asking. "Vince? Do us a favour?"

Too late. "Morning, Khanie." Vince smirked, held the

flowers aloft. "What do you think?"

Oz glanced at Bev, then the bouquet, then back at Vince. Ordinarily she loved that uncertain smile of his.

"Bev won't tell me," Vince teased.

She pursed her lips. Go on, big man: drop me in it.

"Tell you what?" Oz asked, not taking his eyes off Bev.

"Whether I should get the missus some chocolates as well. It's her birthday. Twenty-one again."

Oz's smile was slow in coming. "I'm sure she's sweet enough, Sarge."

"Best crack on," Bev muttered. Oz was already so far ahead she had to run to catch up. When she glanced back, Vince was adding big strokes to an imaginary slate.

The Morriss desk usually resembled a snow globe with paper-flakes everywhere. For once there was just one message. Angela Collins had called. Iris was being buried at Hodge Hill cemetery on Monday. Bev made a note of the time. There'd be a discreet police presence but she'd go along anyway. Paying her respects was the least she could do.

She grabbed a machine coffee en route to the briefing. The room was chocka, though the buzz had nothing to do with the case.

"Hey, Sarge, heard the latest?" Darren New patted the chair next to him. Oz was perched on the windowsill.

"Heard what?" She tugged at the hem of her skirt. It was a bit short for work but the blue linen matched her eyes.

"It's the disciplinary today."

No need to ask whose. Everyone in Highgate had a take on Mike Powell's future in the force. Bev's had shifted slightly in recent days. It was edging towards Better the devil you know, but that was probably down to the woman who'd just walked in.

"Right, listen up." DI Shields stood, arms folded, centre stage. Audrey Hepburn meets Posh Spice. Bev curled a lip. "A stupid mistake was made yesterday which could have cost an old woman her life." The DI let that little bombshell sink, then lobbed another. "If things had been handled professionally, the case might have been cracked. Instead, we're back to square one."

Bev kept her mouth clamped. The squad would have read her report on the incident last night at Maude Taylor's place, so everyone knew where Shields was coming from even if she wasn't naming names.

"Sergeant Morriss. Perhaps you'd like to explain why a vulnerable old woman was allowed to remain without protection in the house of a murder victim?"

Load the question, why don't you? It would never have been asked if Shields had spent any real time with Maude. Bev didn't know how the old woman would be affected by last night, but prior to the break-in she'd had a mind of her own and wasn't afraid to shout it. Despite all Bev's entreaties, she'd refused point blank to stay elsewhere. Bev had compromised as best she could.

When she eventually spoke, Bev's voice was calm and measured. "Precautions were in place." Apart from family liaison, she'd requested local patrols both foot and motor. With hindsight, it wasn't enough.

"Brilliant," Shields said. "So how come an assailant lets himself in with a key?"

"Well, pardon me if my crystal ball's broken."

Shields flapped at the words with a dismissive hand. "Apart from the fact Maude Taylor was lucky to escape with her life, we could have been waiting for him and made an arrest."

Bev was on her feet. "And that's down to me?"

"Enough." How long had Byford been in the room? A dozen heads turned as the guv made his way to the front. Bev was shocked at how haggard he looked. "You're not the only one who should have seen the possibility, Bev. We're supposed to work as a team. The priority now is to make sure no one misses anything else."

He took a seat as Bev resumed hers. Shields, after a nod from Byford, assigned tasks, then asked for input. Bev wanted to see Maude Taylor first thing. A good night's rest might have loosened memories.

"I'll be coming with you," Shields said.

*I'd rather eat sick.* "That'll be nice."

At least the bloody woman used her own wheels. Imagine twenty minutes of small talk with Danny Shields: mission statements and monthly targets. Bev glanced in the driving mirror. Shields was just pulling up behind.

"Your brake light's not working," Shields said.

Bev locked the MG, hoisted her bag.

The DI was waiting. "Let's get this clear. I'm here in a supervisory capacity. I'll take a back seat to observe your technique. And it had better be good."

Bev bit a lip to mask a cynical smile. That was bullshit. The DI was only here so she didn't lose face with the squad. Shields knew she'd be as welcome inside as bird flu.

A uniform was posted outside. It transpired he wasn't the old lady's only company.

"Come in, Sergeant. We're having tea." Maude's invitation didn't include Shields explicitly, but at least she wasn't banned from entering.

"Did you sleep OK, Mrs Taylor?" She certainly sounded perkier.

"Come through, dear. I slept well, considering, and I thought I told you to call me Maude."

Bev was expecting to see Jude Eastwood from family liaison. Instead, Grace Kane looked up from her tape recorder on a low table, Mont Blanc in hand, Hobnob crumbs on her classy ivory blouse.

"Sergeant Morriss. Hello. I didn't expect to see you here."

"Snap."

"Mrs Taylor has kindly offered to help with my series."

"You're a reporter?" Shields's tone suggested the profession was on a par with serial killing.

Maude waved vaguely at a couple of chairs. "She's more of an author, aren't you, Grace? I've been helping with a little research."

Old photographs and letters littered the table and floor. Sophia at various ages was in most of the shots. Bev picked one up, gently fingered its edges. "What exactly are you hoping to learn here, Ms Kane?" She kept her tone casual but the antennae were twitching.

"Background, attitudes, how society treats the elderly, that sort of thing," the reporter offered.

"I thought you were mainly interested in violence against old people."

"That's right." Grace switched off the recorder and capped her pen. "Look, I can see I'm in the way. You need to talk to Mrs Taylor. I've got more than enough for now."

The jade suit was Joseph. Bev followed it through to the hall. "Grace. Perhaps you could let me have a look at some of your stuff? It'll be useful for when we get together."

"We can? That would be so cool. I'll get it in the post later today. Thank you so much."

The girl spoke as if she were in a teen movie. Made Bev

feel quite old.

Maude appeared to have thawed towards Shields; they were chatting about the weather when Bev got back.

"Pleasant girl, isn't she?" Maude's fingers were toying with Grace's business card. Its twin was in the jacket Bev wore yesterday. "Very professional," Maude added. "Awfully thoughtful as well. When I mentioned last night, she got really upset. Asked if there was anything she could do to help."

"Did you talk much about Sophia?" Bev asked.

"A little."

They stayed for half an hour or so. Maude wasn't able to add much to her previous account. She'd had a look around and was pretty sure nothing was gone. Her feeling was that the intruder had only just broken in before he felt the business end of her stick.

"Any idea why he was here? What he was after?" Bev asked.

Maude picked at the skin of her hand. "I've thought about that, but I don't have any idea. All Sophia's money is invested. She had no jewellery to speak of."

"All Sophia's money," Bev echoed. "Is her estate large?"

"Substantial, rather than large, Sergeant. Around £600,000, I'd say."

Bev exchanged glances with Shields. "Do you know who stands to inherit?"

"There are bequests to various medical charities." Maude Taylor's voice suggested more.

"And?" Bev prompted.

"The bulk of it will come to me."

"We'll check it out, natch," said Bev. "But somehow I can't see Maude in the role of killer granny."

Oz nibbled on a curly fry. "How about the DI?"

Bev snorted. "Neither use nor ornament. Barely opened her mouth."

They were in the Kozy Caff surrounded by blue rinses and beige crimplene. The board on the far wall said *Friday special – half-price pensioners.* Tasty.

"That's not what I asked."

Bev sneaked a glance at Oz. Was he being iffy? He didn't share her antipathy towards the DI but it was a fact: the woman's attitude hadn't helped. Interviewing was all about connecting and empathising. Bev knew she was damn good at it. In Shields's presence, Maude had appeared inhibited if not downright intimidated. There'd been a couple of times Bev felt the old woman might have been holding back. Oz was still waiting for an answer.

"Cash is a motive as often as not. Shields ordered the check." And questioned Bev on why she hadn't extracted the information earlier. She took one of Oz's chips, regretted going for the cheese salad. "Like as if I wouldn't."

As every cop knew, good liars practised a lot. And the most plausible practised the most.

Oz took a sip of coke. "Nice time last night?"

Where did that come from? She went for another chip, her other fingers crossed. "Frankie was on top form. How about you?"

"Interesting. I bumped into a friend."

"Talking about bumping into people. That reporter? Grace Kane? She was at Taylor's place, sniffing round."

Her hand reached for another fry. Oz sighed and swapped plates.

"So? That's what reporters do."

She wondered whether to share her thoughts. According to Grace, the man who'd raped and beaten her grandmother was still at large. Was there an unwritten agenda in there as well? She'd run a check, maybe mention it then.

"Don't talk to Danny Girl about journos," Bev said. "She went ape-shit when we left. Asked who else I'd tipped off. Implied I was on the take." She glanced round. There were no ashtrays. Shit. "I'm gonna have to do something about it, Oz."

"What? Danny Shields or your smoking?"

Bev was stowing the roses in the boot of her motor. She'd already recorded her thanks on Tom Marlow's answer phone, and paid off Vince with the promise of a pint or six at the Prince.

A hand tapped her back, a tad too close to the butt. She whirled, eyes flashing, and barely recognised Mike Powell at first. The hair was longer and blonder. But it wasn't that. He was smiling. At her.

"Hello, stranger." Made a change from a peremptory *Morriss.*

"How're you doing?" she asked

Staying at home, suspended on full pay, seemed to be working wonders. Had he had his teeth whitened? And he hadn't bought the suit in a charity shop.

"I'm good," he said. "Yourself?"

"Can't complain."

"Makes a change." He raised a hand. "Joke."

"What time's the disciplinary?" That wiped the smile off his face. For maybe a second she felt sorry for him. Almost. He fell into step as she headed for Highgate's main entrance.

"I see the guv's having a hard time," Powell said.

"It's mainly the *News.* Matt Snow. He's a shit-sack. You know that as well as me." Having said that, they'd left

142

Byford alone for a couple of days. The paper had been going big on a paedo judge scandal.

"Will he go?" Powell asked.

The snort was one of her best. "'Course not. It'll take more than a media mauling to get rid of the guv."

"Not just that, though, is it?" He lowered his voice. "A little bird tells me he's toying with the idea of an early out."

"That little bird?" said Bev. "Shoot it."

He shrugged, apparently indifferent. "The disciplinary's three o'clock, by the way. And it's just a formality."

They were at the swing doors. "Shame," she said. "You'd think they'd at least let you put your case."

"Still a lippy tart, I see."

She opened a door and stood back. "After you, Mike."

The welcoming committee wasn't exactly out in force. Just one friendly face waited to greet him. Bev watched as Powell strode over. "Danny. How're you doing?"


*"Danny! How're you doing?"*

The impersonation was pants but no one was listening. The rest of the squad was either on the knock or touring the streets with E-fits and clipboards. The CID office was empty, bar a cheese plant and a picture of the Queen touching gloves with the Chief Constable. Bev slung her bag on the floor and slumped into a chair. Powell and Shields. What a thought. Just how far back did that go? She closed her eyes, took a few deep breaths. There was no point jumping to conclusions. She sat up and put the odd couple on the back burner. There was work to do.

By the time she'd finished it was gone six. A rare weekend off beckoned but she was loath to leave. She sat back, surveying the screen, her notes and a stack of files. She'd spent nearly five hours going through five days' worth of reports and witness statements.

She ran her hands through her hair, leaving it even more mussed. The case wasn't at a crossroads, it was in a cul de sac. No one they'd interviewed knew anything about the attacks, let alone the murder of Sophia Carrington. They needed conclusive evidence, connections. The diagram she'd worked on hadn't helped. Sophia's name was dead centre, but the links were tenuous: victims' ages, areas they lived, stuff nicked, that was about it. There had to be something else, surely? She screwed up the paper, slung it in the bin; it missed.

"And on that note –" she muttered.

The phone rang as she was on her way out.

"Sarge." It was Oz. "I popped into the Goddard place on the off-chance. Guess what?"

It looked as if the daffodil theory had legs. Way Oz told it, he'd finally found Joan Goddard in; she'd been at her son's in Bath for a fortnight. She'd come across the daffodils in the kitchen sink the day she was released from hospital and assumed a friend or neighbour had left them. Under Oz's gentle questioning, she realised she'd never given anyone a spare key.

The daffodils had long since been thrown out. But a link, however tenuous, remained. It might be a tad premature to crack the Moet, but… She hit a button on her mobile. "Frankie, my friend. What you up to tonight?"

A couple of hours later, Bev and Frankie were ensconced in a Moseley wine bar. With chunky leather seating and fuck-the-diet food, it would be Bev's local if her offer on the Victorian terrace in Baldwin Street was accepted. A good cause for celebration.

And Frankie was another. A night out with her was

better than a week in Rome. Frankie was human Prozac, happy pills on legs. Bev relaxed just listening to her. Frankie's Italian accent was a moveable feast. She laid it on shamelessly for her own ends, and right now she was using a JCB. She'd come up with a solution to the Danny Shields scenario: the final curtain.

"I'm-a gonna send-a the boys round, Bev." She laughed, tossing back a cloud of blue-black hair that Rossetti would have died for. Bev had tried the tossing-hair thing once; she'd ended up in a neck brace.

"What about a horse's head on her pillow?" Bev put in hopefully.

Frankie flapped a hand. "That is so last week."

They laughed, but Bev caught the concern darkening her best friend's eyes. She'd listened to Bev's blow-by-blow account of the confrontations with the DI, the mounting hostility, the constant undermining of Bev's work. Frankie had made all the right noises but, like Bev, couldn't come up with a reason for the woman's arsiness. She tended to suspect Shields was insecure; aware, perhaps, her body was in better shape than her brain.

"Professional jealousy, Bev. No one can accuse you of using female charms to open doors."

"Frankie!"

"You know what I mean," she winked, and grabbed their empty glasses.

Bev watched as Frankie sashayed to the bar, all thigh and cleavage. Christ, the girl turned more heads than an osteopath. Unlike Shields, she had a sweet nature to go with it. Maybe Bev would take Frankie's advice: be *so* nice to the bloody woman she might change her shitty tune.

Bev's mobile beeped a message. It wasn't a number she recognised, but a puzzled frown gave way to a cat-like smile when she read the text: miss u sergeant morriss! when can i see you again? Tom x

Of course she had to tell Frankie: she wanted the full works. They swapped man stories till it was time to hit the road. Frankie was shrugging into a full-length red leather trench coat when she mentioned she'd bumped into Oz in Blockbusters.

"Oh?" Bev's radar was on alert. "When was that, Frankie?"

"Last night. Didn't he mention it? I asked him to give you my love."

Last night. And she'd told Oz she'd been out on the town with Frankie.

It was dark when he arrived. The gates were locked. Not that it mattered. He made sure he wasn't being watched, then shinned over the wall. He knew the way with his eyes closed. No one had been since his last visit. He removed the old stems and wrapped them in paper. He'd bought a bottle of water for the fresh flowers.

The golden petals appeared a dull grey in the blackness of the night.

# 14

Monday, one week since Sophia Carrington's murder, the early brief at Highgate.

"Why leave daffodils at the crime scenes?"

It was the guv's question but Bev had been asking herself the same thing. She'd kept tabs on the inquiry over the weekend via calls to the incident room. Not difficult, nothing had shifted.

"Could it be a ruse? To throw us off the scent?" Bev asked.

Byford sighed. "Are you trying to be funny?"

A Morriss-glare silenced a couple of sniggers. "I mean it, guv. There may be no significance. Just toe-rags trying to be smart-arses. You know, let's take the piss out of Mr Plod."

It was the only conclusion she'd drawn, in between viewing houses and catching up on chores, not to mention a Thai takeaway and a Jude Law DVD. Oz had been playing it cool. So cool he hadn't even phoned. Unlike Tom Marlow, who'd called last night. They'd hooked up for a quick drink. She didn't know if it was going anywhere but it was fun finding out.

"As cunning plans go," Byford said, "it's working."

She smiled. At least the old boy still had a sense of humour. She wondered if he'd heard back from the hospital.

"Either way, where does it get us?" DI Shields's low profile was lifting. She sauntered over to the murder board. "We're no further forward."

"It strengthens the connection," Bev protested. "It's

almost certain the attacks are down to the same gang."

"Is it? I don't see it. We know flowers were found at the homes of two victims. We have no way of knowing who left them. And even if it is some sort of macabre calling card, I don't see any signatures. We're no nearer a name, let alone an arrest, than we were this time last week."

Bev barely heard the phone. DC Carol Mansfield picked up on the second ring. A nod and a note and she replaced the receiver. "I reckon we are now."

Bev wasn't in on the interview but a two-way mirror and covered speakers provided a ringside seat. The guv and Shields were in action but the star had yet to perform.

Fat Boy was one of two yobs hauled in by uniform after a stake-out at a condemned high rise in Edgbaston. They'd been spotted sneaking in. According to the tip-off that prompted the stake-out, the place was a death trap and the stupid buggers were risking their necks.

Officers Flavell and Dilger had turned up expecting nothing worse than a bit of verbal. Two hours and full back-up later, Flavell was in A and E receiving treatment for knife wounds and one of the ugliest kids Bev had ever seen was lolling on an orange plastic chair in Interview One. Think Shrek with acne. His equally aesthetically challenged squatmate was posing in similar fashion next door.

It wasn't threatening looks that had got them banged up. Apart from assaulting a police officer, one of the youths had lit what the response unit imagined was a diversionary fire in a room on the ground floor. Among the ashes, officers had found two wedding rings and a charred scrap of paper with a couple of numbers printed on it. All that was left of a pension book.

"A name would be good," Shields said. It was the sixth time she'd asked. Bev didn't envy the DI. A silent suspect was the hardest to crack. Shields and the guv had been at it for more than an hour. Bev and DC Darren New had fared equally badly with Shrek 2. No one had come up with so much as an initial. Bev squinted at the DI's pad. It had the date in the top right-hand corner. That was it. Shields slowly circled the room, then whacked the table with the flat of her hand. Water sloshed over the side of a glass and a tinfoil ashtray full of butts bounced. The youth didn't bat an eyelash. Bev was equally unmoved. No percentage in losing control.

"It'll be easier if you talk to us, son." The guv leaned a little closer.

The youth ran a slobbery tongue round tombstone teeth and spat in Byford's eye.

By the middle of the afternoon, Ena Bolton and Joan Goddard had identified the rings. The pension book was a no-no, not enough numbers to establish ownership. Thank God pension books were being phased out. Paydays at the post office were an open invitation to light-fingered low-lifes, old dears turned into walking cash dispensers. Not that the Shrek boys were putting their hands up to anything. Neither youth had opened his mouth except to gob or stick in an Embassy Regal.

But as soon as the dabs match came through, criminal records came up good. Or bad, depending how you looked at it. Robert Carl Lewis and Kevin Joseph Fraser had spent more time in court than a magistrates' bench. It was minor stuff: shoplifting, taking without consent, criminal damage. Only tender years and soft beaks had spared them a custodial. They'd just turned eighteen.

"Illegal entry, assaulting a police officer, receiving stolen goods." Shields was pacing the floor "And that's for starters."

Murder and GBH could be the main course. "We've haven't tied them into the attacks yet," Bev said.

"We will. It's only a question of time. They'll crack."

Bev had serious doubts about that. According to records, the youths were borderline special needs. Somehow she couldn't see either of them having the brain cells to run a bath, let alone orchestrate the events of the last few weeks. They might have netted a couple of small fry – there was still a Big White out there. Maybe two.

Davy Roberts's teeth were chattering, his entire body trembling. It was not-so-happy hour in a grotty pub off the Bristol Road in Selly Oak. Jake was getting a round in. How the hell could he stay so cool? Jake had sent Davy a text saying they needed to meet; he had some news. He'd left the paper on the table so Davy could take a closer look. Davy still couldn't believe it.

*Two youths are being questioned by police in connection with the series of attacks on elderly women in the city over the last four weeks…* It was a couple of lines in the stop press. They'd have the full works later.

"Cheers, mate." Jake smiled. "You look as if you need this."

Davy gulped most of the pint, then wiped his mouth with his sleeve.

"How'd the cops get on to them?"

Jake shrugged, checked his hair in the mottled mirror over the bar. He'd certainly got the hang of the spikes now.

"For Christ's sake," Davy hissed. "Kev and Robbie are banged up. It's only a question of time…" He couldn't keep his legs still. A couple of birds at the next table were giving him funny looks. Jake put a hand on the youth's knee.

"Chill, Davy."

Davy put his head in his hands. Yesterday he'd been all ready to tell Jake to take a running jump. Now he needed him like there was no tomorrow.

"Kev and Robbie aren't going to say anything. What's to say?" Jake lobbed a peanut into the air, caught it in his mouth and grinned.

Davy was open-mouthed as well. He watched as Jake did the peanut thing again. Jake offered him the packet but he swatted it away. "You don't get it, do you? The Bill could walk in here any minute."

"Nah." Jake gave a loud belch. "They drink in the Prince."

Davy groaned. It was all right for Jake. He didn't have anyone to look out for.

Jake put his arm round the younger boy's shoulder. "No worries, Davy. Relax. It's just you and me now."

The church wasn't full, not even close. Bev slipped in at the back. She hated funerals, seen too many. Every one brought back her dad's. Given the cancer, most of the family reckoned the end was a relief: no more pain. She closed her eyes; oh yeah?

She sat back and glanced round, breathed the sickly scent of lilies and lavender, caught the faintest whiff of something less fragrant. The ageing congregation was in monochrome: black clothes, grey hair, white faces. Bev doubted there was anyone in the place under seventy, except Iris's daughter. Creaking voices struggled with high notes, then the vicar recalled highlights of Iris Collins's long life. She didn't do a bad job, considering. Iris had never worked outside the home, never travelled abroad, never moved from the house where she'd been born.

That wasn't quite true. Bev put a finger to her eye, surprised at the sudden emotion. It didn't seem right that an old woman who'd spent her entire life under her own roof had died under someone else's, forced out by a gang of fuckwits.

The social reports on Kevin Fraser and Robert Lewis had been emailed to her at Highgate. They were templates for social misfits: both were from broken homes, both had been abused in care and if there were marks for truancy, they'd have been awarded joint firsts. Apart from drugs and booze, the only constant in their lives was each other. The youths had formed a strong bond, even making out they were brothers. They'd been out of care for a couple of years. Oz was back at Highgate trying to fill the blanks.

Bev bowed her head as the coffin was borne past. Angela Collins followed close behind but didn't acknowledge her. Not then. The call came later that evening.

It took all Byford's self-control not to slam down the receiver. He'd forced himself to wait till now before making the call. He might as well not have bothered. *Sincere apologies, Mr Byford. Equipment failure, samples may have been compromised. We'll be in touch.*

The detective rubbed a hand over his neck. He wasn't sure how much more of this he could take. All day he'd expected a call from the hospital; every time he thought of it he'd felt a sliver of ice in his belly. The fear had almost spoiled the fact that two low-lifes were about to get their comeuppance. Fraser and Lewis would be remanded in custody when they appeared before magistrates in the morning. He had no doubt of that. It was everything else he was unsure of.

✳

Bev's hair was dripping. She'd dragged herself out of the shower to answer the phone. It was a tad late for the call in more ways than one: Angela Collins remembered seeing daffodils strewn across the hall floor when she found her mother lying in agony.

"You're in no doubt, Mrs Collins?"

"None. Seeing you at the funeral reminded me. Thank you for the flowers, by the way." The roses had been a god-send. Bev didn't think Tom would mind.

"It should have struck me sooner," said Angela. "But I was so worried about mum."

"That's OK. I appreciate you letting me know."

Bev sat on the bottom stair, towelling her hair, picturing the scene. If Angela had thought about it at the time, she'd have assumed her mother had dropped them in the fall.

So there you go. Three out of three. She'd been right. Big deal. It begged an even bigger question: if they'd made the connection earlier, would Sophia Carrington still be alive? If they'd known the attacks were down to one gang, would they have given the inquiry greater priority, thrown more resources and officers at it? Could they have collared the bastards before they killed?

The thought, and a million others, kept her awake long into the night. She'd never worked a case where there was so little to grab on to. It felt as though they were feeling their way in the dark – one step forward, two back. She turned over yet again, tried to ignore the time on the digital readout: 1.40am. It wasn't just the lack of progress in the inquiry. She was still worried sick about the guv, and the Shields thing wasn't helping. Thoughts of the DI led to Powell. She'd heard a whisper that Powell had left the disciplinary looking like the cat that got the double cream, though there'd been nothing official.

She tried lying on her back, arms behind her head. Not many words from Oz, either. The distance between them appeared to be growing. She wanted him badly, wasn't sure nowadays that the feeling was mutual. He'd barely reacted when she told him about the house. And her lie about being out with Frankie hadn't helped, though Oz hadn't said anything.

She threw off the duvet, angry with herself as much as anyone. Too much wine after dinner; she needed water. She padded down to the kitchen, grabbed her bag on the way back. She paused briefly, smiling at the sounds coming from her mum and her gran's rooms: stereo snores. The envelope Maude Taylor had given her was still there, she'd forgotten about that. She took it out along with the tablets.

She spread the photographs around her. Sophia had been a beautiful woman. Not in-your-face, nothing blowsy about her and if she wore make-up it was subtle. The attraction was in the bone structure, the shape of her eyes, the mouth with slightly turned-up lips as if on the verge of a smile.

Bev sighed. "Talk to me, lady."

She swallowed a couple of paracetamol and drained the glass. 1.50. She gathered the pictures and turned out the light. A noise woke her just as she was drifting off. She knew what it was, couldn't put her finger on it. Of course. The curtains were billowing, flapping in the draught.

As she closed the window, she saw him. A figure all in black in the bus shelter over the road. She moved swiftly to the side, peeping through the gap between the window frame and the curtain. Whatever he was doing, it wasn't waiting for a bus; the last service left before midnight.

Why was a man standing in the dead of night, staring at her house?

Her coat was hanging on the banister. She slipped a torch into a pocket and gently drew back the bolts on the door. The dark form had given her a shock but she'd have the element of surprise. That was the theory. She threw open the door and sprinted out. Not a soul in sight. She came to an abrupt halt in the middle of the road. He could have gone either way. She scanned both directions. Nothing. Could she have been mistaken? Had she seen a shadow? Was it a trick of the streetlight?

She walked slowly to the spot where she'd seen him, peering at the pavement. He'd been there for some time. There were half a dozen butts, and shadows don't smoke.

# 15

The uniform had been posted outside Princes Rise all night. There were coffee-coloured smudges under his tired eyes. He straightened as Bev approached, but didn't quite quell a yawn. She delved into her bag and whipped out an emergency Mars bar.

The young constable's eyes lit up. "Wicked. Ta, Sarge."

"All quiet?" She accepted a bite-size chunk. He already had a mouthful but she got the picture. Her knock on the door echoed in the early-morning street. A blackbird halted its solo but only for a second or so. Bev hoped Maude wasn't still in bed. If her cop's instinct was right, her late-night prowler was the same man who'd paid Maude an uninvited visit. He couldn't get to Maude so he was having a pop at Bev. As to why, she could only hazard a guess.

Maude was in her nightdress, a floor-length white cotton affair buttoned to the neck, the normally regal hair rumpled, a puffy ochre cheek bearing pillow creases.

"I need to take a look round, Mrs Taylor." Bev smiled. "Sorry – Maude."

"It's awfully early, Sergeant. What are you hoping to find?"

*Whatever he'd been after.* Bev shrugged. "Not sure yet."

She searched for two hours. Drew a blank. Everywhere. No false panels, hidden drawers, loose floorboards. She'd worked up a sweat and gathered a stack of dust but as to answers: diddly. Not surprising, really; the place had already been combed by SOCOs.

When she popped her head round the sitting room

door, she found the full-dress version of Maude sorting boxes and crates, parcelling up what was left of Sophia's life; neat packages ready for sale or disposal.

"Can I get a drink of water before I go?" Bev asked.

"Help yourself, dear." Maude was distracted, lost in memories.

Bev ran the tap for an age, held the glass to her forehead to cool down. She glanced round; the kitchen was definitely a room to spend time in. The rest of the house was clinical by comparison. And she did like the hanging wicker baskets –

She narrowed her eyes, then placed the glass in the sink and dragged a stool over, careful not to slip in stockinged feet. The brittle stalks and papery petals were covered in a delicate lattice of cobwebs; grey strands clung to the sweat on her hands as she carefully parted them. Nothing had been touched for months, presumably since Sophia had created this arrangement of dead flowers.

An arrangement designed to ensure that it concealed what lay beneath.


Byford was pacing, head down, hands in pockets. There'd been nothing from the hospital. Again. It wasn't the only communication failure. "We've got two youths in the cells," he said. "And we'd get more joy out of the brickwork."

Fraser and Lewis hadn't even confirmed their own names. A duty solicitor had been assigned but she was getting the same treatment.

"Any bright ideas?" He glanced round. The squad was definitely subdued, affected maybe by the frustration he couldn't hide. It wasn't just arsy adolescents and failures at the General. He'd taken the significance of Angela Collins's phone call badly.

It didn't help that it was purely by chance they had anyone in custody. Uniform weren't actually crowing but the fact was, it was their result. Not that it was all over. A smart brief could probably talk the youths out of serious charges. Being in possession of the stolen jewellery wouldn't automatically convince a jury they'd nicked it, and there wasn't a shred of evidence to suggest they'd been involved in the attacks.

"Sergeant Morriss reckons we've got the monkeys, not the organ grinder," Oz offered.

Byford raised an eyebrow. The phrase was certainly more Morriss than Khan. He glanced at his watch; she was taking her time at Maude Taylor's place. He reckoned she was probably right. He'd read the social reports. The youths barely had a grey cell between them. You didn't need to be clever to beat up old women; you did need a modicum of nous not to get caught. "So where's the organ grinder now?" he asked.

"Not at Winston Heights, that's for sure." Oz had been out with crime scenes to the empty tower block in Edgbaston. Serious squatting had been going on for months. One room on the ground floor was ankle-deep: fast-food cartons, sweet papers, lager cans, enough porn mags to fill several top shelves. Only two sleeping bags, though.

"More to the point, what's he, or they, going to do next?" Oz was thinking out loud.

"Go on," Byford said.

"Joan Goddard and Ena Bolton thought there were three if not four gang members. So in theory there could still be two out there. We need to know why they're doing it. Or we'll not stop them."

"The motive's obvious, surely?" Shields said. The youths

in custody were users; they'd flog body parts for a fix.

"If they need money, why hang on to the rings?" asked Oz. "Why not sell them straight away?"

"Or at least get rid of them." Byford narrowed his eyes.

"Unless –" Oz hesitated, not completely at ease with either spotlight or theory. "Maybe it's not about the cash. Or at least not any more." He glanced at the murder board. "Look at the old ladies, guv. The violence is worse every time."

"A taste for blood? You think it's that now?" Byford mulled the notion over, gave a shrug. "It happens."

It didn't go far enough. Oz took another tentative step. "I keep thinking about Sophia Carrington being a doctor –"

"Don't go there." Shields didn't give him a chance. "I made the checks myself. She didn't bury any mistakes."

"Carry on, officer." Byford was interested. Oz Khan was rarely so vocal. Bev usually had more than enough to say for both of them. The guv registered the fact, filed it for future consideration.

"Maybe it's not Sophia specifically. Maybe it's a general medical thing. I'm wondering if any of the other victims worked in the profession: a nurse, maybe, or a cleaner, a hospital secretary. Carrington trained here in Birmingham. Is it possible there's a link between the victims as well as the villains?"

Byford turned his mouth down. It was a hell of a conjecture. But what else had they got? "Best find out, hadn't you, Oz?"

The photographs had no name on them – only a date on the back of each, February 20th in succeeding years, beginning with 1955. There were sixteen in all, the last from 1971. You didn't have to be an expert. It was the same child, a girl, different ages: newborn, gap-toothed toddler, gangly teenager.

"And Maude Taylor says she's never seen them before?" They were closeted in the guv's office. Bev sat across the desk from Byford. DI Shields leaned against the windowsill, hands wrapped round a mug.

"Adamant," Bev said.

"I find that hard to believe," Shields sneered. "To hear Taylor talk, they were Siamese twins, joined at the hip. I wouldn't have thought they had any secrets between them."

Shields's snide remarks were getting to Bev. Was the DI pissed off because she hadn't come up with the goods? OK, they might not lead anywhere and they certainly raised more questions than answers, but at least it was a new line. Frankie's 'be nice' advice was a bugger.

"We're assuming the date's the girl's birth date?" Byford asked.

Bev held her hands out. "The checks are going in now."

"I don't see the relevance," Shields said. "Even if the old woman had a child. So what?"

"Not if," Bev said. "She did. It's in the PM report." Sophia Carrington had fitted the ageing spinster profile so well, no one had bothered to check. Bev had confirmed it with Harry Gough over the phone on her way in. "As for its relevance, who knows? It needs following up."

Shields shrugged. The casual dismissal infuriated Bev. "You got anything better?"

Byford tightened his jaw. He gathered a few papers and slipped a pen in his top pocket. "If you need a hand, use Darren New. DC Khan's got something on."

"Oh?" She wanted to hear more but the guv was about ready to break it up. She paused at the door. "Know what gets me, guv?" She fanned out the photographs. "If these do mark birthdays, a photo for each year of her life –" she paused – "how come they stop at sixteen?"

Oz glanced over as Bev entered the incident room. He gave her a half-smile as she perched on the edge of his desk while he finished the call, the last of a series. The turned-down mouth was pretty telling, but he filled her in anyway. Joan Goddard hadn't been in hospital as a patient, let alone a worker. Ena had been an office worker, hated hospitals, prided herself on never taking a sickie in her life. Angela Collins confirmed that her mother had never worked outside the house, not even voluntary stuff. And they knew of each other only as fellow victims via the media.

"So another one bites the dust?" Bev commiserated.

Oz sighed and threw his notes into the bin.

"It was good thinking, Oz. Worth following up." It was meant to buck him up.

He rose, pulled on his jacket. "Don't patronise me, Sarge."

Touch-ee. "I didn't mean it like that." She'd been there herself, loads of times. A great idea and it panned out to squat. "I'm getting nowhere fast too."

Sophia had given birth but there was no record anywhere, nothing on paper, no birth, no death. So what happened to Sophia's baby? It was possible the child was stillborn and the girl in the photographs was unrelated, a friend's perhaps, even a patient's. They still had little idea who she was or why the photographs ended in 1971.

Oz ran a finger along his chin. "There must be something. They were hot on records even back then."

"I'm sure the birth was registered. Didn't have to be in

the right name, though."

They exchanged glances. No exactly a piece of piss. Oz was calling it a day. She watched as he logged off.

"Fancy a drink?" She wanted to spend time with him as much as share a few thoughts.

He shook his head. "Nah. I've got something on."

She so wanted to call him back, was sure she could talk him round. She didn't. In case he said no.

Walking always helped Oz think. He was pounding the streets of the city centre. He'd have preferred a beach or the Malverns, even a park, but you can't have everything. It was dry and dark, still early enough not to have to sidestep the late-night delights of drunken yobs and pools of vomit. The young people milling round the Bullring were in good spirits, laughing and joking. Bars and bistros were filling up, snatches of music and scents of a dozen cuisines drifted into the cool air. In a way the buzz and bright lights helped. It was easier to blank out than the sometimes cloying attention of his parents and sisters at home.

He dug his hands in his pockets, crossed into Corporation Street. He wasn't sure how to handle the situation. Actually, it was Bev he wasn't sure how to handle. Clearly he didn't know her as well as he thought. The aggro with the new DI was bad enough. Bev had a beehive in her bonnet about Shields. But it wasn't that particularly. She'd probably work it through. It was the other business. The lying. "Frankie was on top form," she'd said. He could have told her that.

When he'd bumped into Frankie the same night, Frankie had asked him to give Bev her love. He hadn't. He hadn't even mentioned it. He was waiting for Bev to tell him what was going on. Why she'd lied. Who she'd been with. Why she was messing him around. He was accustomed to taking shit from the Highgate hard men, but not Bev. She'd held his hand in more ways than one this past year.

Maybe it was time to let go. The guv had called him in earlier for a chat. Oz still reckoned it was early to be talking sergeant exams and maybe a transfer, but there was no harm giving it some thought.

His mobile beeped a message. Miss you Bev x. His face softened as he pictured her tapping it out, finger hovering over the send button, probably chewing her bottom lip. It was the nearest she'd come to admitting a need. But need for what? She'd never let him get close, maybe never let anyone. He'd picked up on it right from the start: the softer her emotions, the sharper her tongue. And forget serious relationships. She didn't do deep. Too risky. Too much potential for pain down there. You didn't need a psychology degree to work out why. She'd only talked to him once about her father, but it was enough. Losing someone was never going to hurt that much again.

"Give the old girl my love," Frankie had said. Oz sighed, no longer sure he could even give her his own. There was one way to find out. He tapped in a reply. He didn't mind sending messages; he certainly wouldn't be sending flowers. Especially roses.

Tears left shiny trails down Maude Taylor's cheeks, tiny ski slopes in loose-powder snow. Was she crying for Sophia or herself? Maude had never knowingly told a lie in her long life. She'd held back harsh facts from time to time but the sin of omission didn't seem so heinous. When Sergeant Morriss had questioned her about the photographs that morning, Maude had told the truth. She'd never seen the pictures.

She was aware of the story, though, and she'd just read a narrative that filled in the finer points. Maude clutched Sophia's journal to her chest, torn between secrets and lies, loyalty and duty.

Mystery Man was having a night off. Bev checked intermittently all evening. She'd dithered about mentioning the incident at home, reasoning there was little sense worrying them needlessly. In the event she had a quiet word with her mum on the landing before turning in.

"We always lock up, dear. Always double-check as well." Emmy frowned as she laid a hand on Bev's arm. "It's you I worry about."

They'd been through it a million times. Emmy had never understood why Bev had gone into the police service. She'd tried pointing her down the education path, rather liked the idea of Bev following in her dad's footsteps. Bev couldn't imagine anything worse than lecturing bolshie kids on Shakespeare. She shook her head, smiled gently. "Mum, let's not go there again. I know how to look after myself."

"Give it a rest, Em," Sadie shouted. The old girl was probably still reading. So much for keeping their voices down.

Emmy sighed. Two against one was never an even contest.

Bev checked the street a final time from her bedroom window. A police car cruised past. She'd mentioned it to uniform, though she had a feeling the prowler wouldn't be back. She might have imagined the whole thing. Might have jumped to conclusions about a connection with the case. Not surprising, really. It was uppermost in her mind most of the time.

There was a much sexier prospect going round in there

now. She read Oz's message for the umpteenth time. It was more of an invitation, really: a night of wild passion in a place belonging to his mate Zak. She gave a slow smile. It'd be ace; she couldn't wait, was already wondering if she'd have time to nip into Agent Provocateur in her lunch break. She'd kept Oz waiting an age before replying. Best put him out of his misery. She hit the keys: yeah OK.

# 16

The offer on Baldwin Street in Moseley had not been accepted. Bev hung up, mouth down. Back to square one. She ran her hands through her hair, pissed off at the lack of progress on every front. At least there was this evening to look forward to: Oz's mate's place. But there was a stack of stuff to get through first. The phone rang as she was about to lift the receiver.

"Bev?" She frowned, couldn't place the voice for a second. "Hope you don't mind a call at work." Of course. Tom Marlow. She jotted his name on her desk pad, added a few curly embellishments. "A meeting's fallen through and I'm only round the corner. I wondered if we could meet for coffee?"

"That'd be great." Her voice held a smile. "Can you hold on a tick, the other phone's going."

It was Maude Taylor. Bev told the old woman she'd be right over, then switched back to Marlow, still on the line. "Sorry about that, Tom. I'd love coffee but no can do. I've got so much paperwork, it's a fire risk in here."

He laughed. "How about tonight? There's a great film –"

"I'd really like to, Tom, but I've got something on." An ivory silk camisole, if they had it in her size.

"Not to worry. Another time?"

"You bet."

"Cool. Well done, by the way. The attacks on the old ladies? I see you've got someone in custody?"

The remand had attracted a fair bit of news coverage. It was still quite rare for defendants to refuse to utter a word in court. Political prisoners, maybe, but not a couple of shit-for-brains. The magistrates had ordered yet more reports while the Shrek boys developed a taste for prison food.

"Way to go yet, Tom. Look, I really have to cut this short. Can I call you back?"

She reached for a file, managed to knock a tray full of paper clips all over the floor. Sod it. The road to hell was paved with good intentions. What about the way to Kings Heath? Twenty minutes later she was at Maude Taylor's place.

Oz tapped the door, popped his head round. He checked the office for Bev's jacket or bag. He must've just missed her; the seat was still warm. She needed the address for tonight. He had a pen and reached for the pad, then paused. So Coffee Man was still in touch. He jotted down the number and street-name of his friend Zak's place in Selly Oak. Tom Marlow was something else they were going to have to thrash out.

Bev hadn't had the heart to play the heavy. Maude Taylor's eyes, when they eventually made contact, spoke volumes. Bev read guilt there and, even as the old woman handed it over, doubt that she was doing the right thing. The journal had been hidden within the hollowed-out pages of a medical textbook. It was now, figuratively speaking, burning a hole in Bev's bag.

She was so focused she barely noticed the media scrum outside Highgate, just about took in that Danny Shields was doing a turn. While the DI was looking to make the news, Bev had her eye on the past. She'd leafed through a few pages of the journal at Maude's, registered the potential importance of the words. Every entry was in the same neat hand, written in black ink, probably with the same fountain pen. Maude had confirmed it was Sophia Carrington's handwriting. And definitely not the script that appeared on the back of the photographs.

"What's up, son? You look as if you've seen a ghost." Gert Roberts looked up from her latest romantic dalliance. There was a greasy thumbprint on the cover and the kitchen stank of fish and chips. Davy wrinkled his nose. At least there was no washing up. Gert reckoned they tasted better out of the paper, regretted they didn't come wrapped in yesterday's news any more.

He shoved the note in the pocket of his jeans. It had been delivered by hand. Just. The regular post had arrived hours ago. "Nothing. I'm right as rain, gran."

Gert's smile didn't reach her green eyes. Call her an old witch but she knew something was wrong with the boy. "You never mention that mate of yours these days, Davy. What's his name?"

Perhaps they'd had a falling-out. It'd be a shame, that. They'd got on really well. It had been a worry to Gert how much time Davy used to spend hanging round at home with only his old gran for company. He didn't seem to have many friends till this other lad came on the scene. Davy'd really come out of his shell since then.

The boy glanced at his gran, eyes narrowed. "Jake. Why?"

"Jake what?"

Davy opened his mouth, hesitated. "Dunno. What's it matter?"

Gert shrugged massive shoulders. "You ought to ask him round. Get a pizza in or something." She saw the look

168

on Davy's face. "You needn't worry about me. I'd make myself scarce. I wouldn't get in the way."

Davy struggled to keep a calm voice. "He's not around. He's gone away for a few days."

Gert spied a chip she'd missed, popped it into her mouth. "When he gets back, then. It'd be nice for you, Davy love."

Nice as shit pie. "Sure thing, gran. I might just do that." Davy fingered the note in his pocket. He didn't need to take it out; he remembered every word.

*Tonight. I'll see you there. Reckon Gert needs to die…t?*

# 17

*No one knows yet. Dear God, let no one ever find out. I've prayed so hard these last few weeks. Prayed to a God I'm not sure I believe in for a child to die. A child who's yet to be born. I'm shaking and feel shame even as I write the words. My only excuse is that I won't do anything to jeopardise the pregnancy. An unborn life is precious but precarious. If the foetus isn't viable, the pregnancy will abort spontaneously. What a coward I am, what weasel words: foetus, viable, abort. I won't hide behind them, not here.*

*I am having a baby and I pray to God that I'll miscarry.*

*How could I have been so careless? How could I have been so stupid? If the truth comes out it will ruin me. It will kill my mother. I can barely live with myself. Dear God, let this baby die.*

*Shame is a corrosive emotion. Secret shame the most corrosive of all. It's been burning into me like acid. I had to talk to someone. Did Maude suspect before I told her? I think she may have. I've caught her looking at me in a certain way. She's never asked about the baby's father. I could never tell her. It would destroy his marriage. Adultery is a sin. I finally told Maude I was expecting because I couldn't – I can't – do this alone. I can't carry off this pretence, this charade, without help. Weasel words again. This isn't pretence – it's deceit. I'm living a lie away from home, amid strangers who know more about me than my own mother and father.*

*I cry every night. The tears aren't for me: my isolation, my duplicity, my shame. They're for the growing baby. I feel him – I'm sure it's a boy – kicking and moving in my womb. I cried before because I wanted him to die. I cry now because I can't bear the thought of losing him.*

*They've located a respectable married couple. Sister Bernadette stared at me coldly as she stressed the words respectable and married. Or did I imagine it? I seem to live in a dream world these days. Sometimes I even picture myself keeping the baby and bringing him up on my own. Impossible. Ludicrous. Maude's right. I'm an unmarried woman. What sort of a life would it be with a child?*

*What sort of a life will it be without?*

*It's Patrick's birthday. I baked a cake. He blows out the candles – all six. He smothers me with kisses and my cheeks are damp with little-boy love. I smile as I reach to stroke his hair. The movement wakes me and I open my eyes. I cram my fist into my mouth to stifle a scream. Sister Angela will move me if I disturb the others again. I taste blood as I bite down on my fingers and feel the tears cooling as they trickle down the back of my hand. This is the cruellest dream so far. There's less pain in the ones where the baby's born dead. I rub my belly, feel the outline of a tiny heel. Dear God, let him live.*

"What the hell are you doing? I've been looking all over for you."

Danny Shields was framed in the doorway of the rape suite. It was about the only part of Highgate where you could get a bit of peace. Bev sighed, gearing up for yet another bloody battle. It looked as if the media turn had

171

gone well; the DI was still flushed from the performance. Bet the cameras loved the power dressing and the big hair. Bev blinked, realised her eyes were damp and turned her head from the DI's glare.

"You're not paid to sit round reading. Everyone's working their balls off out there."

Bev opened her mouth to explain but was sick of justifying her existence to a woman who seemed intent on making her life a misery. Anyway, she needed time to think, to work out the significance, the relevance, if any, of Sophia Carrington's secretive past to her violent death.

"Well?" Shields planted her hands on her hips, her feet apart. Christ, if they were in the Wild West, she'd be going for her gun.

Bev shrugged. "Whatever." She closed the journal, slipped it back into her bag and got to her feet. There was more to read but she'd finish it later. She felt strangely protective of the old woman's secrets, certainly wasn't inclined to share them with Shields. Sophia had never meant anyone to read her words, Bev was sure of that. There were no dates, few names. Weeks, sometimes months, went by between entries. It seemed she wrote when she hurt the most. It was a painful thought. Shields was still in the doorway. Bev barely noticed.

"Where are you going?" The DI moved aside at the last moment.

"To have a word with the guv."

"Check visiting hours, then. He's in the General."

# 18

"You probably misheard." Byford grimaced as he took a sip of orange liquid masquerading as tea. Even in profile, Bev looked as if she needed something stronger. She'd jumped three red lights and the MG was parked on a double yellow.

"Shields said you were in the General. Said I should check visiting hours." Her lips were tight, the folded arms and tapping foot far more informative of her feelings.

Byford tried to keep a bemused smile from his face. Bev's concern was touching, if a little intense. "In a manner of speaking, I am."

Bev snorted. "You're at, not in. Seems to me there's a difference there."

Any clarification from Shields had been cut short by Bev's hasty departure. She and the guv were leaning against the wall outside the hospital's main entrance. Bev had needed nicotine, was on her third Silk Cut. She wasn't the only addict. Lines of smokers were propping up the brickwork, puffing away like there was no tomorrow. Which for some of them was probably true. Bev took a last drag and ground the butt into an industrial-sized ashtray. Her panic was giving way to ice-cold anger.

Byford poured the dregs of his tea on to a sick-looking shrub and cast round for a bin. "Maybe it was wishful thinking on her part."

"Nah, guv. She was pulling my strings." It had been spiteful and sly. And it had scared the shit out of Bev. She'd asked around but no one else, not even Vince, knew where

Byford was, let alone what was wrong. She'd discovered him visiting the sick. Gerry Flavell, the officer knifed during the standoff at the Edgbaston high rise, was only supposed to have been kept in overnight but a wound had become infected. Byford was doing the decent thing. He always looked out for his men. And women.

A long sigh lifted the fringe from Bev's troubled eyes. "Why is she doing this, guv?"

He didn't need to ask who or what. You'd have to be blind not to read the body language, feel the hostility.

"She's gunning for me. And I don't know why." Bev stared ahead, chewing a thumbnail. It was a minefield. Byford trod carefully.

"She seems a little insecure to me." Echoes of Frankie there.

"Shame."

"It can't be easy."

*Don't* say *being a woman in the police.* "What?"

"Being a woman in the police."

The sweaty gropes in the locker room. The dyke porn on your computer. The tampons in your drawer. It wasn't good. It wasn't smart. But that was the reality.

Shields would have gone through it as well. "Tell me about it."

"Maybe it's easier for you."

"No, it isn't, guv. I just get on with it." Anyway, the shit from the neanderthals was sugar-coated compared with the vitriol Shields slung. Ironic, really. "You have to give as good as you get."

"You certainly do that." He smiled but she wasn't playing. "Maybe that's it, Bev. Maybe you should hold back a bit."

"How does that work, then?"

"She's just arrived at Highgate. It's her first DI post.

She's finding her feet."

Bev sniffed. "They're usually in my teeth."

"She's wary of you, Bev."

Byford was currently uneasy as well. He was out of order discussing a senior officer but Bev deserved a hearing, if not the full picture. "Have you ever thought she could be jealous?"

More shades of Frankie. Still, the guv's take would be useful. "Excuse me. I banged my head on the way down."

"I'm serious."

"You're gonna have to spell it out, then, guv. 'Cause I don't know where you're coming from."

He couldn't tell her everything. He couldn't prove it all. Byford had replayed the scene several times since the DI boards. He wouldn't have witnessed it at all if he hadn't left his phone lying around. He'd found it in the interview room – where he'd also come across Danny Shields. During the lunch break. The table was littered with appraisal sheets and interview notes. Took the wrong door, she'd said. He had no way of knowing how long she'd been there or how much she'd read, but it would have taken only minutes to pick up the strengths and weakness of the other candidates; especially Bev's. She was Shields's closest rival and Shields was next in.

"You're a good detective, Bev. You're young, bright, snapping at her heels."

"Give me a break, guv. If I was that hot, how come I'm not in her shoes?"

Because in the interview Shields had emphasised team-work and procedures, derided the sort of officer who acts on initiative. "She's a good officer, Bev. And she had the vocabulary."

"Anyone can talk the talk."

Not about ethnic minorities. Not as convincingly as Danny Shields. And admit it or not, the police service everywhere was desperate not to be perceived as racist. The Stephen Lawrence inquiry cast a long shadow. He didn't believe Shields had deliberately played the race card. She hardly needed to, not with the other aces up her sleeve.

There was another explanation, of course.

"Could just be she doesn't like you," Byford offered.

"Thanks, guv. I'm feeling better already."

He flapped a hand at the smoke. "I'm glad someone is. Come on, let's get back before I need oxygen."

The ivory silk camisole was laid out rather fetchingly on the bed. Bev was doing her Cop Idol bit in the shower. She'd segued from *Angels* to *Sympathy for the Devil*. It was going to be a wicked night. Her water was never wrong. She wrapped a towel round her hair and fashioned another into a toga. The body lotion had cost a small fortune and it was going on every inch of flesh she could reach. She gazed into the mirror: could you pout and smoulder at the same time? Nah. Looked as if she'd had a stroke. She flashed a smile instead. The chat with the guv had bucked her up no end. Bright young snapper-at-heels was fine by her.

A shout from below broke into her thoughts. "See you later, Bev."

"You bet." Her mum and Sadie were off to see a man about a dog. Literally. Talk about excited. They were like a couple of kids. They'd done their homework since Humph: contacted the Kennel Club, recced reputable breeders. The puppies were six weeks old. Bev had a feeling it would be love at first sight.

"Don't do anything I wouldn't do." Was that a cackle from Sadie? Bev grinned; much as she loved the old girl, that didn't give a deal of scope. She slipped into the camisole. Well, it was almost her size.

# 19

"It had better be good, Oz." God. She sounded like her mum.

"I'm really sorry, Bev. I'll explain when I get there. I'll grab us a bite to eat."

Bev had already added the feminine touch of a soft candle or two to Zak's bachelor pad in Selly Oak. Having slipped into something less comfortable, the camisole being a tad on the tight side, she was now chomping at the bit. By the sound of it, she'd not be getting her teeth into Khan's dish of the day. Oz cooked like a dream but there'd be no time now for him to knock up anything in the kitchen. He was probably hoping she'd say she fancied an Indian. Tough.

"Chinese, preferably. Pizza at a push." The flat delivery contained more than a food order. How long was he going to be? She wanted to chuck the mobile across the floor, aimed it at the settee instead. 8.30. She'd give him an hour, then she was off. So much for a night of passion; he couldn't even get here on time. At least she could have a drink. She'd brought booze as well as candles. She wandered, chilled Chablis in hand. Zak had left a note on a pin board: make yourselves at home. She sniffed; gift horse in the mouth and all that, but Zak's pad was a bit boring: all chunky chintz and Athena prints. Except for the floor. The carpet tiles were black and white; she was beginning to feel like a chess piece.

"Checkmate." Talking of mates… She'd give Frankie a bell. A girlie whinge about unreliable blokes would pass an hour or six. A recorded voice put the mockers on that. And the point of a mobile not on, is? She slung the phone settee-wards again.

The telly was a turn-off; the sound system was cool but she wasn't in the mood for soft music. She'd spotted a pack of playing cards on the side but she hadn't the patience. Sod it. She'd nip out for a ciggie. She delved into her bag, frowned as her fingers closed round the edges of a book. Sophia's journal. Not quite how she imagined a night of passion panning out. She started to read, smoking forgotten.

*I saw them this afternoon. It's not allowed, of course, but I watched from the walled garden as they parked. I can still smell the rosemary on my dress, still picture the couple in every detail. Perhaps I hoped they'd be unsuitable, brash and common and stupid. Would that have given me the strength to say no, to send them away? Foolish thought. They were none of that. She looked like the actress from Brief Encounter. He reminded me of the manager at my father's bank: portly and pompous in a pin-stripe suit. He cupped her elbow in his hand as they walked. They exchanged nervous glances and tight smiles.*

*Maude forwards my post. I shake with shame when I read my parents' letters. They think I'm a saint. I had to lie. I told them I was nursing a dying friend, a woman with only months to live. I can tell them exactly when she'll die – after I've given birth. I've considered countless times whether to reveal the truth. I can't do it. It would hurt them too much.*

*The pains are coming regularly now. The contractions are two minutes apart. It won't be long. I won't cry, however much it hurts. I keep telling myself that if I endure the physical pain, God will help me cope with the mental agony later. Strange how I long to see the baby's face.*

*She's perfect. Wisps of dark hair feather the tiniest skull I have even seen. She has huge blue eyes that gaze into mine and seem to read my thoughts. I can't decide on a name. Elizabeth, perhaps? Or Isobel? How could I ever have imagined giving her up?*

*I couldn't do it. I'm not strong enough. I was swayed by what was said and afraid of what others would think. It wasn't for my sake. I must hold on to that thought. Children need both parents. I want her to have a normal happy life. People can be so cruel to a baby born out of wedlock. I've heard the words they use, witnessed the contempt, as if it's the child's fault. I leave here tomorrow and will try to forget everything. That way I may be able to survive it.*

*I saw them from the window. They're here to take her. I kiss her head, stroke her face, whisper I love you. Her baby scent lingers in the air. It breaks my heart. Dear God, let her be happy.*

Bev had a crick in her neck and her right foot had gone to sleep; the rest of her was coming round slowly. She rubbed her eyes, couldn't remember where she was at first. Oz was sitting opposite. Why the hell hadn't he woken her? Gone midnight and he was curled up with a good book. She took a closer look. Actually it wasn't a good book; it was real life. And it was sad. Judging by the expression on his face, he was near the end.

She yawned and swung her legs round, instantly aware of the camisole's shortcomings. Apart from which, she was frozen. Oz was on the last page when she returned from the bedroom looking slightly less like something off page three. She nodded at the book. "And they all lived happily ever after. Not."

Sophia certainly hadn't. She'd lived a lie and died a lonely violent death. Bev was sure there was a connection there, was struggling to make it. They'd try to trace what happened to the kid, of course, but thousands of illegitimate babies were given up for adoption in Sophia's era. It was a heartbreaking story, a shameful secret, but it was two a penny back then.

Oz closed the journal. "Amazing."

So was he. You could do breaststroke in those eyes. She moved across, took the book from him, snuggled close. The arm round her shoulder was good, the peck on her cheek could be improved. OK, Oz, in your own time.

"I feel sorry for the baby, Bev." He was still in the past.

"I suppose she did what she thought best." The thigh-stroking was designed to catapult him to the present. A sort of strangled sound emerged, which was highly encouraging until she registered it as a snort. Not unlike one of her own.

"Best for who, Bev? The baby or Sophia Carrington?"

She removed the arm, turned to face him. "That's a bit harsh, isn't it? Imagine having a kid, then giving it up for adoption, never seeing it again."

He picked up the journal. "I don't have to imagine. It's all there in black and white. Lots of pain, loads of angst, woe is me, then hey! Where's the sink? She washes her hands of the whole mess, walks away and gets on with her life." Heated or what? The diatribe left her almost speechless, not that there was a chance to join the debate. "And I'll tell you this for sure: there's no way on God's earth I'd give my own flesh and blood to strangers."

"Best hope you don't get up the duff, then, hadn't you?" OK, it was childish but he'd asked for it. She knew he was big on family, but that didn't make him right. Nothing was ever that black and white. "Come on, Oz. The poor bloody woman made one mistake –"

"Three." He ticked them off on his fingers. "She had sex with a married man. Failed to take precautions. Had a baby."

Sexist prig. She could barely get the words out. "It's a damn sight better than getting rid of it."

A muscle tensed in his cheek but he kept his voice calm. "Isn't that exactly what she did?"

The silence was broken by a muffled sound neither recognised at first. She looked round, located the source, dashed over. The mobile was jammed down the back of one of Zak's chunky cushions.

"Shit." Half a dozen missed calls. All from Highgate. One unopened message.

She read the words. "Double shit."

# 20

Oz drove. The nine-minute journey took five. There was a uniform on the door and a cluster of gawkers in the street.

"Better late than never." DI Shields looked up from her notes. A quick glance suggested she'd been called out in a rush. No make-up, hair could do with a comb, the outfit had been thrown together. Not exactly catwalk cool; more cop under pressure.

Bev ignored the crack, concentrated on not throwing up. The stench in the small space was horrendous; it filled every inch. Her stomach lurched; the retching made her eyes water. It was partly the rank odour, partly the pitiful sight. Oz succumbed to both and headed outside for air.

The terraced house in Kings Heath was in the street next to the first victim's, though Bev reckoned Iris Collins would turn in her grave at the state of this place. It was a dive: dirt-poor and dirty; bare floorboards, paper hanging off the walls, a one-bar electric fire, not switched on. Thank God.

"What have we got?" Bev asked. She nodded at a couple of SOCOs who were waiting for a green light from Shields.

"Dolly Machin. Seventy-six. Widow. Man next door hadn't seen anything of her for a while."

Bev held a tissue under her nose and got down on one knee. "How long's a while?"

Shields shrugged. "He admits to three weeks. Darren New's there now, trying to get a firmer fix. But by the look of that, it'll be a damn sight longer."

Bev tightened her lips. *That* was an old woman who'd

once been a little girl, somebody's daughter, maybe somebody's mother. She'd lived in appalling poverty and died in her own waste with a colony of hungry rats for company.

She rose, regretted buying, let alone wearing, the camisole. "I'm going to have a quick look round."

Shields didn't object. Bev couldn't put her finger on it but there was something not quite right about the DI. It went deeper than the new look. She hadn't exactly deferred to Bev but she'd seemed relieved to have her there, anxious almost for her input. Maybe thinking on her feet wasn't the DI's forte? Mind, if she saw this as her first big test as lead detective, that'd be a shame. Bev wasn't convinced they even had a case.

The recce confirmed her suspicions. The kitchen looked as if it had been fitted in the fifties and not touched since. Other rooms were virtually empty. Maybe Dolly Machin had sold the lot; maybe there'd been nothing to sell. Bev went back to check the bin and ran her hands under the tap before joining Shields in the front room. Oz had returned, looking a tad shame-faced. No reason. Everyone had been there, done that, got sick on the T-shirt.

Shields turned to face Bev. "Well?"

No sense in rushing it. "What's Harry Gough said?" She'd spotted the pathologist's Range Rover pulling away as they arrived.

"You know what he's like. He won't commit himself until he's sure."

Not in Bev's experience. Harry might not set his initial thoughts in stone but he generally offered them. "Guess it makes no odds, really."

Shields stiffened. "What do you mean?"

"Well, there's nothing for us here, is there?"

"Nothing for us?" The DI struggled to keep her voice down. "This has to be the scene of the first attack. Iris Collins wasn't the first victim. This woman was."

Bev shook her head.

The DI persisted. "Machin fits the profile perfectly. This is a crime scene, Sergeant."

Crime, maybe, but not the sort you find in the law books. Getting old. Not having two pennies to rub together. Living next door to people who watch *Neighbours* but can't be arsed to look out for their own. "Look around, DI Shields. There's nothing worth nicking."

Shields swept the room with a perfunctory glance. "No one would know that until they were in. The place has been turned over."

Bev shuddered. The place was a tip all right. "No one broke in here, Inspector." Certainly not the shits they were after. It was all wrong. Dolly's wedding ring was still on her finger. There was a pension book on the side in the kitchen. Bev had even found a few bob hidden in a Charles and Di tea caddy. One thing she hadn't come across? A floral tribute. There wasn't so much as a dandelion, let alone a daffodil.

As for Dolly Machin, she'd been a sick woman. There were so many prescription drugs, the kitchen looked like a pharmacy. Bev nodded in the direction of the bloated, blotchy corpse. "It's a bloody awful way to go, but I'll be amazed if it's not natural causes."

Shields ran a hand through her hair, acutely aware the crime lads were listening to every word. She lowered her voice. "Are you undermining my authority?"

A single lifted eyebrow expressed exactly what Bev was thinking; she wasn't stupid enough to say it. "You're in charge. Do what you think best."

"That's ex –"

Who the hell was ringing at this time of night? Bev lifted a finger to stem the DI's flow as she took the call. She felt the colour drain from her face, the blood rush to her head. She was about to pass out. She staggered, must have reached out a hand. Oz was there, arm round her shoulder.

"What is it, Sergeant?" Shields's voice held concern. Bev tried to speak but her mouth wouldn't work. Her mother's screams were still ringing in her head.

## 21

*Dear God. Let her be all right. I'll do anything you say if you let her be all right.*

It was a pact she'd made before. It hadn't stopped her dad dying. *This time, God. This time...*

She glanced at Oz, willing him to drive faster. Familiar roads flashed past in a blur, wet pavements reflected orange streetlight. Maybe Oz had heard her silent plea. Or maybe she didn't need to voice it. The body had its own language and hers was shouting. She couldn't stop her right leg jerking. She clamped it with a hand, still felt the tremor through her fingers.

"Pull over." She stumbled from the car, threw up on a grass verge, then sucked in lungsful of fresh air. The stink of death in her nostrils also clung to her clothes, her hair. It wasn't why she'd vomited.

*Dear God. Let her be all right. I'll do anything you want if you just let her be all right.*

She was aware of Oz strapping her into the seat, wiping sweat and tears from her face. He gently placed a ball of tissues in her hand.

"She'll be fine, Bev. Just fine."

*How the fuck do you know?* If she'd been in the house, it would never have happened. She couldn't speak, couldn't look at him, just wanted to get home. She closed her eyes, clenched her fists, counted the seconds. She was halfway up the drive before Oz was out of the car.

Muffled voices came from the sitting room.

"It's me," Bev called. The last thing they needed was

another shock. She stopped just inside the door. A bruised and bewildered-looking Sadie was lying on the sofa propped up by cushions, sobbing her heart out. Without her glasses she seemed smaller, more vulnerable. Emmy had pulled up a chair and was holding Sadie's hand. They turned at the same time, their faces taut with fear and hurt. They both tried so hard to smile it broke Bev's heart.

"Can't leave you alone for five minutes, can I?" Her voice quivered and the tears welling in her eyes spilled down her cheeks. She ran to comfort her gran, froze halfway across.

Sadie's beautiful hair. The bastard had hacked it off. Long grey hanks littered the carpet. Clumps had been casually tossed around the room. The senseless act, unbelievably callous, took Bev's breath away. She'd brushed Sadie's hair a million times. It wasn't just part of her gran's appearance, it was part of her identity. Sadie hadn't got a vain bone in her body but she'd been proud of her hair. Slowly she went to Sadie and knelt at her feet. For once, she couldn't find the words.

Sadie stroked her head, whispered, "I'm fine, Bev. Don't fret. Everything'll be OK."

"Yes, gran, it will," she breathed. *Because I'm gonna fucking kill the bastard.*

It took an age to coax Sadie upstairs. And a promise they'd stay with her until she fell asleep. Oz's offer of a policeman's lift finally swung it; he carried her as gently as if she were spun sugar. There were no broken bones; the doctor had confirmed that. But a crushed spirit? Sadie looked old and frail. The remaining hair, too short to pin up, looked like a badly fitting bathing cap.

Bev closed the door and perched on the edge of Sadie's

bed. Her mum sat in a chair opposite. The silence didn't last long. Some victims of violence withdraw, can't think about it, let alone talk. Sadie could. Bev fought for calm as she listened to the story. She glanced down, wondering why her palms were stinging, noted absently her nails had broken the skin. It was nothing compared to the red rawness round Sadie's wrists, and it hurt just to look at the bruises on her gran's face. Sadie was trying to play it down but when she thought no one was looking there was absolute terror in her eyes.

The intruder had appeared out of nowhere. Her gran had been dozing in front of the TV. "I thought I was dreaming, Bev. A masked man in front of me like that." The rope and gag were real. She'd screamed once before he smacked her in the mouth. Unwittingly, the old woman lifted a hand, stroked the swelling on the side of her face.

"No one's ever laid so much as a finger on me, Bev. Not once. Not even when I was at school."

Bev closed her eyes, had to swallow a couple of times. "No one'll ever hurt you again, gran." *Not if I can help it.*

Emmy passed Sadie a tissue. Bev waited while her gran wiped her eyes. "Did he speak at all, gran? Can you remember anything about his voice?"

She put a shaking hand to her forehead. "I'm just trying to think –"

It hurt to see Sadie so confused. The old woman was normally bright as a box of buttons. Emmy wasn't thinking straight either. "I should never have gone out."

While Sadie was being attacked, Emmy had been playing the Good Samaritan, ministering to strangers.

Bev shook her head. "Don't go there, mum. It's not your fault." *Nor mine.* She'd changed her tune on that score. The untold damage here was down to a piece of low-life scum masquerading as a worthless shit.

"Bitch." Sadie never swore.

Bev widened her eyes. "Excuse me?"

"That's what he said. When he heard the knocking. He called me a bitch."

Thank God for neighbours, thought Bev. The husband of the Crime Lovers' Book Club hostess was pint-sized and hen-pecked, but had a bruiser's baritone and strict instructions from his wife: Sadie Morriss had left her glasses after the meeting and he was to return them. He'd been hammering away a full five minutes before he finally gave up and shoved the specs through the letterbox. By then the attacker had taken flight.

"He was scared, though," Sadie said. "I could see it in his eyes. He went as white as this sheet."

Not scared enough. He'd already used Sadie as a punch bag and hacked off her hair, and before leaving he whacked her in the mouth again. Bev shuddered. She'd speak to the neighbour later. He'd probably saved Sadie's life. Broken glasses, cracked dentures, the kitchen scissors the bastard had nicked, they could be replaced. Her gran was a one-off.

"I kept thinking he'd come back," Sadie's voice quavered. "That was worst of all."

She'd had three hours of fear while bound, gagged and tied to a chair. Sadie closed her eyes. Bev dreaded to think what was going on behind them.

She stroked the old woman's hand. "Try and get some sleep, gran. I'm just nipping downstairs to have a word with the guys." To see if Oz and crime scenes had come up with anything to point them in the right direction. And if the signpost was marked Sophia Carrington, Iris Collins, et al. Coincidences happened. But this close to home?

Bev didn't think so.

Her hand was on the door when the thought struck. She stood stock-still, narrowed her eyes. She must have misheard. "Gran?" She turned round slowly. "The man's face. You said it went as white as a sheet."

Sadie nodded. "That's right."

Bev fought to keep the fear out of her voice. "So the mask? He'd taken it off, had he, gran?"

Sadie didn't pick up on it. She even had a stab at a joke. "Yes, dunno why he bothered. He was no oil painting, if you know what I mean."

Bev walked slowly back to the bed. He'd let Sadie see his face, didn't care if she could describe him. That meant two things: Sadie was now a prime witness. And she was lucky to be alive.

# 22

It was mid-morning, Highgate. Byford, perched on the edge of a desk at the front, was taking the briefing. "At least we know what we're dealing with." He looked round. "The attack on Sadie Morriss was no coincidence."

Bev ignored concerned glances from members of the squad, concentrated on harsh reality. SOCOs had found eight daffodils at the back of her mum's house. They'd been scattered at random, almost certainly dropped by the attacker as he fled. The thug had clearly intended to say it with flowers. Add the floral message to the initial description provided by Sadie, and every officer at the briefing shared the guv's conclusion: Operation Streetwise had claimed another victim.

"Bastards." Darren New voiced what everyone was thinking. Targeting a cop's family was like shoving two fingers up at the police. The attack on Sadie was an act of defiance. Or revenge. Probably both. The arrest of Robert Lewis and Kevin Fraser must have pissed the gang off no end. Another bout of mindless violence was a way of saying up yours. These and other theories had been floating around for the last half-hour. Bev had listened without comment. The *why* was for later, right now she wanted a *who*.

She clasped her hands in her lap. She'd had three hours' sleep and been first in. It was her way of showing it was business as usual. Except it wasn't. The case had a renewed urgency. And a possible lead. She nodded at the murder board. "We need a name to go with that."

Heads turned. In the early hours, they'd compiled an

artist's impression of Sadie's attacker. It stared back now, and hopefully would soon be splashed across a few front pages. Bev shuddered. Helping to elicit details from Sadie had made her blood run cold: late-teens-early-twenties, pasty complexion, facial piercings and dark spiky hair. Déjà vu or what? Tom Marlow had painted an identical picture.

Byford rose, took a closer look. "Someone must know who he is."

Bev sighed, shook her head. The Shrek boys certainly hadn't provided any pointers. They were still banged up and buttoned down. Oz had called in first thing from the prison. They'd been asked to look at the latest likeness and, according to Oz, neither had narrowed an eye, let alone opened a mouth. As performing monkeys went, they'd perfected non-speaking roles. Who was the trainer? That was the big question. And how many others were in the act? Six weeks down the line and they still didn't know for sure the size of the gang.

Bev glanced across at the sound of paper rustling. DI Shields was leafing through sheaves of printouts. "We've had that description before." Her finger paused halfway down a page. "A witness called Tom Marlow phoned in early last week. We need to speak to him again."

Bev stifled a yawn. "It's under control. I'm waiting for him to get back to me." She wanted to check out a couple of things Sadie had mentioned. It might even be worth getting the two of them together, see if it sparked any thoughts.

Shields nodded, said nothing. Bit like the note she'd left on Bev's desk: *Dolly Machin. NFA.* No further action. SFA as far as thanks or even an acknowledgement went. She'd saved Shields from a load of grief. Dolly Machin's diabetes had killed her, not the scum they were after. Talk about ego on face.

Byford indicated the image on the murder board. "Is it possible you've seen him before, Bev?"

She shrugged. Every street, every day. It was uniform for a lot of youths. Appalling thought though it was, the attacker had found out where she lived, probably tailed her back, and DS Morriss, shit-hot detective, had failed to notice. Logic told her he had to be the same figure she'd seen lurking in the shadows the other night: a figure she'd dismissed so casually. She couldn't believe she hadn't taken it more seriously.

"There's no point beating yourself up." She widened her eyes. How did the guv do that? "You did everything right, given what you had to go on."

She'd be doing a hell of a lot more now. Sadie had been assigned more minders than a royal crèche. The old woman had been targeted because of who she was. Bev was finding that difficult to deal with.

# 23

"I need a quote, love."

*You need castration.* Bev's red ballpoint had already scored through several sheets of paper, in the process of eviscerating a pen portrait of Matt Snow. Luckily for the *Evening News* reporter, he was at the end of a phone.

"No comment." Her voice was surprisingly calm as she added a rather artistic cluster of weeping pustules round his mouth. *Eat your heart out, Tracey Emin.*

"Ah, come on, love, it needs a bit of human interest."

Human interest? Sadie getting smacked around? Bev concentrated on the addition of warts round his genitalia. "It's still no comment."

It begged the question, though: who had opened their big mouth? She glanced round, hoping it was no one here. The squad knew the score. A bland media release had been agreed. It carried bald facts: no name, no address, certainly no connection to Bev. Apart from respecting Sadie's insistence on no publicity, no one at Highgate wanted the finer points broadcast, literally or metaphorically. The idea was to get a steer on the attacker, not lead the media pack to the Morrisses' front door.

"As I understand it, the latest victim's related to you. And the assault took place in your mother's house. Is that right?"

"Which part of 'no comment' is difficult for you, Mr Snow?"

He paused, probably revising tactics. "She must be quite a woman, your granny."

Bev rolled her eyes. The little shit had the bones anyway.

He was after the flesh. As for the matey chat approach, it had to be the oldest trick in the journalist's book. Bev was on a different page and definitely not playing. Didn't stop Snow, though. Guy must be playing with himself.

"Fighting back like that. An old woman taking on a vicious thug." The voice was an embossed invitation to comment. It provoked only a deep sigh. Bev knew Snow was making it up as he went along, flying kites. She made a few strokes with the pen; his neck looked good with a noose.

"Bet you'd like to get your hands on him, wouldn't you, love?"

She snapped. "I'd like to get my hands on the fantasist who's feeding you this crap."

"It's not true, then?"

It was a lose-lose scenario. She cut her losses and broke the connection. The phone rang within seconds.

"Hey, love, I s'pose a piccie's out of the question?" Snow's snivelling persistence almost made her relent; she could always furnish him with his own portrait, warts and all. She settled for another grand slam instead.

Boy. Did this guy never give up? She snatched at the receiver. "Back off, Snowie."

"Nice one, my friend."

*Frankie.* Just the voice made Bev smile. "Sorry, mate. I'm really up against it." What with the poor man's Paxo and other assorted time-wasters, her list of things-to-do had fewer ticks than a bald sheep.

"Wow!" Frankie enthused. "Lucky you. And they pay you as well?"

The smile broadened. "Only when I'm good."

"Bev, my friend, you're so damn good I'm going to whisk you away for a treat. Café Rouge. Half an hour."

"Babe, I'd love to –"

"That's a no, isn't it?"

"Sorry." There was a shedload to get through. The early media coverage had prompted a stack of calls that needed monitoring and prioritising, same with the material coming back from house-to-house. And she was waiting on Tom Marlow. He could ring any time. "I would if –"

"Say no more. I suppose you're dumping your old friends now you're famous." There was an arch quality to the voice that could span a canal.

Bev laughed. "What are you going on about?" If anyone made it on to *I'm a Celebrity* it'd be Frankie. The girl had already turned down a load of modelling agencies, though she'd kill for a recording contract. Think Aretha Franklin meets Nina Simone. Only Italian.

With mock awe dripping from every fractured syllable, Frankie added, "Could I possibly make an appointment? Would you have a five-minute window between Trisha and Parkinson?"

"Have you stopped taking the tablets?" The bemusement was genuine. She hadn't a clue where Frankie was going with this.

"You are so easy to wind up, my friend." She dropped the banter, adopted business-like. "I clocked you on the telly news. Actually, I'd've missed you if I'd blinked."

"When was that, then?

"They were interviewing some woman outside the nick about that murder in Kings Heath? And there's my mate Bevvie striding past, looking all serious and important. How come you don't get to do the exciting stuff?"

Some woman? That was the DI doing her media appeal. "That was Shields, Frankie."

"The woman I'm gonna send the boys round to sort?"

Frankie laughed.

"What did you think of her?" Bev asked.

"The boss lady? Didn't really notice. Not once I'd spotted my best mate."

"Bull." Knowing Frankie, she'd have been glued to the screen with a points card.

"Come on, Frankie," Bev urged.

The pause had been dramatic. "Never trust a woman with skinny lips and shifty eyes. Guaranteed to be a pain in the arse." Head. Nail. On. Bev grinned; that was so what she wanted to hear. "Whereas you, darling," Frankie continued, "looked a million dollars."

Talk about flannel. Pass the butter. "Thought you only caught a glimpse?"

"Must be your very presence, Bev. Your charisma, your –"

"Hold on a min, Frankie."

The girl had loosened a thought or two; Bev needed to tie them. One was a shot so long you couldn't see the end. Or perhaps you could.

Bev had been in frame the other day, caught unwittingly on a wide-angle. It must happen all the time. Had it happened in Cable Street? Was it possible the BBC crew had filmed more than Marty's ugly mug? Cameras attracted ghouls like moths to a light show. At the very least, the footage could reveal potential witnesses; people who'd been around but hadn't come forward.

"You're a genius, Frankie. Have I ever told you I love you?"

"Not unless you want to get arrested."

The chance of capturing the perp on tape was infinitesimal, Bev knew. Even so, killers were cocky. Some killers were so damn cocky they cried out to be caught.

Bev found Oz in the canteen. An empty plate, apart from a few smears of ketchup, suggested a full stomach. Going by the papers spread across the table, he was now digesting more than a policeman's lunch.

"What you up to?" She perched on the seat opposite, wondering why he'd swept the papers up and turned them face down on the formica.

"Nothing important." He sounded casual but there was no eye contact. She didn't pursue it.

"Good. I have. Got something important." Well, potentially. She'd stopped to make one phone call after the chat with Frankie. It should be set up by now. "If you've finished –" her nod took in plate and papers – "we can push off."

Oz rose, slipped into his jacket. "Where're we going?"

"I'm taking you to the pictures."

There was no popcorn and definitely no adverts. Bev and Oz were in an edit suite at the BBC's new canal-side studios in the city centre. The Beeb had only just moved into the Mailbox from its old premises at Pebble Mill. And it wasn't the only occupant. In a previous life the Mailbox had been the Royal Mail's main sorting office. Now it boasted prestige business names, exclusive bars and restaurants, luxury hotels and posh shops. Not so much upmarket as celestial.

In edit suite six, the ginger ponytail pushing the buttons was an old mate, Steve Rock. The hair, like the flashy earring, was a recent affectation. Bev didn't care if he was into leopard-print thongs as long as he could still do things with video.

"This what you're after?" Steve nodded at the left-hand

monitor where the news footage from Cable Street was running: Marty Skelton's impromptu and decidedly unofficial press conference. "Christ. That bloke's ugly." Coming from Steve, that was harsh.

"It's not pretty boy I'm interested in." She rolled the chair forward, hunched over the control desk. Marty was centre frame, shooting off like it was soapbox corner. Thank God for volume control. The soft hum of technology from a bank of classy-looking kit was just about the only sound in the booth; a full-scale orchestra wouldn't have distracted Bev as the action moved on. There were exteriors of Marty Towers: yawn; a wobbly-vision pan across the railings at the back: boring; a piece-to-camera from the boy wonder. The end shot was a bunch of daffodils, all moody and soft-focus. It had obviously been planted, but not by Monty Don or any other gardener. Journalistic licence, it was known in the trade.

"Is that it?" Bev slumped in the chair, arms folded.

"What do you want? Tom Cruise?"

She rolled her eyes. It was a good-natured tease but the timing was bad.

"That's just the rushes, isn't it?" Oz asked.

Bev stared, not quite open-mouthed. Steve's features clouded over, his thunder stolen. "Not just a pretty face, are you?" He turned, missing a face even Mrs Khan wouldn't describe as pretty. Seconds later the editor was inserting a tape into a player.

Bev's eyes reflected the glow from the screen. This was cutting-room-floor stuff. Only digital. At first it was more of the same: exteriors and gvs. The fluffed pieces to camera were a hoot. They fast-forwarded after a few duff takes from the Beeb's boy wonder and nearly missed it.

"There!" Her finger was almost on the monitor, heart

racing. No wonder this hadn't made the final cut. The interview was just getting under way; Marty was in mid-shot and full flow, oblivious to the figure behind.

She was on her feet, jabbing at the screen. "That's what I want." The next second it had gone; her groan was involuntary. She raked a hand through her hair, glanced despairingly at the editor.

Steve was already rewinding the tape. He punched a few buttons and nodded at the right-hand screen where the crucial clip, brief and tantalising though it might be, was materialising. He winked at Bev. "Don't worry, petal. I can play with it now." The finger-flexing was a tad over the top but she gave a weak smile. For the moment Steve was the maestro and she needed a touch of magic.

Half an hour on, the magic tricks were more Tommy Cooper than David Copperfield. Bev bit her lip, fury vying with frustration. A face with pale skin and dark hair, almost filling the monitor. Was it the youth they were after? She stared, muttering obscenities under her breath. The picture quality was so poor, Bev doubted the youth's mother would pick him out of a line-up, let alone Sadie or Tom Marlow.

It wasn't Steve's fault. He'd tried every which way. Enlarging the image was easy. But the quality was crap; all definition gone. She screwed her eyes, willing regular features to emerge from the distortion. Talk about blurred vision. No wonder pixillation was used to disguise identity. Ironic or what?

Steve played around with the image a while longer, then sat back, fingers linked behind his head. "That's the best I can do, Bev. At the end of the day, I can only work with what was shot."

She nodded, bitterly disappointed. "Let me have a copy anyway, will you, mate?" He'd wire her the file. There was an anorexic chance a police techie might have a bigger box of tweaks.

Apart from a few sighs, the silence lasted till they were at the motor. She shrugged as she unlocked the door. "Sod it. I thought we had a goer there."

"Still might." He turned to fasten the seat belt, but not before she caught the look on his face. She hated it when he went all enigmatic.

"Christ, Oz. He's not a miracle worker. We just viewed everything they shot."

He was doing it again, with eyebrows this time. "That's right. *They* shot."

A slow smile spread across her face. *Of course.* It hadn't exactly been an exclusive. The media, to coin a phrase, had been out in force at Cable Street.

"Come on, Einstein. Let's hit the phones."

# 24

"You'd best look at this, Sarge." The door very nearly took the Dulux off the wall as Darren New strode in to the incident room.

Sod it. It was home time. Bev's feet, figuratively speaking, hadn't touched the floor tiles since the trip to the Mailbox. Her size sevens were currently taking a short break on a desktop while she lounged back with a Curly Wurly. Her smile was down to the call Tom Marlow had just returned. Saying he'd be happy to meet with Sadie any time – and Bev. Like tomorrow for a drink.

Reluctantly she swung her legs down and took the tape Dazza was thrusting in her face. She was impressed with the quick turnaround. It was only a couple of hours since she and Oz had put the requests in. All the picture desks had promised help, though none had given it priority. "Where's it from?"

"It's not from anywhere. It's one of ours," he said.

She licked chocolate from her fingers, waiting for enlightenment. It didn't arrive.

"Come on, Daz. It ain't Twenty Questions, what's on it?"

Why was he looking at his feet? "I went to fix that puncture of yours."

Puncture? "No diss, mate, but it's been a long day..."

"There's a chunk of glass there. The tyre was slashed." He nodded at the tape. "It's all on that."

"DC New sussed it, guv." Bev hit pause on the remote, froze the tape. They were in Byford's office, having just viewed it for the third time. So much for an early out.

Dazza's assertion that it was 'all on that' was unfounded. The CCTV footage was not a complete picture. A furtive hooded figure crouched at the bike's front wheel. There was no doubt what was being done. As to who was doing it…? There was no mug shot and due to the high camera angle there was no sense of the youth's size. Christ, it could even be a girl. Not that Bev thought so for a second.

"And there's no other damage? Nothing else touched?" Byford tapped a finger against his top lip.

She shook her head. The implication was clear. It wasn't random vandalism. It was a deliberate act. As she saw it now, there'd been a shadow on her tail far longer than she'd suspected. Shame she hadn't seen it back then. By walking home that night, she'd inadvertently played into his hands. It was as good as opening a door with Sadie's name on it.

"I know what you're thinking," Byford said. "It doesn't necessarily follow." She watched as he adopted his favourite stance by the window. Shame. She was dying for a drink and the booze was in his bottom drawer. "We're cops. We've all had run-ins with kids. It could just be little Johnnie's idea of payback."

Nice try. She'd given it a passing thought herself. It didn't stand up. "I don't buy that, guv. Not given the timing." The big question was why they'd targeted Sadie. Byford asked it.

Bev ran a hand through her hair. It sounded fanciful even to her. "I think it was a trophy thing, guv. Bag a cop's gran, show the pigs how smart we are."

His face said it all. She hadn't finished yet. "Look. What if we've been going about this the wrong way? We started off looking to nail a gang of toe-rags who duff up old dears for a few quid –"

He sighed. It seemed a lifetime ago. "Operation Streetwise."

"Yeah, well, maybe it should be Street sodding Genius."
She leaned forward, elbows on knees. "I don't think we're
dealing with a bunch of brain-deads. We'd have got a fix
on them by now. Yobs into granny-bashing are stupid.
They're cowardly. But they're not killers." She caught a
flicker in those grey eyes, pressed on with the argument.

"We've never really got to grips with this case, guv.
There's no evidence, barely any forensics, a serious lack of
witnesses and descriptions so vague they couldn't catch
cold. Christ, we don't even know how many perps we're
after." Her outstretched palms underlined the point.
"Strikes me that's either a run of fucking good luck or
someone's way ahead of us at every point."

He raised a hand. "Aren't you forgetting something?"
She frowned, closed her mouth. "Shouldn't you be asking
Lewis and Fraser if they feel lucky?"

"And what good's that going to do? They've been in
custody four days and haven't uttered so much as a prayer.
Why's that, d'you reckon?"

He started circling the room. She swivelled to keep him
in sight, restraining her impatience.

"Whatever they say is going to incriminate them,"
Byford countered. "They're scared to open their mouths."

"Come on, guv. They could spout the complete works of
Shakespeare, they're still going down."

Byford halted, sat on the corner of the desk. "So tell me."

"They're scared. You got that right." She held his gaze.
"They're scared because they're ASBO kids. Not killers.
And I reckon right from day one that's what this has been
about. It's about Sophia Carrington – and everything else
is a smokescreen."

Byford closed the pages, laid down the book and drew his

dressing gown tighter. It was cold and he was dog-tired. He should never have gone. "Drinks on me, guv," Bev had trilled. Boy, was he paying the price now. It hadn't even been a late night. Bev had been keen to get back to Sadie, taking the old girl a tin of Roses and a Des O'Connor CD. Painful.

The cramps had worsened the minute Byford's head hit the pillow. It was now 2.11 and he'd spent more time in the loo than under the duvet, eventually decamping downstairs where it was easier to read.

She'd handed him the journal as they were leaving. It hadn't taken long to get through. Not your average bedtime story. He wondered what today's kids would make of it. Laugh their designer socks off, most like. Or wouldn't believe a word. Not now, when women avoided marriage like the plague yet went out of their way to get pregnant. Anyway, who needed a man? According to Bev, all you needed these days was an empty yoghurt pot. He wondered vaguely whether the flavour mattered.

He took up the journal again, flicked through the entries. Poor Sophia. She'd had a love-child and spent a lifetime hiding the shame. Had it come back to haunt her? Bev seemed to be heading that way. He wasn't convinced. There were no photographs of Sophia's daughter after her sixteenth birthday. Besides, it was all so long ago. Tracking anyone involved back then was a fine-needle-in-a-field-of-hay job.

He stretched his legs, winced at a sharp pain in the gut. He'd felt the first twinges late afternoon. Bev had picked up on it in The Feathers. She'd been incensed about the continuing delay at the General. He smiled as he recalled her nagging. With hindsight, he reckoned she'd manoeuvred the session just to give him a grilling. She'd wanted the low-down on the tests, slipped in casual remarks about early retirement and wondered idly about Powell's disciplinary. She'd even asked if he'd heard her latest nickname. He'd not given much away, certainly not what a few of the men had started calling her behind her back.

# 25

The sun had got its shades on. It was more mid-June than late March. Bev closed the door and looked out, relishing the early rays. Baby-blue sky, clean air, dew glistening like fairy lights. She rolled her eyes and suppressed a grin. Much more of this and she'd launch into her Julie Andrews: not that there were many hills in Highgate.

The moment lasted till she clocked the MG. A young bloke in black jeans and a dark bomber jacket was bent double, peering in through the driver's window. Bev halted alongside, arms folded, tapped a Doc Marten.

The figure unfurled and flashed a smile across the top of the car. "Hi. I was hoping I'd catch you."

It wasn't a stranger. And it wasn't a bloke. The trade-mark hair was scooped up under a baseball cap but this close the face was unmistakeably female. Bev nodded. Apart from a feeling of having been wrong-footed, she was trying to work out how Grace Kane knew where she lived. As to the doorstep approach, Bev had a hunch already.

She watched as the writer made her way round the car, stroking the bonnet with a finger as she passed. "Low mileage. Good bodywork. You must look after it. I wish I'd held on to my Midget. I loved it to bits."

Bev narrowed her eyes. *Top Gear* auditions she could do without. Though an explanation for the small bunch of freesias the reporter was carrying would be nice.

"I heard what happened to your grandmother... I thought she might like these."

So that was it. Grace and favour. Under that flawless skin and wide-eyed flattery, the reporter was little better than Matt Snow. Presumably it was the dog turd's exclusive in the *Evening News* that had pointed Grace in the right direction. Bev was struggling to keep a civil tongue. It was bad enough for reporters to go round dabbling in the souls of strangers but no one, not even Grace Kane, was getting anywhere near her gran's.

"Thanks," Bev said briskly. "I'll make sure she gets them." She took the flowers and turned to exit, aware it wasn't in the script. Not Ms Kane's copy.

"Actually…" A winning smile.

"Yes?" A straight face.

"I was rather hoping to talk to her." She was doing that Princess Di thing with her eyes.

"Really? Why's that, then?" Surely Kane knew she was taking the piss?

The Di eyes darkened. Pique? Anger? Bev couldn't tell. The writer held her hands out. "Look, I hate intruding. But sometimes it helps, talking it through… with a stranger like me. It can be really cathartic."

"Helps?" The word struggled through clenched teeth. "Helps who? It certainly won't help my gran. Your bank balance, maybe."

"This isn't about money."

Yeah, yeah, yeah. "Don't make me laugh. Next thing it'll be 'I'm only doing my job.'"

"I am. I believe I can make a difference." There was something in the voice; she'd quit laying verbal bait. "Have you even bothered to read the stuff I sent?"

What stuff?

"You haven't, have you? Look, I know you don't like what I do. But we're not all Matt Snows."

Bev ran a hand through her hair. Had she been quick to judge? Maybe. "It's not you personally, Grace. But Sadie's not up to it at the moment. It's a shit time. I'll have a look through your stuff, let you know. Maybe in a few days?" If she could find it.

The writer looked ready to argue but didn't. "Of course. I understand. It must be awful." She held out a hand. "Thanks for your time anyway."

Grace Kane set off towards an Audi convertible parked a few doors down, then turned. "How about if you have a word with Sadie about me? At least give her the option. If she says no, fair enough… You've got my number. I'll be moving on at the weekend. But feel free to call me. Any time."

The phone box stank as usual. It had better be a quick call. He already had the number for the cop shop. No point talking to the bint on the switchboard. He drummed his fingers, waiting for connection to the incident room. He told the posh tart at the other end to listen up.

"The old lady who bought it down Cable Street? Got a pen?"

Bev's desk was covered in large brown envelopes sent from news desks all over the Midlands. But had Christmas come early? She slung her bag over the back of a chair and set her coffee on a beer mat. Oz was already making inroads into a mountain of calls he'd lined up. *Cherchez la femme*, Sophia's mystery daughter, was the name of the game. Except it was deadly serious.

Oz shook his head. No joy yet. Daz appeared to be the only one else around. He was hunched over a computer, two fingers worrying the keyboard. Bev took a seat, mental fingers crossed, while the real ones started on the morning's mail.

Five minutes later the bin was full of junk. She sat back, angrily brushed her fringe from her eyes. Christ. It had been bugging her for days now. There was barely time to wash it, let alone cut it. Sod it. That was one thing she could do. She headed for the loo, pocketing scissors en route.

The mirror confirmed she was no Nicky Clarke. But at least the eyebrows were evident, even though Caz, her regular crimper, would throw a hissy fit when she saw the effects. Bev stood in front of the glass, pulled her hair into a minuscule ponytail and posed, turning her head from side to side. She gave a pout or two, aiming for the elfin effect. She missed. More heartburn than Hepburn. Mind, her Quasimodo was to die for: she crossed her eyes, stuck her tongue out, hunched a shoulder and swung a lifeless arm.

"Nice one, Sarge."

Bev swirled round. DC Mansfield was just disappearing into a cubicle.

"Catch you later, Carol." She put as much authority into the voice as she could muster and headed back.

It was the first thing she saw on her return: an edge of brown envelope poking out from under her desk. The missing link? She snorted. Given the results so far, the weakest link was more likely. The cappuccino was cold but she swallowed a sip anyway and opened the envelope. Among the twenty or so stills there were two glossy black and whites that had her heart racing. The smile spread slowly until it covered her face. "Gotcha!"

If she was right, she had a killer in her sights.

The police lab worked fast. Mainly down to having Bev on their back. She refused to leave until they came up with the goods. And they were very good indeed. The techies had done their tweaking and a shadowy figure lurking on the edge of the originals was now in the limelight. Make that candlelight. The mug shots were well grainy, not perfect by any means, but both pics showed a youth with a pale face, black spiked hair and piercings. The last thing Bev needed was to go off half-cocked, so she'd popped back to let Sadie see the photos just to be on the safe side. Which was why, by the time she finally made the briefing, she didn't even apologise.

"Where the hell have you been?" Shields snapped. The DI had adopted that Annie Oakley pose again but this time Bev was calling the shots.

Maybe if she hadn't been so focused she might have picked up on the atmosphere, the tone in Shields's voice. She didn't. She headed straight for the murder board and pinned up both prints. "That's the bastard we need to nail."

She swirled round, not exactly expecting applause. But why the blank looks and open mouths? Except for Danny Shields. The DI was smiling, an amused glint in her caramel eyes. Bev glanced round, at last sensing the uneasiness. She'd misread the signs. The faces weren't blank; they were embarrassed. For her.

"And what makes you so sure, Sergeant?" The amusement had spread to the DI's voice now.

Bev felt a trickle of sweat race cold down her spine. She looked again at the dark hair, the pale skin and the piercings. She was right. She had to be. Anyway, Sadie was sure. As sure as an old woman shaking like an orchard could be. Bev stuck to her guns. "He's been identified. We just need a name."

Shields gathered her papers from the desktop. "Oh, we

have a name. In fact we have the killer. He's in a cell. I'm just about to charge him."

Bev felt the flush rise. No wonder people were sniggering. She'd produced a black and white print when apparently the original was banged up downstairs.

"Just one tiny anomaly, Sergeant Morriss." Shields was halfway to the door, didn't even turn to finish the sentence. "The youth we're holding bears as much resemblance to your pin-up boy as I do to Jordan."

# 26

There were too many muttered asides and sneaky looks going round Highgate. Bev had retreated to the caff down the road to lick her wounds. Not that she was into humble pie. Shields might be trumpet-blowing; it didn't mean she was playing the right tune.

"Are you listening or what?" Oz was keeping her company.

Or what. She managed a half-smile, noticed a table full of Chavs giving Oz the ogle. He was oblivious, mind on other matters. And that didn't include the downmarket décor or low cuisine. Stan's café was greasy knife, fork and spoon. Even the iceberg was deep-fried.

"Amazing, isn't it?" Oz enthused. "I mean all that shoe leather and it comes down to the DI's witness appeal. She was over the moon. Took the call herself, you know."

Bev chewed desultorily on a chip. Everyone this side of Uranus knew by now.

"Talk about getting it on a plate," Oz shook his head. "A name would have been good. But the address as well…"

She was incredulous too. Different reasons. "Shame he didn't come forward a bit sooner."

Oops. He didn't like that. The fork paused momentarily on the way to his mouth. "I heard he'd been out of the country."

"Shields should have got a number. A name at least."

He didn't like that either; the eyebrows were knotted. "We got a result. What's the problem?"

"Have you seen him?" Bev had, still could. Cowering in a corner; eyes like a rabbit's at a floodlit racetrack. Black hair was the only similarity. Other than that, Davy Roberts

214

was too small, too young, too scared. "He didn't do it, Oz."

She met his gaze but was unable to read it. She watched as he pushed his plate to one side. Either the cheese pasty was as flaky as it looked or she'd had an adverse effect on his appetite. Oz leaned forward, carefully positioned elbows to avoid unidentifiable spillages. "Then why's he saying he did?"

She sighed. Couldn't argue with that. It sounded as if Davy Roberts was going to put his hand up to every charge slung his way. Not that a confession was crucial. Not given what SOCOs had come up with. The bloodstained clothing and old-lady handbags found at his home would incriminate the Archbishop of Canterbury. So why hang on to the stuff?

"It just doesn't stack up." Davy Roberts didn't have so much as an acne scar, let alone a face full of studs. Whoever he was, whatever he'd done, she had serious doubts that he'd killed Sophia Carrington. And he hadn't attacked Sadie.

Oz scraped his chair back. "So prove it."

The murder room was doing a Marie Celeste. Daz had stuck a post-it on Bev's desk: *We're in The Feathers. Catch you later.* She lobbed the note in the bin, didn't see jack-shit to celebrate. Not that, strictly speaking, she'd been invited. She slung her jacket over the back of a chair. Oz had issued a challenge: put up or shut up. She flexed her fingers. Criminal records was as good a place as any to start. She logged on, tapped a few keys. Davy Roberts had barely cut a demo: a couple of cautions for retail levitation. Since when had lifting a pair of Nikes led to grievous bodily harm?

She raised her head, glanced at the grim gallery on the

murder board. The leap to offing old women was almost inconceivable. It just didn't work that way. And it severely holed her fledgling theory as to why Sophia Carrington had been killed.

She riffled through a sheaf of papers, looking for the youth's social report. OK, Davy Roberts hadn't been in the running for a school-attendance award. Who had? Christ, Bev had bunked off any number of times and she'd had both parents around back then to keep her grounded. Davy hadn't had so much as a name for his dad, let alone a bit of paternal support.

She read on. The lad's mother had no trouble bonding: with smack, heroin, Charlie. A five-year-old Davy had been found alone with the body – syringe still attached – and the poor little sod had been rewarded with a place in care.

Given the background, he should be doing a hell of a lot worse. So why wasn't he? A few lines further on and a possible answer emerged. Davy Roberts, a youth staring at a life sentence for murdering an old woman, appeared to have had his life turned round by another old woman. Bev tapped a biro against her teeth. How did that work, then? Kill or cure?

"Mrs Roberts?" Bev hoped her revulsion didn't show but keeping it under wraps was nigh on impossible. The fattest female she'd ever seen virtually filled the doorframe. Gert Roberts had taken her time getting there; wonder was she'd made it at all. Bev pocketed her ID. She didn't want the neighbours in on the action but seriously doubted whether Gert was physically capable of manoeuvring her vast bulk back inside.

"Can I have a word?"

"Where's Davy? What've you done with him?"

Bev's eyes widened; where did that come from? The little-girl voice was thin and reedy. Bev paused slightly, not sure what Shields had told the old woman or how much she'd absorbed. "He's helping with a few inquiries."

It was hard not to stare. The Cher-piece had to be a cheap wig and she must have had planning permission for the foundation. Christ knows what she'd had for the blusher. Not a mirror.

"What you gawping at?"

"Sorry. I…" Couldn't possibly say. "I need to talk with you about Davy."

The old woman clapped a surprisingly tiny hand to her massive… bosom was the only word. Oh, God. A wobble. Bev shot out a steadying arm, simultaneously aware it would do a fat lot of good if Gert went down. Talk about shoring up the Great Sphinx with a pin. It was touch and go, then panic over. Gert was hanging on in there. Bev breathed again and caught a whiff of rancid body odour laced with pee. Compassion vied with contempt. How could anyone get in such a state? Then again, she chided herself, what did she know of this woman's life?

"Can we go inside?"

Gert's swaying rump, encased in a dull grey frock that could have doubled as a duvet cover, just about glanced off the hall walls. Bev trailed in its wake, weighing up the place. The sitting room was all swirly carpets and flock wallpaper; MFI meets Pound Shop. Cheap and cheesy pottery animals lined a dusty mantelshelf. Bev feigned fascination in a purple hippo sporting a grass skirt and straw hat. It passed the time until Gert, now beached on a settee, had enough laboured breath to speak.

"Put that back where you got it. I don't want it smashed."

Really? Bev did as bidden, then perched on a chair next to Gert. A pile of paperbacks in pastel covers had already bagged most of it. "Tell me about your grandson, Mrs Roberts."

"He's a good lad. Never done nothing wrong."

Bev raised an objection with an eyebrow.

"Nothing serious," she added hastily. "He got in with a bad lot a couple of years back. Did a bit of shoplifting. I'm not excusing it. It's wrong. But you know what kids are. He got a load of stick from the others 'cause he didn't have the proper labels and that."

Designer fear. Bev nodded, noncommittal. "Does he still hang with the same crowd?"

"No. There was a falling-out."

"Who's he knock round with now?"

The huge shoulders shrugged. "He doesn't go out much."

It didn't answer the question. And it was bit late for that sort of protection. "He must have mates, Mrs Roberts."

The lines of her mouth went down.

"It could be important," Bev persisted. She counted to twenty, keeping time with the hiss and plop of a gas fire. Maybe it was the stifling heat or Gert's apparently cool indifference. "OK. Stuff it. If you don't want to help the lad …" She reached for her bag.

"He's mentioned some fella recently. Jake."

"And?"

"I don't know his other name."

"Where does he live?"

"Haven't a clue. Davy'll tell you."

"Davy's in serious trouble, Mrs Roberts." She broke the news as gently as she could. Not easy, given it encompassed murder, assault, theft, breaking and entering.

The great head shook. "Never in a million years."

"It's what he's saying, Mrs Roberts."

Gert stared into space, trembling fingers kneading rolls of thigh. Poor old dear. The shock was doing her head in. Bev waited and watched. Kids' laughter drifted in from the street. Maybe that was the catalyst... She jumped a mile as Gert pummelled the arm of the settee, sending up a cloud of fine dust.

"It's all lies. He'd not harm a living soul. He's too soft for his own good."

Bev moved in closer; elbows on knees. "There's evidence, Mrs –"

"Then he's been framed!" Gert's eyes were the colour of over-ripe limes. "And I'll tell you this for nowt, if you lot have harmed a hair of his head – " The rest was lost in huge shuddering sobs as tears coursed down flabby cheeks and collected in the folds of her chins.

Bev rummaged in her bag for tissues. "Here you go."

Gert dashed at the tears. The make-up smeared and ugly red blotches stood out against a sickly pallor. "What do you want, anyway? Why are you here?"

Bev paused, adding weight to the words. "I'm trying to find the truth."

The eyes almost disappeared as her face creased in... what? Disbelief? Doubt? Hope? Gert lowered her head, started shredding a damp tissue, scattering the tiny scraps in her voluminous lap.

"Hates seeing anything in pain, does Davy. When he was a kid, he'd bring birds home, try and fix their wings so they could fly off. Dog we had got run over. The lad cried for a fortnight." She looked up, willing Bev to believe. "He couldn't have done them terrible things. He just couldn't."

She would say that, wouldn't she? But she'd also said something a lot less predictable. "What do you mean, 'he's too soft for his own good,' Mrs Roberts?"

Gert flapped a hand. "He'd never fight back. I told him he'd to stand up for himself. But he never would."

Bev eventually elicited the full version of the persistent bullying Davy had endured at school. A gang of older kids inflicting daily beatings and verbal abuse. Davy's only retaliation had been to take countless sickies. It was another note that didn't ring true with his alleged crimes, unless she was tone-deaf. Or was it possible the prolonged attacks had brutalised him? If you can't beat them...

Gert dismissed the notion with a snort. "Brutal? Don't be so bloody soft. Look at him."

Bev followed Gert's indulgent smile. She'd already registered the photograph on top of the telly; assumed the old woman had other grandchildren. The blond-haired blue-eyed boy linking arms with Gert at first bore no resemblance to the kid back at Highgate. Bev moved nearer, looked closer. The eyes had it.

"How long's he been dyeing his hair?"

"He's only done it the once. A week back, maybe. Why?"

Bev was pretty sure she already knew the answer. "Can I borrow the pic for a day or two, Mrs Roberts?"

Davy Roberts was a dead ringer for Baby Face. No angel, definitely. But a killer?


It was all over the front page but Jake was reading between the lines.

*Detectives are questioning a youth in connection with the murder of Birmingham pensioner Sophia Carrington. The body of the retired doctor was found...*

Yada-yada. Get on with it...

*The youth, believed to be from the Kings Heath area, is also helping police inquiries into a series of attacks on* *elderly women in the city. Two other youths have already been charged in connection with the investigation and will appear in court again next …*blah blah…

*Operation Streetwise is headed by Det Supt William Byford…*

Jake folded the paper, caught sight of his reflection in the mirror behind the bar, barely recognised himself at first. Certainly didn't realise he'd been smiling. Still, why not? Mission accomplished. One or two loose ends to tie, then he'd hit the road. He drained the glass, ordered another pint. Talk about making a killing. This called for a toast: absent friends.

"Is this the midnight oil or are you still burning two-ended candles?"

Bev glanced up from a desk buried by paperwork. How come he never knocked? Guv's perk, she supposed. She replaced a grimace with a weary smile. It was good to see a friendly face. "Nah. I need the overtime to work on my expenses."

"Very droll."

It wasn't that late. Just after eight. The meet with Tom wasn't till nine. This early, Friday night, Highgate wasn't exactly buzzing; it was a good place to get her thoughts in some sort of order. There were too many conflicting theories in her head. Just as she thought she saw a connection, there'd be a bunch of anomalies in the way. All she knew for sure was that she had serious doubts about Davy Roberts's culpability. He was definitely involved; they had a forensics match on the hair recovered from the mask at Maude Taylor's place. But murder? DI Shields wouldn't even give Bev's misgivings a proper hearing. Oz was generally a decent sounding-board but he'd gone out to play. Indoor cricket, as it happened. Until the guv put in an appearance, she'd been talking to herself.

"You got a min, guv?" Given the briefcase and buttoned coat, he was on his way out; she pulled a chair over before he could say no.

He sighed, took a seat and gave her a look. "Have you done something to your hair?"

She tugged at a fringe that was more Siegfried than Vidal. No one else had commented; maybe no one else had dared. "I gave it a trim. Stop it getting in my eyes."

"Seeing things straight now, are you?"

There was an edge to the voice you'd have to be blind to miss. She had an idea where he was coming from but there was no harm in asking. "Your point being?" Pointedly, he waited for a 'sir'.

"I've had Danny Shields on my back. She says you don't have Davy Roberts down as our man. That you're undermining her authority. That your negative attitude's bad for the team."

She felt the twitch of a muscle in her cheek, counted to five in her head. "Fuck that." Should have made it ten. "Maybe I don't want to be in a team that bends the rules."

Byford rarely shouted when he was angry. The reverse. "You'd better have grounds for that."

It had been a struggle to catch what he said. "That came out wrong; rule-bending's over-stating it. What I'm saying is you can't claim a victory if the game's not over." Impatient, she scratched her head. "Look, guv, Shields is going round like she's pulled in Bin Laden. The sound of backs being slapped is making me puke."

"Davy Roberts has confessed to killing Sophia Carrington, admits the other assaults. What more do you want?"

She slumped in the chair. "I don't buy it. I don't think

he's capable and I don't see the why."

His fingers drummed the desktop. "We know why."

She shook her head. "I don't think so. OK, at first it looked as if it was about nicking a few quid, slapping old dears round a bit. But Sophia's murder doesn't fit the pattern. It was savage, guv. Christ, you saw the damage." She could have added, "And she'd been cleaned up by then." But they both knew that. She outlined her recent visit to Gert Roberts; told him of Davy's troubled past, reiterated why she didn't see him as a murderer.

Byford listened. The occasional nod didn't mean he agreed. "Violence escalates, gets out of control. That's why it's called mindless."

"What if it wasn't mindless? What if it was meticulously planned?"

"I'm not with you."

She wasn't sure where she was headed herself. But wherever her thoughts strayed, they invariably returned to the same starting point. "What if the murder of Sophia Carrington is what this is all about? Has been all along? DC Khan thought her profession might have had something to do with it. I reckon it was because of her past."

"Not sure I go along with you." He reached for his case. For a second she thought he was leaving. He ferreted around, found what he was looking for. The journal. "Her story wasn't unusual. It happened. People moved on. Buried the past. Made new lives."

"And the shit death?"

He sighed. "Look, as it stands, we've got three youths in the frame, evidence and forensics that's coming together. We've got a case. If you're not convinced, do something about it."

Bev narrowed her eyes. He must know Shields had

ordered her to drop it, to concentrate on tightening what they had, not following leads that didn't exist. "You're saying I can dig around?"

"It's the weekend. You can do what you like." He got to his feet, a glint in his eye. "Just don't put it on your over-time."

Two days to trace a baby born half a century ago. No records, no name. Piece of piss.

She called it a day, grabbed her bag and caught up with Byford in the corridor. Five minutes later they were in the car park. The guv was raving about some new Thai restaurant in town. Bev listened with half an ear, simultaneously working out a list of priorities for tomorrow. Maybe she could sweet-talk Oz into lending a hand.

"So what do you think?" Byford asked.

Oops. "Sorry, guv, run it past me again."

She frowned, almost asked him to repeat it a third time. He'd asked if she thought Oz was ready to take sergeant's exams.

Which was more than Oz had.

On the other hand, Bev had a card or two close to her chest these days. She tamped down a flash of anger. Pique shouldn't figure in her response. Her initial thought was that he'd make a shit-hot sergeant. But...

Was the hesitation professional or personal? Was it head or heart saying *too soon*? The guv obviously thought the timing was right or he wouldn't be pushing.

"Well?" Normally he couldn't shut her up.

"Off the top of my head, guv..." She paused, pictured Oz, bit the bullet. "He should definitely go for it. Not a shadow of doubt."

She was still doing the hard sell when they reached Byford's Rover. She waited as he unlocked it. He looked tired but not unwell. The question slipped from the tip of her tongue. "Any news from the hospital, guv?"

She thought he was about to tell her to back off but his expression changed once, twice, maybe more before he spoke. "The results are inconclusive."

Inconclusive? Sounded like a cross between fudge and fuck-up. She was desperate to know more, dying for him to tell her what'd happen next. She was holding her breath, hoped her "Oh yeah?" sounded more laid back than she felt.

She watched as he got into the car, placed his case on the back seat. Bastard. How could he do that to her? She dug her hands into her coat pockets, stamped a foot primarily against the cold. Next thing she knew, he was leaning across and opening the passenger door. "I'm going into the Nuffield. First thing."

Private, then. She didn't blame him; probably do the same herself. She turned to face him. He looked just the same, sounded upbeat, but his hands were strangling the wheel. "Anything I can do, guv. Anything you need. You only have to ask."

He nodded and smiled. It was all he could manage; it was more than enough.

# 27

The Angel was one of those classy wine bars in the Mailbox designed to attract the city's coolest customers. Must be fucking freezing, if you asked Bev. There was so much naked flesh on show, she'd spent the last thirty minutes counting goose bumps. Her bar stool in the far corner was an ideal vantage point. She swerved to avoid a bony elbow and a trail of stale smoke. Bridget Jones had a lot to answer for. From what Bev could see, the place was an upmarket Smithfield's: a load of scantily clad singletons swigging Chardonnay and looking for Mr All-Right-On-The-Night-In-A-Piss-Poor-Light.

Bev sank a last mouthful of Sauvignon. She wasn't pissed, just pissed off. If this was Tom's idea of a joke, ho bloody ho. The purpose of the meet was ostensibly professional; it felt like she was being stood up. She glanced at her watch yet again. Sod this for a game of solitaire. Time waits for no man. And neither did Morriss.

"I'm so glad I caught you. I was sure you'd have gone." She felt Tom's hand on her arm. He managed a profuse apology even though he was out of breath. "I'm so sorry. Please. Let me get you another drink."

Fulsome though it was, it wasn't an explanation.

"Bitter lemon," she said. "And I can't stay much longer. I've got things to do." Churlish, but she didn't appreciate being kept hanging round. She was knackered, starving and had a seriously busy weekend ahead. A group was grabbing its Armani jackets and heading for the door. She slid off the stool. "I'll see you over there." The bar was no place to talk.

She watched him closely as he waited to be served. She'd seen him cool, casual and concerned. She'd be hard put to define his current state. He kept looking over his shoulder, darting glances at the door. As he handed her the glass, she thought she noticed his hand shake slightly. She didn't comment, just took a sip. The bitter lemon was exactly that; she pulled a face, regretted eschewing more grape.

"Look, Bev, I honestly don't make a habit –" he started.

"Has anything come to mind?" If he'd been on time there'd be no need to grovel. That was the trouble with good-looking blokes; thought they could get away with murder.

"Sorry –?" Confused? Clueless? She couldn't tell from the voice and refused to meet his glance.

"The youths. Near the park," she said. "We're particularly interested in the one with spiked hair. Dark."

The silence went on so long it forced her to make eye contact. Only she couldn't. Tom Marlow was staring at his hands. He mumbled something but she must have misheard. "Say again."

"I saw him tonight."

"You did what?" She couldn't believe it. Neither, it appeared, could the couple at the next table. She lowered her voice, leaned in a little, watching as he halved the large scotch in a single gulp.

"I gave chase. It was so stupid."

Incredibly. Number One: the youth was almost certainly carrying. Number Two: it was a collar opportunity, cocked up. She was about to erupt again but something about his voice, the expression in his eyes stopped her. He was trying to hide it but the failed heroics had left him badly shaken.

"I should have called the police. I know that now."

She nodded. There was no point rubbing it in.

"He had a knife." Marlow opened his coat gingerly. He'd staunched the flow of blood with a wadded-up handkerchief.

"Jesus H," Bev gasped. "What's the fucker done?"

Marlow attempted a weak smile. "I'm sure it looks worse than it is."

Bev reached for her keys. "I fucking hope you're right."

An overworked, under-stress A and E doctor agreed. Tom Marlow was lucky. The wound wasn't deep but it was close to the heart. His blood pressure was low; they'd keep him in overnight.

Bev nodded. It was a vindication. She'd virtually had to force Tom to visit casualty. She'd done the driving while he filled in the details. Highgate was acting on them now. They just might get lucky. Tom Marlow had been in the back of a black cab when he spotted the youth getting off a 35 bus in town. The area of the chase was pretty well covered with CCTV and the tape from the bus was being biked back to the nick. Officers were on the street searching for a weapon, seeking witnesses. According to Tom, there'd been a number of people around though none, predictably, had intervened.

She popped her head round the cubicle, relieved to see the colour back in his face. Even in this lighting he looked good. "I'm off," she smiled. "Catch you later."

He lifted a hand in farewell, pain and delayed shock accounting for the obvious exhaustion. "Thanks for everything, Bev." He looked down but she sensed he had something to say. "I'm really sorry. Maybe if I'd –"

"No sense beating yourself up. He's out there some-where. He'll cock up sooner or later. And when he does, we'll get him."

She flashed him a bright smile, kept a dark thought to herself: Marlow was attacked because he'd recognised the youth. Did the assailant also know Marlow? Was it possible the scumbag had actually engineered the encounter? Was it, like the attack on her gran, a warning? Did it mean she was getting close? Or was she getting paranoid?

It doesn't come easy. Sleep, that is. Not when your thoughts are doing a Schumacher. She put a pan of milk on to boil; hot chocolate might encourage the zeds. She rubbed the back of her neck, tried to smooth out a few knots. They'd been so close to a collar tonight. Close but no cigar. If only Tom Marlow hadn't tried to play the hero. He'd ended up as an extra in *ER* and the runaway now had the lead in a road movie. She slumped and sprawled, too wired to unwind, too knackered to make connections.

She glanced round in need of diversion. She took a paper from her mum's re-cycling pile on the dresser, wondered if she dared light a ciggie. Nah. It was too cold to keep the door open. She flicked through the pages, froze, flicked back. A familiar face stared out from page three. God knew when they'd snatched her pic but it had to be during the last force ten. The headline screamed:


**STREETWISE GANG TARGET COP'S GRAN**

The story bore even less relation to the reality. According to *Evening News* Crime Correspondent Matt Snow, *West Midlands Police hunting a vicious gang of street thugs are confident of further arrests...*

She raced on, spotting two spelling errors in the next paragraph. Frigging hell. If Snowie couldn't even get the names right... She went back over the story to see how he'd fared with the facts.

*Detective Sergeant Beverley Morris, whose grandmother Saddie is recovering from her ordeal, was hopeful that new evidence would lead police to the killer 'within days'.*

Bev wiped a hand over her face. Fuck the facts, but what a scoop: a poop scoop. So exclusive was the report, Matt Snow had the copyright. She read it for a third time. Cunning sod. It was implication and suggestion. He hadn't actually stated the police had new evidence and of course they were confident of an arrest. Eventually.

She tore out the article, slipped it in her bag. It wasn't just Snow's lurid imagination bugging her, but she couldn't put her finger on what else was wrong. She gave a wry smile. Maybe she'd ask 'Saddie'.

"Shit!"

Bev's mad dash to the cooker was too slow. The bubbling milk had the edge. Had the hot ring, top of the stove and kitchen floor as well.

Sadie was crying over more than a drop of spilt milk. The noise sounded like the mewling of a sick frightened animal. Bev heard it on her way to bed. She paused on the landing, cocked an ear. Her gran was sobbing her heart out and Bev's was in bits. She dithered outside the bedroom door. Sadie would be mortified if Bev, or anyone come to that, witnessed her distress. Her gran's generation regarded 'letting it all hang out' as something you did with washing.

Bev closed her eyes, pictured Sadie, tear-stained cheeks, bewildered, confused. Diminished – that was the word. A shadow of her pre-attacked self. Bev bit down hard on her lip. Unbidden, an image of the yob with spiked hair flashed before her. The anger was physical; she felt the heat running through her veins. She'd be no use to Sadie feeling like this. Anyway, she was bone-tired. She walked away, heading for her room. Then made a detour.

"Fancy a nightcap?" The Armagnacs were probably large enough to anaesthetise, let alone induce sleep. "Best not tell mum."

She forced a conspiratorial grin into the whisper, giving the old lady a few seconds to dry her tears. But Sadie didn't bother. Maybe there were too many. Bev sat on the edge of the bed, took one of her gran's hands between her own. The bones were brittle and trembling like twigs.

"Want to talk about it?"

Sadie kept her eyes down. Bev sneaked glances, waited for the right moment. The tears, the silence – it was so not Sadie. Some people could light up a room; her gran could light up a castle. She loved life, loved people, always had a good word to say. She'd had knocks before. Bert, her fireman husband, had died fighting a blaze at a block of flats. Bev glanced at the wedding photograph that never left her gran's bedside table. In a certain light you could catch the outline of Sadie's lips where she kissed his through the glass. Worse was when Sadie buried her only son, Bev's dad. Even that hadn't crushed her like this. She squeezed her gran's hand, almost at a loss.

"It's OK to have a good cry, you know. No one thinks any of the less of you."

Sadie looked up. "I do, Bev." She turned her head. "He's made me feel weak and worthless. Like as if I don't matter."

"Don't let him, gran. He's not worth it." Easier said than done. Violence wasn't about the scars you could see.

"I'm frightened. Every minute of the day and night, I'm frightened."

"Anyone would be, gran. It's nothing to be ashamed of."

Sadie shook her head. The clock ticked. A horny cat was on the prowl out back. A couple of times, Sadie opened her mouth to speak, finally got round to it on the third attempt. "Every time you go out the door, I wonder if you're ever coming back."

Where did that come from? "Gran," she soothed. "Gran…"

"I never thought about it before. Em always did enough fussing for the both of us. But I've seen it now. People hurt each other. You're out there on the firing line, Bev."

"Don't go worrying about me, gran. I can take care of myself."

It was true. She had more self-defence courses under her belt than Bruce Lee. She embellished a few tales to try to reassure the old lady. Maybe it was the alcohol or the anecdotes, but it didn't take long before Sadie nodded off. Bev brushed her gran's forehead with her lips and slipped off the bed. She turned at the door. Sadie wasn't asleep; she was looking straight at her.

"I always thought you were making a mistake, Bev. But I see it now. You made the right choice."

Bev gave an uncertain smile. Maybe she'd overdone the Armagnac.

"No getting married, no kids," Sadie went on. "You've got your job. You can't have it all. You've always said that."

*Have I?* Then the penny dropped. Saint Joseph's Junior School. Double feature: sex and childbirth. She could see it now. She'd got home that afternoon swearing eternal celibacy and vowing never to bring up so much as a guinea pig.

"I –" She broke off. No point putting Sadie straight this late in the day. The little-wife thing wasn't based on the pressures of being a cop. Before this case, she'd never wanted kids or commitment, full stop. Now? She wasn't so sure.

She nodded, hoped the smile reached her eyes. "You said it, gran. Try and get some rest now, eh?"

# 28

"Here you go, Davy." Bev placed a mug of chocolate topped with marshmallows on the metal table. She'd have added parasol, cocktail cherry and a couple of 99 flakes if she'd thought it would oil the wheels. She held out a hand. "I'm Sergeant Morriss. Bev." She reinforced the gesture with a warm smile. Neither elicited a response of any kind. *Suit yourself.*

Shame that, because this wasn't a 'he said, she said, who gives a fuck' sort of interview. This mattered. Or it should. Not that Davy Roberts was aware – not by the look of him. He'd barely glanced at Bev. She was less interesting than the stainless steel toilet bowl and the almost certainly semen-stained mattress. The cells at Highgate were not five-star.

A quick sip of Cadbury's didn't count as an indication of gratitude, but it was the youth's only acknowledgement of her existence. Another slurp added to the nascent chocolate moustache. Bev restrained an urge to dab his top lip. It wouldn't do much for his ego, which was clearly struggling as it was.

"Gonna tell me about it, Davy?" Bev's faded denims and bomber jacket said cool rather than cop, but maybe Davy wasn't listening. His expression could have turned cream. But it didn't reach the lad's startled, and startlingly blue, eyes. She caught a flicker of something else there: vulnerability? Fear? She registered the same unwitting conflict in his body language. His legs, in baggy black combats, were sprawling-wide-boy but those skinny hunched shoulders were curled in on themselves. She mirrored his stance with her own legs, glanced round ostentatiously. "Nice place you got here."

He sniffed. Not something she'd recommend, given the competing odours. Floral disinfectant was no mask for urine, stale sweat and the ghosts of a thousand farts.

She waited a while, taking covert glances at the lad, but the laid-back approach was going nowhere.

"Why're you doing this, Davy?" She didn't mean biting his nails, not that there was much left to chew; all ten were down to the quick; a couple were bleeding. "You'll go down big-time. Know that? When you come out, you'll not need to nick pension books. You'll have one of your own." If you're lucky.

It was no bedtime story, though he'd closed his eyes. Bev bit her bottom lip. The silly little bugger was going to take the rap for something she was convinced he hadn't done. She had no idea why, or who was behind it, but when it came to piling on the pressure she'd just been to the pressure shop.

"Who's bullying you this time, Davy?" She'd clocked the bruises when she'd sneaked a butcher's at the lad last night. Butcher's was right; skinny pale arms blotched the colour of liver. "What bastard's scaring the shit out of you now?"

A toilet flushed along the corridor. She waited. And waited. It wasn't going to work.

She itched to knock some sense into him, opted to hit where she sensed it hurt most. "'Course, they'll probably let you out for Gert's funeral." So that's what eyes snapping open looked like. Carry on, Beverley. Go for the closed mind now. "Poor old soul looked like death yesterday. Doubt she'll last till the trial."

His eyes were pleading but the mouth was still clamped.

Trouble was, she had no time for finesse. The minute he was formally charged, there'd be no more little chats like this. What was happening now wasn't just off the record, it was off Bev's own bat. And she had no intention of being caught out. She lowered and softened her voice, pulled the chair closer. "This isn't a game any more, Davy. It's big boys' stuff."

Half a minute's grace for him to take that in then, slowly, casually, she outlined the evidence they'd uncovered in his room: the handbags, the bloodstained clothing. She had a feeling it was news to him: bad news. "It couldn't be more serious, Davy."

He opened his mouth, then swallowed hard, as if to stop words he'd later regret. But the urge to speak was there. She'd read the signs, seen them before. It was a question of finding the right button. She found a possibility in her bag, pushed the photograph across the table.

For a heartbeat or two, she thought he was going to throw up. His body tensed, he darted wild glances round the cell walls, anywhere but on the bloody battered face of the murdered Sophia. Not that it mattered. The split-second glimpse was enough. He covered his eyes but the image was recorded forever. The brain could play it back any time. And would, if Bev's experience was anything to go by. She felt a momentary pang of conscience. The picture show had been well out of order. Tough.

"Gert doesn't believe you did that, Davy. She reckons you're a good lad." She reached across, slipped the still back in her bag. "Poor old dear was crying her eyes out when I left. She'll not cope on her own. I guess the Social'll find her somewhere."

His face was wet but the tears weren't enough. She had

to get the lad to talk. She was up against the clock and fresh out of buttons. She re-ran the scene with Gert, desperate for a lead-in. There was only one avenue she hadn't gone down. She frowned, walked it mentally again. Came across a thought that sparked an idea. Stay cool. It was too crucial to blow.

"I'm wasting my time here. You'd best have this." She chucked him another photo, a copy of the picture she'd borrowed from Gert. Davy and his gran linking arms; smiles wider than the old girl's girth. "It'll give you something to remember her by."

She gathered her bits, headed for the door. It was a throwaway line; she turned to see if he caught it. The lad had his head down, cradling the photograph in both hands.

"Hey, Davy. Where's Jake get his piercings?"

"Dunno." It was only one word. But it told Bev what she needed to know.


Talk about busking it. Jake could have had a peg leg and been on nodding terms with Rolf Harris until Davy Roberts had uttered that single word. Unfortunately, that was as far as it went. The lad hadn't uttered another syllable. Bev had been forced to call in the cavalry. She and it were having coffee and croissants in the canteen at Highgate. She licked a finger to gather the crumbs off the plate, simultaneously indulging in fantasies of Oz in riding boots wielding a whip. Though delicious, it was a touch distracting. Reluctantly she reined in her thoughts and finished running through the Roberts interview.

"It wasn't so much a leap in the dark, Oz. More head-first into a black hole." She waited for the verbal pat on the back.

"Sure it was the head?"

She bridled. "Meaning?"

"This chat? Who OKd it?"

A one-shouldered shrug.

"The photo? What possessed you?"

Another shrug. She sneaked a glance at his face. He shook his head slowly. "Out of order."

Maybe he was still miffed over her meeting with Marlow. She'd filled him in on it last night but only because she'd had to put it in a report. Or maybe the sergeant-wannabe was keeping his nose clean? Shame the guv had told her to keep it buttoned on that front. She'd a good mind to tell him to shove it but she needed his help.

"Come on, Oz. It paid off. We've got a couple of steers now."

As it happened, the emergence of a youth called Jake had pushed her pet theory off the boil. Sophia Carrington's past might turn out to be a diversion, but Bev wasn't yet ready to discount it completely. Oz appeared unmoved. She held out empty palms.

"I can't do it on my own." Not rifle a haystack the size of a planet for a couple of thin needles: Doctor Carrington's missing daughter and the youth with spiked hair.

Oz looked unconvinced. "Can't see why you're so keen on this Jake character. Lots of kids have face studs. Stupid hair. We're making a hell of a lot of work for ourselves if he turns out he's just a mate of Davy's."

He was right. But then Oz hadn't been there. Davy had only said one word but she'd never forget the look on the lad's face. If Jake was a friend, Davy Roberts sure had no need of enemies.

Jake was late. Unexpected delay. Best not to rush it anyway.

He deliberately slowed his step, cast surreptitious glances down the street. It was empty apart from a few motors, a couple of kids kicking a football round. He pulled his hood up, then paused to light a Marlboro. No sense in attracting an audience, not when the final act was so near and he'd soon be staging an exit. He moved on, slipped a hand gingerly into his pocket. The blade was lethal; he'd sharpened it. It was a different knife, but Kitchen Devils were easy to buy. Not that he'd be prepping veg.

He was approaching the house now. Was he going to kill her? Hadn't made up his mind. Could go either way. Personally he didn't give a shit. She was a bargaining counter. He had a bit of loose change in his back pocket. Maybe he should toss for it? On one hand, it was always good to see the knife go in, the flesh parting; but if the old girl was dead, Davy had nothing left to lose. He brightened at the prospect of another thought. What if the old lady lost something? An ear, maybe, or a finger? He pictured Davy opening the parcel. Jake smiled. Oh, that was good. That was very good.

A car pulled up behind. Fuck it. Don't look back. He didn't break stride, walked straight past the house, turned as he reached the corner. Thank God he'd carried on. It was the cop with the big nose and even bigger mouth. His eyes narrowed as his fingers tightened round the knife's handle. He might have doubts about offing Gert Roberts; he had none whatever about getting rid of Miss Piggy.

## 29

By late afternoon Oz reckoned he'd drawn the short straw. Make that miniscule, with excrement. He'd been stuck in Highgate while Bev was paying house visits and calling in favours, flashing a photo of Davy Roberts and the TV still of Jake whoever-he-was to tame snouts. Informants loathed granny-bashers almost as much as paedophiles. Could be they'd supply a name, a break, at least put the word on the street. She planned running the pics past the old ladies as well. It was a long shot but it just might jog a memory or two. Despite the odds, it had more going for it than Oz's share of the workload.

He'd been left holding the baby. Or not holding it, trying to get a fix on it. It'd be easier tracing Lord Lucan than Sophia Carrington's offspring. Antecedents were no problem; Sophia's lineage went back generations. But post-Sophia: nothing. The family tree appeared to have contracted Dutch elm disease.

He lounged back, legs sprawled, hands on head. He'd checked every which way: family records, general register office, adoption society. The information had to be there. But clearly not under Carrington. Without the right name, it was like trying to breach a firewall without a password.

"DC Khan? I didn't know you were in today."

Oz shot up. DI Shields was framed in the doorway behind him. The woman moved like a stealth bomber. How long had she been standing there? He lifted his mobile. "Just making a few calls." He reached for the mouse to clear the screen but thought better of it.

"Don't let me stop you. I'm out of here." The salute was

obviously mock, he was still wondering about her smile when the phone rang.

"Wotcha." It could only be Bev.

"How's it going?"

"It's not."

"That good, huh?"

He talked her through it; listened as she reciprocated. "I've put the word out. Have to wait and see. Ena and Joan? Not brilliant. They're keen to help but neither's a hundred per cent."

"I know the feeling."

"Do us a favour, Oz?" He thought he already was. "I need another look through Sophia's journal. I think I left it in my top drawer. Can you bring it tonight?"

"Tonight?"

"Your call. My treat." She owed him for all this. Big time. Owed him the truth over Marlow as well. Anyway, there was catching up to do; they never did get that night of passion.

"You're on," Oz said. "What you up to now?"

"I'm nipping in to see Gert Roberts, then I'm calling it a day."


"I'd help like a shot but I never met the lad. I told Davy he should bring him home, like. He never did. Sorry, love."

Gert Roberts looked glum; sounded it too. Life without her grandson was taking its toll. She relinquished the photograph of the pale-faced spike-haired youth with a grimace of regret. Bev sighed, should have known it'd be a waste of time. She'd already spent the better part of an hour up in Davy's room. No point, really, not when SOCOs had given it the works. Anything vaguely useful had been removed: clothes, computer, letters, books.

"You look whacked," Gert said. "Shall I make us a cuppa? It'll only take a minute."

No way. "Yeah, go on then." She couldn't resist the child-like plea in the old woman's voice. Must be lonely as hell for her without the lad. Gert was struggling to raise her bulk from the chair. "Want me to do it?" Bev offered.

"Smashing. The fixings are on the side. Can't miss them."

She was beginning to regret the impulse. The kitchen stank: stale fat, sour milk, unwashed flesh. Gert's little-girl voice wafted in from the sitting room. "Can't stop thinking about him. Wondering what he's up to. How he passes the time."

"He's got books, magazines." The dishcloth was teeming: bacteria heaven. Bev ran it under the tap and dabbed half-heartedly at a surface or two.

"Takes after me. Loves reading. Has done since he was a kid."

"Oh yeah?" She sniffed her fingers, chucked the cloth in the sink and washed her hands.

"You'll find a bit of Swiss roll in the tin."

It was next to the chip pan: vintage Charles and Di, beaming couple, golden carriage. Bev's snort said it all.

"Here you go." She plonked the tray on a low table.

"You not having cake?" Gert's incredulity suggested Bev was cutting back on oxygen.

Bev shook her head. "Trying to give it up." They drank PG, talked Davy. Bev listened, made the right noises. Gert's strained face shed a few years in the reminiscences. Nothing like being in denial. Barring a miracle, the lad would be in court on Monday, remanded in custody. Forget the fatted calf. Davy wouldn't be home any time soon. The old girl lapsed into silence, staring into space.

Bev shifted forward on the seat. "You gonna be OK,

Mrs R?"

"I reckon." She ran a hand over her face. "Sister's coming down from Liverpool. She's widowed. On her own now. We're gonna muck in together. See if it works."

Bev nodded. "Sounds good." She put her mug on the tray and rummaged in her bag for a card. "Anything comes to mind, give us a bell, OK?"

Gert was reaching for another dog-eared paperback before Bev had reached the door. She turned to smile, spotted one of the old dear's reads on the floor in imminent danger of disappearing under the chair. The book was sticky as well as tacky. Bev handed it over and wiped her hand on her jeans.

Gert frowned. "This isn't mine. I've never seen it before."

Bev took a closer look. The stickiness wasn't down to Gert's sweet tooth. The book had been stuck to the under-side of the chair with masking tape that had lost its grip. She opened the pages and her eyes lit up. Whoever had hidden it had taken great care. The cut-out was virtually undetectable. The floppy disk fitted so snug she broke a nail easing it out.

"Hey, Khanie, you heard?" Big Vince was on the desk at Highgate. There was a faint whiff of cheese and onion in the air.

Oz was halfway down the stairs, in a hurry. "What's that, Sarge?"

"They've found the knife."

The blade used on Marlow last night? Had to be. "Prints?"

"Full set. Name tag on the handle."

Oz widened his eyes, the mouth already O-shaped.

"Had you going there, didn't I?" The big man winked.

"Nah. It was clean as a bishop's conscience, 'cept for the blood. Dumped in a bin down Bolt Street." Vince reached in the drawer, tore open another pack of crisps. "Want one?"

Drawer. Journal. Bev. Shit.

"No, ta. Just put one out."

He took the stairs two at a time. Where was the damn thing? She'd said top drawer.

He pulled out everything but the sink unit: tapes, black tights, property details on half of Birmingham and two squares of fluff-covered dairy milk. He smiled, shook his head. She'd be a nightmare to live with.

It was wedged in. He tugged the handle gently. Not gently enough. The cover was well torn. Bev'd kill him. The sodding thing had survived unscathed for half a century until Oz got his clumsy mitts on it. Or maybe not. He moved nearer the light.

The journal's original cover was intact. Not a mark on it. Little wonder. It had been protected by another cover on top. Oz glanced round for a ruler, letter-opener, anything to prise open the rip he'd made.

Very gently he extracted the cutting. It hadn't even been folded. He held the tiny scrap of paper between his thumb and forefinger. Protected between the two covers, it hadn't got brittle and faded. It would have looked like this the day it appeared in the *Evening News*: 10th March 1985.

Two lines of print, eleven words:

*Collison, Sara. Beloved daughter of George and Hannah. Rest in peace.*

So Sophia Carrington's murder happened on the twentieth anniversary of the death of someone named

Sara Collison. Someone whose death notice was hidden in Sophia's journal. Oz tapped a finger against his lips. Like Bev, he didn't do coincidence, not when the connection was staring him in the face.

Jake hadn't factored it in – the cop turning up out of the blue like that. Obviously he'd be taking her out, that was a given, had been almost from the start. Doing her now was tempting but it'd throw the timing right out. Nah, he'd stick to the plan. It had served him well so far. Jake double-checked the blade and took a last deep drag on his cigarette before moving off. The old lady was gonna lose a bit of weight. As for the pig, he'd settle for a shot across the bows for the time being. The snicker was involuntary; *shot across the bows...* That was good, Jay, my son. That was very good.

"Shit-for-brains fuckwits." Bev halted outside Gert's house, hands on hips, fury incarnate. Her MG had gained a go-faster stripe: badly executed and fucking unbelievable. The deep gouge had penetrated right through the new paint-job. Now a jagged line of the original dull yellow ran the entire length of the black re-spray. She dashed to the passenger side; if anything, it was worse.

She scanned the street, fists clenched. Given the area, she was lucky the motor was still there. With a sinking feeling, she checked the tyres. Thank you, God. There were still four, none slashed. Last thing she needed was a hold-up. Not with Davy's floppy burning a hole in her pocket. Even so, a cruise round the block on yob-watch couldn't do any harm. She completed two clear laps before heading home.

It took twenty minutes to get there, slinging her bag on

the kitchen table and snatching up yet another note from her mum. Emmy's missives usually rambled stream-of-conscious style, but this offering was to the point, more or less.

*Hi love, We're seeing a man about a dog. Again! Check the answerphone. Loads of messages for you. Have a nice time tonight! Love, mum. PS Found your earring so you can stop looking!*

Bev pulled a face. Stop? She hadn't started. Anyway, the little earring looked more like one of Sadie's. She made for the box room that Emmy grandly dubbed 'the office', and played back the answerphone tape while the computer was booting up.

Frankie had landed a gig at the Jug of Ale next Friday. "Be there, Beverley – or else." Bev smiled, jotted details.

Baldwin Street was back on the market; the agent with a lisp and a wandering eye asked if he should resubmit her offer. You bet!

Maude Taylor wondered when Sophia's body would be released for burial. Bev's smile faded. She ought to pop in, bring the old girl up to speed on the inquiry. "Oh, and Sergeant Morriss, I think that young man telephoned again. *Simon?* He said it was a wrong number but I feel sure it was him."

Bev tensed for a second or two. The 24/7 police presence out there had been called off. On the other hand, patrols were still keeping an eye open and Maude was too canny to take risks. She jotted down Simon, underlined the name twice. He'd never been traced, remained just a voice on the line. She frowned. Come to think of it, there'd been quite a few of those. She added a reminder. It had to be worth a check.

Another addition to the To Do list…

There was a hang-up, then the guv. His voice brought a smile to her face until she registered what it was saying. Shields had been on to him. She'd found out Bev was still sniffing around. Tight-lipped, she punched in the guv's number: no reply. She'd keep trying. As for Shields, the woman could take a running jump.

She reached in her pocket, urged herself to stay calm. The disk could contain Davy's geography essay for all she knew. But she'd stake a month's salary on it going further than a bit of course-work.

She tapped the mouse, held her breath. There was only one file. She speed-read it, then went back to the top, taking her time. At last she leaned back, gave a low whistle. Should have made that a year's salary.

# 30

"Are you showing off?"

Oz wielded chopsticks in one hand and a hard copy of the contents of Davy Roberts's disk in the other. Bev was attacking crispy bashed duck with knife and fork. She preferred to eat while the food was still hot.

"I'm ambidextrous," he said without looking up.

"Must be a cure for it."

He rolled his eyes, nonchalantly plucked a tiny prawn from a mound of rice. She was playing it cool, but her voice told him how wired she was. He'd managed to get a word in about the concealed cutting, the fact that for the first time they had a name to go on. But it was Davy's hidden disk that was sending out sparks.

"What you reckon, then?" Her fork indicated the printout.

"He's no Adrian Mole, is he?"

"Hope not." Mole's diary was fiction; she was counting on Davy's words being fact. Oz needed a tad longer to take in the details. Bev poured another glass of Pinot, absorbed the ambience. The Happy Gathering heaved with city-chic types gearing up for a Saturday night bop. She'd have been up for it herself if she'd had time to change. Oz was in black: silk shirt, linen trousers. Tasty. He placed the sheets of A4 to one side. She wondered how long he'd been looking at her.

"Why did he record it all like this?"

She shrugged, not sure. It seemed simple, at first. The excited outpourings suggested Davy was having the time of his life. A chance encounter in the street had led to a new best mate and Davy revelled in the attention. Jake's largesse extended to cash handouts, cool gifts, regular treats and, above all, she suspected, making Davy feel good.

'Course it came at a price. When Jake suggested picking a pocket or two, how could Davy refuse? Turned out to be good training. Soon Jake had taken on a couple more recruits and the gang graduated to street robberies. Kev and Robbie, the Shrek boys who'd taken a vow of silence, provided the muscle. Bev couldn't shake off the image of a Fagin-style operation with Davy as the Artful Dodger. It was sad in a way; the lad was besotted. She understood why he needed someone to look up to but as role models go, Jake sucked.

"My guess is, it was exciting, cool, wicked. Little Davy in with the big boys at last."

"Cool?" Oz said. "Knocking old ladies about?"

The names were there: Ena Bolton, Joan Goddard, Iris Collins, a couple more Bev didn't even recognise. It was Operation Streetwise writ large.

"Money for old rope." Not the best choice of phrase. She pushed her plate aside. "Until the doctor's murder."

Sophia's name was missing. The entries ended a couple of days before her death. As it happened, the hero worship was beginning to tail off as well. It was another guess but Bev reckoned Davy was beginning to regard the diary as more than a record of events. Maybe he saw it as an insurance policy. It could explain why he'd taken to following Jake – so he could fill in a few blanks. Thank God he had. Like Davy, they still didn't have Jake's last name but now they did have an idea where he lived. A spot of surveillance should narrow it down.

She watched as Oz rubbed a hand along his jaw. Could

he be less enthusiastic?

"Come on, Oz. It means we're nearly there. Soon as we haul the bastard in, end of story."

He swallowed a sip of Highland Spring. "What does the DI reckon?"

"Haven't a clue." Bev flashed the waiter a smile as he cleared the table, aware of Oz's open-mouthed stare. They both knew the information should have been referred up. She ordered coffee, but going by Oz's expression should have opted for something stronger.

"You are joking, right?"

Obviously it needed checking, but assuming Davy was on the level the main player was still out there. Going in mob-handed would be as good as a tip-off. The last thing she wanted was the bastard legging it. "Couldn't get hold of her." Which was true, since she hadn't put a call through.

He made a big deal of proffering his mobile. "Be my guest."

"Later." When she had a collar. When she could look Sadie and Ena and Maude and Joan in the eye and say it's over.

"Bev!" His dark eyes flashed. "Davy Roberts has provided chapter and verse. You can't sit on it."

There was no need to sit on it; she'd already hatched the next move. "It's not enough, Oz. We need the whole book."

He knew exactly where she was coming from. "No way." His arms were folded, lips clamped.

"Twenty-four hours." She put her elbows on the table, leaned in closer. "If we don't get a result. Fair enough."

He shook his head. "It's professional suicide."

"Scared it'll stymie your promotion?"

The sudden silence was broken by a peal of laughter from the next table. Oz's glare didn't waver an iota until he flung his napkin on the table and pushed back the chair. Bev wasn't the only one watching as he stormed out.

Fired up was an understatement. Oz was ballistic. A brisk walk might have had a calming effect but thin drizzle was turning into a heavy downpour. He cabbed it home through near-empty streets slick with rain. Still undecided whether to call it in or not, he twice started tapping the DI's number before angrily jamming the mobile back in his pocket. Bev was often out of line: on this occasion she was out of her mind.

"Here you go, mate. £8.50."

Cheap night, considering. Oz handed the driver a tenner, made a dash for the front door. The hall was all soft lights and scented candles; his mother was a sucker for makeover programmes. He shucked off his jacket and froze on the spot. A high-pitched scream was coming from the sitting room. Almost immediately it was accompanied by screeching violins. He gave a half-smile; the hellish cacophony was a sure sign his parents were out. Shulie and Amina would be watching a movie and knowing his kid sisters it wouldn't be *The Sound of Music*. Dracula and copious amounts of gore was more to their taste. He toyed with the idea of joining them but wasn't in the mood.

A hot shower helped but Bev's jibe still rankled. He lay on the bed, hands behind his head, listening to *Let It Be*; recalled the earlier scene, wished he could. There must be a whisper about his application going round the Highgate rumour mill. Shame she'd only garnered half the story. She never sodding listened, anyway. She was so blinkered about her own thing she'd barely taken on board his news about the cutting. giving them the name of Sophia's child.

It might not have the same urgency now, but it was still worth a look.

Oz narrowed his eyes, his attention caught by a daddy-long-legs lurching drunkenly across the ceiling. No wonder. Poor thing had lost a leg. If it went any nearer the light, it'd lose a few more. He rose, cupped it gently in his hands and released it into the night.

Turning, he caught sight of Bev's picture on the table by the bed. He couldn't recall the last time she'd smiled like that. *Yesterday* was playing now. Talk about 'all my troubles'. Oz knew the feeling.

It was why he'd have to make the call.

# 31

Saturday night. Viewing room, Highgate. Bev headed for the audio equipment, carrying reels of tape under her arms containing incoming calls to the nick on Monday and Friday. Maude's message on the answerphone about the mysterious Simon had planted the seed. It struck Bev there were more mystery voices in this case than at an international convention for mystery voices. Unless the same one was being thrown.

She gave the late show downstairs a miss. She'd seen the 3-Ds loads of times: drunks, dossers and druggies, wall-to-wall. Uniform could cope well enough. She was here for the sound show.

She flicked switches, stifled a yawn. No time for tiredness. Oz's arsiness had stiffened her resolve, increased the urgency. It was glaringly obvious to her now that Jake was no organ-grinder; he was head of the strings.

The suite was empty but she slipped on headphones anyway. It cut out extraneous noise like the drunken chorus of *You'll Never Walk Alone* from below. It was a comforting thought but a touch distracting. Anyway, she needed all the concentration she could muster. He wouldn't have made it easy. Not if he had any sense. All the calls were logged; it didn't take long to pinpoint the relevant sections. She cued both from the beginning then listened back-to-back. Repeating the process confirmed it.

"You arrogant arsehole," she whispered. The first voice reported intruders at Winston Heights, the tower block in Edgbaston where the Shreks had been squatting. The second gave the anonymous tip-off that led to Davy

Roberts's arrest. It was the same voice. No attempt to disguise it.

Bev shook her head. Cocky or what? She had no doubt it was Jake dobbing in his mates, creating distractions from the main man. And it had almost worked. She rubbed a hand over her face. Dear God, don't let him do a runner.

She made copies of the recordings. Maude needed to hear the voice as well. She secured the suite, then headed up another flight of stairs.

The murder room was deserted. Moonlight cast a pale glow over empty desks. The picture board was still in situ. The victims. That was what it was all about. She stood, arms folded, ran her gaze over the gallery of battered old faces, eerily leeched of colour in the silvery light. In a way, it exacerbated the horror. Bev closed her eyes, saw the spike-haired sicko who'd orchestrated the attacks. Why do it? What was in it for him? Surely more than a bit of cheap jewellery and a few quid?

She focused on the face of Sophia Carrington. Recalled her initial conviction that everything stemmed from Sophia's murder. Had her instinct been right all along? Thoughts racing, she ran her mind back over the conversation in the restaurant. Oz had mentioned a cutting, a death notice in a false cover of the old woman's journal, maybe her daughter. The name had rung a faint bell but she'd dismissed it in the face of Davy's unwitting revelations. Unless...

She checked her watch. 12.15. She had to speak to Oz. It couldn't wait. Her mobile was at the bottom of her shoulder bag. It rang as she reached to make the call.

"Twenty-four hours, right? Not a nano-second over." It was Oz. No preamble. No need.

She punched the air, mouthed a silent yes! "I owe you."

"What's new?" he sighed.

"What changed your mind?" Not that it mattered.

"You'll do it anyway. I don't want you hurt."

She didn't comment on that. There wasn't time. "Where are you now, Oz?" The phone was no good. There was work to do. She tapped her foot. *Come on, Oz. Not difficult.*

His voice was tentative. "I've still got the keys to Zak's place."

She narrowed her eyes, quickly calculating. As long as they had access to the net, it was as good a place as any. She pictured Oz, gave a slow smile. Make that better than most.

They'd been hunched over the laptop for the better part of an hour. At this rate Zak's bachelor pad in Selly Oak wouldn't be seeing any action in or out of the master bedroom.

"It's no good, Oz. It's not going anywhere." Bev had already kicked off her shoes. Now she was itching to put a boot through the screen of the laptop. Instead, she paced the carpet, sucked on a biro, craving a Silk Cut.

She'd firmed up a theory on the way over. If Sara really was the baby Sophia Carrington gave up for adoption, what if Sara had kids of her own? Maybe a son? Called Jake?

But guesswork and gut instinct could only go so far. Bev had been banking on the adoptive parents to provide some quick answers. Problem was she'd need a medium. The Collisons had been dead nearly five years. With a shortcut no longer on the cards, Bev and Oz would have to take the long route. Davy Roberts had recorded a road name. They needed the house. They'd start surveillance at first light.

Oz sighed and rubbed the back of his neck. He'd been accessing the news archives that told the Collisons' story. George and Hannah had died in a fire at their home in Solihull. No suspicious circumstances. No police involvement. No surprise it had passed Bev by. She was right about Collison ringing a bell, though. George had headed up one of the Midlands's biggest transport companies. Back then, the name had been plastered across a fleet of HGVs.

Oz tapped a couple more keys, pulled up the *Birmingham Post*. It was the only version that carried a picture of the couple. "She looks a lot older than him."

Bev stopped pacing, gazed at the screen over his shoulder. George and Hannah, snapped at a CBI fundraiser six months before their deaths, looking as if they didn't have a care in the world. "Poor sods," Bev sighed. "It's a good job we don't know what's round the corner."

Oz turned to face her, an unreadable glint in his eyes. "Yeah. But we can usually find out what's next door."

She smiled slowly as comprehension dawned. Maybe one of the Collisons' neighbours could shed some light. They'd have to go on the knock. They could split it, take turn and turn about. Stake-out *and* shoe leather.

"Pass us those cards, Oz." She'd noticed the pack on her last visit. It was still on the side. "Cut you for first surveillance." It was a damn sight better than knocking doors in Solihull at some ungodly hour on a Sunday.

Oz drew an ace and a happy face when Bev turned over the three of hearts.

"Sorry, mate," she sympathised. "I'll take Moseley."

"Aces – "

"Low." She winked. "Still, you know what they say…

'Unlucky at cards, lucky in love.'"

"Do they?"

She held out a hand. "They do now, Ossama."

# 32

Richmond Green in Solihull was all detached properties and gleaming people carriers, long drives and tall hedges. Oz had cruised round a couple of times, clocked the Collisons' former pile. Even with a lottery win, he'd need a mortgage to buy the outbuildings. He parked, locked the motor, zipped his leather jacket. Door-to-doors were the pits, but the sooner he started...

Twelve houses later he wished he'd stayed in bed or at least brought gloves. The temperature had taken a dive along with his high hopes. It was fewer than five years since the fire but so far everyone he'd questioned appeared to be in the latter stages of collective amnesia. Either that or they didn't do Neighbourhood Watch, let alone Speak. Mind, given the distances between the ivory towers, they'd need binoculars and megaphones.

Hopefully Bev was having more joy. The thought of her brought a lazy smile. She was right. He wouldn't mind losing at cards more often. Like every night. At the moment he needed a win. He lifted yet another gleaming brass knocker, stamping his feet to remind the blood there were toes down there. The young woman who opened the door spoke little English; the plain black dress and white apron were more vocal. Oz watched as, behind her, a much older female descended the sort of staircase the National Trust preserves.

Margot Whittle brought with her the scents of lavender and peppermint. Steel-grey hair was swept back into a loose bun; intelligent eyes a shade lighter. She took Oz's ID and studied it at close quarters through half-moon glasses.

The slight nod indicated readiness. He had the questions off pat by now. Had she known George and Hannah Collison?

There was a slight narrowing of the eyes. "A little."

Hoo-flipping-rah. He smiled encouragement. "How did you know them, Mrs Whittle?"

Slight hesitation. "We attended the same church."

"We're keen to trace surviving members of the family." He lifted expectant eyebrows, received a blank look. The woman was probably too well-mannered to tell him to naff off but for some reason she was wary. Oz had the distinct impression she was holding back. She was. She said nothing.

"Was anyone else living there at the time of the fire?" he prompted.

Another delay. "Not that I'm aware of. Why are you asking, after all these years?"

Strange question. "Just routine inquiries, Mrs Whittle." He should have known the casual fob-off wouldn't work.

"I'm sorry. I can't help." She made to close the door.

"Please. Mrs Whittle. If you –"

The slam echoed in the still morning air. A crow took off from the lawn, wings beating furiously. Oz watched it disappear, stood a while longer, debating whether to try again. He was convinced the woman could tell him more but, then again, maybe she already had.

Ding bloody dong. Bev curled her lip. Church bells pissed her off. Always had, always would. On the other hand, if Jake were a God-botherer, how good would it be to nab him on the way to worship? Yeah. Like that was going to happen. That'd be a sodding miracle. She lowered the car window a couple of inches, blew smoke through the gap.

Despite what she'd said to Oz, a stake-out could take days. Assuming the little shit hadn't legged it already, and assuming Davy had pointed them in the right direction. She glanced in the driving mirror: nada.

The initial recce had been promising. It was the sort of area she could imagine Jake staying. The occasional skip and scaffolding suggested gentrification was on its way, but most of the three-storey properties were still split into dingy bed-sits where keys changed hands faster than dodgy tenants. Front gardens resembled used-car lots. Here and there dusty greenery sprouted at roof level from cracks in grimy brickwork. Wentworth Close was short on aesthetics, big on anonymity.

Which sucked. As did sitting round freezing her butt. Still, she was well ready. The passenger seat resembled a tuck shop: a prawn-and-mayo sandwich, beef-and-onion crisps, a Picnic bar and a flask of caffeine. Tucked underneath somewhere was a picture of Jake. Not that she needed the visual reminder.

"Come to Bevvie, you little shit," she murmured. Another glance in the mirror; still nada.

The sudden rap on the window could have led to a head-shaped dent in the roof. She spun round, ready to mouth off. Tom Marlow was standing there, looking as good as she'd seen him. He lifted a hand in mock surrender, a wide grin on his face. She opened the window all the way and gave a token smile but felt a muppet. Maybe he picked up on it; he dropped the stance and lowered the hundred-watt beam.

"Sorry, I didn't mean to make you jump, Bev."

Slightly flustered, she flapped a hand. "How're you doing?" There were sepia circles under his eyes. She wondered if he was still in pain.

"Stitches are a bit tender but I'm getting there." He ran a finger along the scar in the Midget's paintwork. "What in hell happened here?"

*Don't remind me.* "Blade job," she snarled. "If I get the fucker, he's dead."

Marlow shook his head, still inspecting the damage. "Mindless."

"Anyway, what're you up to?" Stupid question. Judging by the Sunday papers under his arm, he'd bought a newsagent's.

Marlow cocked his head at a two-skip property over the road. "A friend of mine has a flat on the top floor. I keep an eye on it while they're away."

"Where are they?" It was small talk, her eyes on the bigger picture.

"She, actually." Tom switched the papers to his other arm. "In the States, visiting family. Why?"

It would be ideal, kill two birds with one outlook: great vantage point, no prying eyes. She opened her mouth, then thought again. Marlow was already one of the walking wounded; it wasn't fair to drag him in further. "Just wondered."

He gave that half-smile. "Not after a place to rent, then?"

She dithered. It was tempting. A quick butcher's couldn't do any harm. "Actually, Tom, I'm desperate for the loo…"

Oz headed for the nearest phone box. Empty. Completely. No phone. No book. He'd try one more, then maybe think again. In the next one the directory was torn and tatty but it was there. He cast an eye down the listings, noted the details of six churches. Back in the motor, he checked addresses against the A-Z, mapped out the best route. Saint John the Baptist's was in the next road. Oz gave a wry smile, envisioning heads on plates. In reality he knew it was never that easy. It wasn't. The vicar at Saint John's had no recollection of the Collisons. Oz left a card on the off chance.

Five cards later, he was still drawing blanks. Margot Whittle appeared to be the only worshipper in the galaxy who'd heard of George and Hannah. He was toying with the idea of a return visit when his mobile rang.

"DC Khan? Jane Cater here. Saint Mary's."

He frowned; he'd have remembered that voice: melting chocolate. "You spoke to my father," she prompted.

Of course. Funny little man with a beard. "The Reverend..?"

"Cater. But he's not the vicar. I am." He sensed a smile, guessed she was accustomed to people jumping to conclusions. "You were asking about the Collisons."

"Still am. Did you know them?" A mental crossing of the fingers.

"Not personally. We moved here several months after the fire. But my predecessor often spoke of them."

"We're keen to trace surviving family members."

"Yes. Dad mentioned that. Alan Protheroe would be the best person to speak to."

Oz jotted down the name. "Where can I find him?"

"They're in Bath. He's retired. Got a pen?"

It was a tough call. The flat was ideal for surveillance: top-floor front, unrestricted views of the street. The place wouldn't be appearing in *Ideal Home* any time soon, but who'd be looking at the interior décor? Bev flushed the toilet, washed her hands, leaned on the sink, gazed in the mirror. OK, here's the deal: it's too good to pass up; tell Tom the score, then get him the hell out of there.

Marlow glanced up from sorting a pile of post as she

entered the sitting room. An envelope drifted from his fingers as she passed. She knelt to retrieve it but he was already there, face almost touching hers. Had he choreographed the encounter? It was hardly subtle. Neither were the slightly parted lips. The eyes were less easy to read but she reckoned 'smouldering' came close.

"Oops!" She backed away, laughing.

"Ditto." He laughed too. Maybe she'd misinterpreted. "Do you want to take a pew?" he said. "I shan't be a tick."

"No rush." She moved to the window, scanned the street again. Yep. It'd be spot on. "Tom, can I ask a favour?"

Marlow listened with interest, asked the odd question. He was happy to help but she sensed his doubts. Bev shrugged. "I know it's a long shot but it's all we've got."

He rubbed a hand along his chin, then gave that half-smile. "You've got a deal."

"Deal?"

He held his hand out to seal it. "You can use the place as long as you want, if I can take you out again."

That she could manage. "You're on."


Alan Protheroe liked the sound of his own voice. It was growing on Oz, too; he'd listened to it for almost ten minutes. The old buffer had gone round more houses than a rent collector. Oz suppressed another sigh. "To get back to the Collisons, sir?"

"Good people, very good people." There it was again. A pronouncement followed by a nervous giggle, a cross between a whinny and a guffaw.

"In what respect, sir?"

Protheroe clearly needed a few seconds to think about that. Oz fiddled with a paper clip; at least it was warmer now he was back at the nick.

"Always willing helpers. Church funds. Parish activities."
Again the curious laugh.

"They had a daughter. Sara. Did you know her?"

This time the pause was so long, Oz began to think they'd been disconnected. "Sad. Very sad."

Blood. Stone. "What can you tell me about her?"

Oz strained his ears. Was that hum coming from the old man? "Can you tell me what happened, sir?"

"Hold on a moment, there's a good chap." A senior moment, presumably.

Oz waited, caught the odd word from a muffled conversation.

"Eileen Protheroe. Can I help?" A woman's voice: clipped, authoritative. Oz pictured Joan Bakewell but realised that was probably wishful thinking. He ran through it all again. After an initial pause, Eileen Protheroe turned out to be as direct as her husband was divergent. "Sara Collison was a tortured soul. Whether that was anything to do with her being adopted, who knows?'

Hallelujah. Oz flicked the clip bin-wards, grabbed a pen.

"What I do know is that she broke Hannah's heart. They were both at their wits' ends. Sara rebelled from an early age. She ran away, lived on the streets, almost died from a drug overdose."

"Almost?"

"The hospital pulled her through. George and Hannah took her back. Lavished love and money on her all over again. It didn't last. As soon as she was fit, she took off. Five years later they buried her."

"Another overdose?"

Oz waited for her to elaborate. "I don't know the details. It all happened long before they moved to the parish."

Oz frowned. This was quality, but how come no one else had breathed a word? "Do you mind my asking how you know all this, Mrs Protheroe?"

The pause was minimal. "Neither Hannah nor I could have children of our own. It was an abiding sadness and it brought us together. George was away a lot building up the business. Hannah was painfully shy with most people but we became close. We confided in each other. Unlike the Collisons, we never went down the adoption path. Though given how Alan is now..." Oz caught the Alzheimer's drift, didn't comment.

"Do you know who the birth mother was?"

"No idea. We never discussed it." Rapid answer but it held the ring of truth.

"Does the name Sophia Carrington mean anything to you?"

"Should it?" Again he didn't think she was lying or with-holding information. Not when she'd been so candid and up-front.

"Tell me, Mrs Protheroe, did Sara have children?" It was the big one. Oz held his breath.

The answer came after a long pause. "There was a child, yes. A son. Simon. He was about five when his mother died. He'd be in his early twenties now."

"So where is he?" Bev asked.

"Don't know. He moves about a lot. I've traced an address in Worcester." Oz was on the line bringing Bev up to speed. She'd been static for a couple of hours. Wentworth Close had less life than some brands of yoghurt. She'd clocked two dog-walkers, an ageing hippy and a couple of teenagers pushing prams. Next door's bonfire had been the hottest item around until Oz's revelations.

"And you can't get a fix on him in Birmingham?"

"Nothing."

Not surprising. It didn't cost a fortune to change your name and if it did, Simon Collison probably had one. George and Hannah's inheritance was a box they'd still to tick but it wasn't unreasonable to assume he'd got the lot. She sucked on her pen, blew imaginary smoke. "So it's odds-on this Simon Collison and Jake whoever-he-is are one and the same?" Changing persona to fit the bill. Or fuck The Bill. A cert too he was the Simon who'd called Maude Taylor. Hadn't even bothered with a fake name. Why bother if he assumed she was only some senile old biddy?

"Works for me," said Oz. "And the timing's spot on."

She watched absently as next door chucked more rubbish on the bonfire. "The Worcester guys are definitely in position?" An element of surprise was all they had. It was crucial Collison didn't know they were on to him.

"Watching brief," Oz said.

She ran it through her head again. Sophia Carrington has a baby who's adopted by George and Hannah. Sara goes off the rails, has a kid of her own: Simon Collison. Sara dies twenty years ago and Simon's brought up by his adoptive grandparents. Five years after the fire that killed them, he unleashes a series of attacks on old women, culminating in Sophia Carrington's murder.

She rubbed her temple, hoped the niggling pain wouldn't develop into a full-blown headache. "Why, Oz? Why kill his own grandmother?"

*Unless he didn't realise who she was?* Sophia had gone to massive lengths to hide Sara's birth. As far as they could tell, contact had ceased more than thirty years ago. "Oz. What if he didn't know she was his grandmother? What if

266

Simon or Jake or whatever his sodding name is had no idea he was related to Sophia Carrington? What if he went after her because of what she did, not who she was?"

The ready answer suggested he'd been there already. "Doesn't explain the others, Bev. We've been down the doctor-stroke-patient route before."

She sighed. The pen was no substitute for a baccy; she needed a smoke. Wreaths of the stuff drifted listlessly from the bonfire next door. She watched it swirl like lazy fog. Christ, if it got any worse she wouldn't be able to see the other side of the street.

She froze, thoughts racing. "It does, you know." She paused, thinking it through. "It does explain the others – if they were a smokescreen." *A diversion. Like the tip-offs.*

"Eye-off-the-ball job?"

The snort was classic. "Except it was never on in the first place."

Oz gave a low whistle. "How callous would you have to be?"

To attack old women at random to conceal not just the intended murder victim but the genuine motive?

"I'm heading back, mate." She'd already gathered her bits. "See you soon as." There was no point hanging round. Jake wasn't going to show now, maybe he never was. As for Simon Collison, there were a million checks to run. He might be unaware that the woman he'd killed was his grandmother; Bev was still in the dark as to why.

When she knew, she'd bury the bastard.

# 33

Essence of bonfire with a hint of Silk Cut permeated the interior of the MG. Bev pulled a face and wound down the window. Her glance fell on Jake's picture, still partially obscured by the untouched edibles on the passenger seat. She squinted, trying to imagine the little shit minus the spikes and piercings. Should have an idea soon enough. Oz was on the case, trying among other things to track down a visual.

Traffic was light, pewter clouds heavy with threatened rain. She slipped a Van Morrison into the CD player, helped him out with a few bars of *Brown-Eyed Girl*.

"Shit." She'd overshot Tom Marlow's place. By the time she'd reversed and parked up, he was on the doorstep. Judging by the coat over his shoulders, he was on his way out. "Not stopping," she smiled, handing him the keys. "Thanks a million."

"That was quick." He looked surprised. "All over?"

"Bar the shouting."

"That's good." He must have seen her expression. "Isn't it?"

'Course it was. Especially if she was the one hauling Collison's sorry ass into custody. She so wanted to see the look on DI Shields's face. "Sure is."

He slipped the keys into his pocket. "I was nipping into town but I could rustle up a latte if you like."

She remembered it from the first visit, latte to die for. Bummer; she was pressed for time. "Got to crack on or I'd be in like a shot." Another pressing matter was the flask full of Fine Blend she'd already quaffed. This was getting to be a habit. "But can I just nip to the loo?"

268

*

Still at Highgate, Oz checked his watch, fingers tapping an urgent beat on the desk. He made a grab for the phone, changed his mind, sent a text instead, wishing he could see Bev's face when she read it. Armed with a name and a specific timeframe, he'd run a fresh check with the Guildford papers. Keeping an ear cocked for the fax, he now reread the printed articles.

Back then the local weekly had gone big on the drugs angle. Sara Collison had died from a heroin overdose, her emaciated body found in a graveyard in Surrey. There was a bunch of statistics and a warning about the dangers of drug abuse. Oz had struggled to make sense of it – until the final paragraph.

*Ms Collison had recently been discharged from hospital. A spokesman at the Guildford Royal Infirmary refused to comment.*

He wandered to the window. Still no sign of Bev's MG. He wanted her take on it, but the fact was: Sara Collison had been a patient in the Surrey hospital where Sophia Carrington had been a doctor. It had taken two phone calls to establish that link. But what was a raddled heroin addict doing in Maternity?

Oz'd had no joy tracking down anyone who'd been round at the time. There were still blanks and he was busking, but he reckoned Sara Collison had been pregnant for a second time. Given there was no record of a birth, presumably she'd lost it. The euphemism covered a couple of possibles: abortion or miscarriage.

The niggling pain was now a throbbing headache. Bev splashed water over her face, stroked her temples. The makeshift massage didn't work. She sat on the loo seat and delved in her bag: Polos, matches, pen. The paracetamol was at the bottom. Natch. Four should do the trick. She wiped her mouth, looked round for a bin to chuck the strip. She raised an eyebrow at the condoms and gel already in there. Tom had clearly been entertaining a ladyfriend. She was heading for the door when a glint from the floor caught her eye.

She knelt for a closer look. A cufflink was trapped between the edge of the tiles and the skirting board. She broke another nail teasing it out, but knowing Tom, it had cost an arm and a leg. Mind, he didn't strike her as Cufflink Man.

He wasn't.

She rose slowly, eyes narrowed. It was a silver stud. *The kind kids wore if they couldn't afford piercings, or they hadn't got the bottle for the real thing.* She touched the back. The glue was still tacky. She turned it over, rolling it in her palm. She'd seen one before: its identical twin. She pictured it now, nestling on her bedside table.

The lost earring her mum had found. But not an earring. Not lost. Not by Bev or Sadie anyway. Dropped by Jake during the attack on her gran.

She perched on the edge of the bath. Chill, Bev. Think it through. What did it mean? Was it possible Jake had been inside Tom's house? She dismissed the thought with a snort. For fuck's sake, it didn't have to be Jake's. It could be anyone's.

"Fuck's sake." Oz chucked his pen across the desk. Moseley to Highgate was twelve minutes max. He'd kill her if she'd stopped for a drink.

"OK, mate?" Darren New looked up hopefully, any distraction from report-writing welcome.

Oz nodded a *no problem*. But there was. There were countless loose ends to chase and Bev was AWOL. He knew she had little time for follow-up and phone-bashing. Even so, they were supposed to be splitting this stuff.

Daz was wolfing a second pork pie, vestiges of the first still scattered across the desktop and keyboard. Oz shook his head, made his way over to the fax again. About time.

He frowned. The sender's name meant nothing. Mind, he'd put so many irons in the fire he felt like a blacksmith. The address made more sense: Clunes House in Shropshire. Collison's school. Hallelujah. He waited impatiently as the picture gradually appeared, thought for a heartbeat the school had cocked up. The surly schoolboy, eyes almost hidden under a dark fringe, couldn't be Simon Collison. Oz snatched the sheet of paper, swore under his breath. He'd seen the features before, but never with a scowl. They'd always been set in a smarmy smile.

Bev twirled the stud between thumb and forefinger, her thoughts focused elsewhere. The idea was so off the wall she couldn't get her head round it. If Collison and Jake were one and the same – could Collison also be masquerading as Tom Marlow? She almost laughed out loud, yet it made twisted sense. Collison – as Marlow – had given them the original tip-off. It would mean the whole Marlow/Jake thing was yet another distraction. Christ. How cocky was that?

She ticked off comparisons. Both were roughly the same height, build and age. As for the spiked hair, the make-up, the piercings – they were cosmetic. Literally. A peek in the bathroom cabinet confirmed it; the hair-gel she'd seen in the bin wasn't some woman's, but Marlow's. Everything about him was skin-deep.

*Skin*. That reminded her of something. Of course. Sadie's crime novel, *Beneath The Skin*. That's where they should have been looking.

She grabbed her mobile, ignored the missed calls, bashed out an urgent message to Oz. If she was right, she needed back-up. If she was right, they'd been played a blinder. If she was right, Sophia Carrington's killer was waiting downstairs.

Oz took the stairs three at a time. Was Bev still at Wentworth Close? He tried her number again. Pick up, for fuck's sake. He flung the mobile on the passenger seat. It was raining in sheets, the wipers could barely cope; the inside of the windscreen was fogged. He dashed a hand across, but only added sweat to smear. What if she'd already left? He glanced at the clock on the dash. Forty minutes since they'd last spoken. If she wasn't there, he'd check out Marlow's place. If no joy there, he'd have no option but to call it in.

He mouthed a silent prayer as he turned into the Close. Cars and vans were double-parked, no gaps. He eased the speed, anxious not to miss the MG. He did a three-point-turn, drove back even more slowly. He needn't have bothered. It wasn't there.

"Sure I can't get you a coffee?" Marlow's coat was draped over the back of a chair. He was flicking through one of the Sunday supplements; it looked like the *Observer*.

Bev mirrored his smile. "Why not?" She watched him leave the room. Try as she might, it was impossible to imagine Tom Marlow as a piece of scummy street life. She'd never seen him with a hair out of place, let alone a head of spikes.

"Doing anything later?" His voice carried through from the kitchen. She tried matching its nonchalance.

"Grabbing an early night, I hope." There was no proof. A silver stud and a tube of gel wouldn't get past the prosecution service, let alone stand up in court. She prowled a circuit of the room, keeping her ears pricked for noises off. Come on, God. Give me a break: bloodstained balaclava, dripping knife. *Yeah, right.* "How about you? Anything lined up?"

"Business meeting. No peace for the wicked…"

"Coffee smells great." Keep him sweet. The slightest inkling she was on to something and it'd make pear-shaped look perfect. She slipped a hand into the pocket of Marlow's coat and gasped. Not quite a signed confession. But getting there.

It was the post from Wentworth Close, every envelope addressed to Simon Collison. The toe-rag did have a pad in the city. By using it for surveillance, she'd virtually handed him a copy of her movements.

"Milk. No sugar. Right?"

She raised her voice. "You got it."

Her mobile beeped a message. Oz. Her personal fast-response unit. A faint smile morphed into a frown. His words didn't make sense and why no reference to back-up? She reread the text and began to get the picture. *sara collison heroin overdose. abortion/ miscarriage prior to death.* Tweaking a few mental knobs brought another blurred edge into sharper focus. It looked like a motive to her.

As for the cavalry, Oz wouldn't have pissed round with another message, he'd have hit the road pronto. She'd bide her time, play it by the book. They'd take Marlow in for questioning, establish a hundred per cent he was the killer.

Priority now was to make sure he didn't pick up on her thinking.

"Here you go." Marlow placed a tray with coffee and Amaretti biscuits on the table between them. "Shan't be a tick, I left something in the kitchen."

She took a seat on one of the chesterfields.

"There's an ashtray on the side," his voice drifted through. "You can smoke if you like."

He re-emerged carrying a crystal vase. She watched, stunned, as he placed it in the centre of the tray. But it wasn't the daffodils alone that stopped her in her tracks. Marlow was talking again. The voice she'd likened to a Silver Ghost had gone. In its place, a nasal twang she'd recognise anywhere.

She had it on tape in the back of her MG.

"Letting you spark up's a nice touch, right? Everyone's entitled to a last request, aren't they?" He sat opposite, casually crossed an ankle over a knee.

"Sorry?" An uncertain smile.

"A last request." He flicked a speck of dust from his immaculate trousers. "As in before they buy it."

He knew. It changed everything. *Think. Feet. On.* She forced herself not to show a reaction, felt her heart hammer her ribs. Split-second decisions, a million darting thoughts. Contain and control. How to play him? She tried an indifferent shrug. The arrogant shit didn't like that. Fury flitted across his face. For a split second she saw him for what he was. And for what he'd done.

"Did Sophia have a last request?"

"I guess that's something you'll never know." He gave the half-smile she'd found so appealing. She wanted to rip his face off. Images of his victims – battered, brutalised old women – flashed in her mind's eye. Christ. This was the sick bastard who'd hacked off Sadie's hair. The horror increased with each passing second, each realisation like acid in an open wound.

"Why did you do it?"

He shrugged. "Why not?"

"You can do better than that. Clever bloke like you." He might fall for it; he was ego-on-a-stick.

Her mobile rang. She jumped a mile. Marlow didn't bat an eyelid. "Answer it, you're dead."

"Piss off." She took the phone from her pocket, recognised Oz's number. She shouldn't have taken her eye off the pus-ball. Marlow rammed the table into her shins and shot out of his chair. She gasped in pain as he snatched the phone from her grasp. He towered over her now, face distorted in hatred, fist raised. She braced herself for the blow, still trying to free her legs. It didn't come. Marlow slowly lowered his hand, hurled the phone against the wall and sauntered back to his seat. What the fuck was he playing at?

She rubbed her shins, flesh already swollen. Hurt like shit. Her eyes shone in defiance. "Don't come near me again."

He ran his gaze over her body. "You should be so lucky."

"Too young?" she snarled. "Old women more to your taste?"

He sniffed. "Whatever."

"What I can't work out is why someone so shit-hot cocked up big time." She sensed a first glimmer of interest.

"My mistake was not taking you out earlier. You and your stinky grandmother."

She counted to ten. Then twenty. "You are so going to regret that."

"Am I? Your time's running out, babe."

She snorted. "I'm trembling in my boots."

But she stiffened as he extracted a black-handled knife from a sheath strapped round his ankle. A blade put a different complexion on things. She needed to keep him talking, preferably at arm's length.

She made a big play of examining his face. "Yeah. It just might work."

"Fuck you on about?"

"The insanity plea." She pursed her lips, making out it actually mattered. "Mind, you can't always tell with juries."

"Mad? Don't be ridiculous. Killing that old bag was the sanest thing I've ever done. The bitch killed my mother."

"I'm listening."

Maybe he liked an audience. He circled the room as he spoke. He'd idolised Sara. She was young and beautiful. It had been him and her against the world. Make that against the Collisons. And the quack who killed her. Bev followed him with her eyes. It was clear he'd created a fantasy around Sara; he'd lost the real thing when he was a small child.

His grandparents told him he'd been abandoned. It was years before he discovered the truth. He forced it from George and Hannah before they perished in the flames. He considered it a suitable death for religious fanatics who'd shown his mother no mercy and made his life hell. They'd thrown her on to the streets when she got pregnant again. She'd been forced into an abortion and butchered by an incompetent doctor. Anyway, he needed his inheritance. Revenge would be sweet but it wouldn't come cheap.

Bev listened, unmoving and unmoved. It was a tragic picture. But inaccurate and incomplete. An abortion hadn't killed Sara Collison. Her heroin addiction had done that. Had the Collisons lied? Was a so-called medical blunder more palatable than a drug overdose?

"And the other attacks –?"

A smokescreen to save his pathetic skin, ditto Davy and the Shreks. Bev shook her head; being right was no consolation. She had a zillion questions, asked just one.

"Why the daffodils?"

"Week after week, I had to stick fucking daffodils into a poxy vase at the grave while my mother rotted under the earth." The half-smile was revolting. "Seemed a nice touch."

She'd listened carefully to every self-serving word. Not heard a syllable about adoption. He had no idea what he'd done.

"Ironic, isn't it?"

He stopped pacing, focused on her. "What is?"

"Doctor Carrington didn't kill your mother. She didn't do abortion. She gave her own baby up for adoption rather than get rid of it."

"Bullshit."

"I've read her diaries."

"Congratulations."

"Why do you think Sara went to Sophia Carrington? A doctor practising miles away?" She waited, hoping the words would sink in. "Sophia wasn't just another medico. Sara sought her out. Sophia wouldn't have recognised her. How could she? Sara was only a few days old when they took her away. Think about the irony: the daughter Sophia gave up for adoption coming back to ask for an abortion." She searched his face. "One thing I'm not clear on is whether Sara told the old lady about you. Because, at the very end, while you were sticking her like a pig, she'd have worked out you were her grandson."

He was there already. A case of shoot the messenger. Thank God he wasn't carrying a gun. Still had the knife, though. She leapt to her feet, better prepared this time. During the talk show, she'd worked on moves. He slashed out wildly, maybe hoping she'd panic. But Bev was icy calm. He wouldn't be the first knife-wielding maniac she'd disarmed.

The training kicked in. She kicked out. Collison made a grab at her. Missed. He circled; she sidestepped. He thrust; she parried. He feigned a lunge; she mirrored it. It was a deadly *pas de deux*, badly choreographed with no music. Panting and the occasional gasp punctuated the tension. She was out-stepping Collison at every move.

Frustrated and in blind fury, he took a sudden run, lunging at her with the knife. She stuck out a foot. It was all it took. He fell badly, on to his knees, in obvious pain. She kicked the knife across the floor, then lashed out and sent him flying.

"Bitch." He tried to get up.

She kicked again; heard a crack. Hoped it was a rib.

"Is that what you called your gran when you stuck the blade in? How much of a fight did she put up, big man?"

She could have left it there, slapped on the cuffs, walked away.

"Fuck you," Marlow snarled.

She snapped. In a second she was straddling him, smashing a fist in his face. "That's from Sophia, arsehole."

She could have left it there.

"Fuck you." He spat blood, flecks spraying with the words. Angrily she dashed them away, swung another punch. And another. And another.

She was vaguely aware of a presence behind her; guessed Oz had finally arrived. She took a final swing at the fucker...

And couldn't work out why her head was exploding with sudden agonising pain.

As she went down, she caught a glimpse of a vaguely familiar face. Couldn't put a name to it.

Was the hammering in her head? Bev opened an eye; the one that still worked. How long had she been out? Seconds? Minutes? Hours? Collison was still down, his battered face a hand-span from her own. He was bleeding heavily. She tensed. Another sound. Close. Mustn't move. Not sure she could. Hammering again, louder. Not in her head. She tried the other eye. Daffodils lay strewn, water pooled on the floor; her clothes were drenched. No broken glass.

"Police! Open up!"

Oz. Thank God. She risked a slight movement of her head towards the door. Well, well. Collison's lady friend was standing there. Another distraction, another dupe. The band of merry men included the delectable Grace Kane.

Bev watched as she turned the handle and stood back to admit Oz. He barely gave her a glance, certainly didn't register she was clutching a vase, as he dashed across to Bev. Kane's approach was stealthier, armed with the same lethal weapon that had knocked Bev out cold. Oz was about to get the same treatment. Unless Bev headed it off. Timing was all. She waited till the last second, then tripped him. Sorry, mate.

Oz's fall left Grace Kane open to attack. Bev rolled on to her back, brought her knees to her chest and kicked out. Kane doubled over. A Doc Marten in the stomach does that. But her recovery was swift; she swung the vase up and let fly. It shattered against the table, showering Bev's face and hair with splinters of glass. She never knew how it missed her. It had missed Collison too, although he looked as if his face had taken the full force.

Bev sat on the floor, head in hands, while Oz cuffed and cautioned Kane. It didn't stop a verbal attack. "That woman should be locked up," Grace screamed. "Look at him. Look what she's done. She's insane."

"Shut it," Oz snapped. "What happened, Bev?"

I lost it. "I don't know."

The broken bleeding skin across her knuckles told Oz what she couldn't. Collison's shattered face added detail. She glanced up, registered a revulsion Oz couldn't hide. Directed at her.

"Oz, I –"

He lifted a hand. "I don't want to know."

She heard him call it in to Highgate. She knew what she had to do; she took a long hard look at what she'd already done. Collison's face was a bloody mess: not dissimilar to how his grandmother had looked.

# 34

The letter hadn't taken Bev long to write. Byford took even less time to read it. He folded the single sheet of paper, laid it on the desk between them.

"I think you're making a mistake," he said.

Bev shook her head. They'd been through it before. It didn't matter what anyone else thought; she couldn't fool herself. It had taken nearly a week to make up her mind, the longest of her life. She'd been going through the motions, acting a role: Detective Sergeant Normal.

"It was self-defence, Bev. The man had a knife."

She snorted. It was self-control. Lack of. And if Collison had pressed charges, she wouldn't be sitting here now.

Byford leaned forward. "There were extenuating circumstances."

This time. Maybe.

"You have my support. You know that." He'd already spoken up for her; she'd been hauled over more coals than a pit pony. That's when supposed mates weren't shit-bagging her or taking the piss. She knew what they called her now, it wasn't behind her back any more.

*Lonely. Fucking felt it, too.*

"Yeah, right." She examined her nails. "That'll be your full backing from some beach in Bermuda?"

An envelope had appeared at the front desk. She'd added a tenner to the leaving collection. She couldn't blame him. Take the money and run. The only bright spot since the Collison debacle had been the guv's relatively clean bill of health. The tests had revealed IBS. He'd even joked the B stood for Bev.

"Are you really packing it in, guv?"

"Are you?"

She'd asked herself the same question a thousand times. She wanted to talk it through with Oz, but had barely seen him since Bloody Sunday. He was keeping his distance. Or was it her imagination? Her judgement was shit at the moment.

"I've had enough." She was knackered, barely sleeping; like Sadie, just different nightmares.

He brought out a bottle of malt and a couple of glasses from the filing cabinet. Bev took the largest measure and swallowed half. A belated *Cheers* was anything but. She slumped in the chair, legs stretched out in front. The body language said a lot and Byford was listening.

"It was a result, Bev. He'll go down."

"He'd have gone down for good if his girlfriend hadn't decked me."

She was scared. Scared how far she'd gone; scared there'd come a time when she wouldn't stop.

"We've all been there, Bev. We're only human. We get pushed to the limit. It's not surprising we falter now and again."

"Falter? Is that big boy for fuck-up?

He held his hands out. "You went too far. It happens. You're not the first and you won't be the last."

"Can't imagine you taking a pop, guv."

"I've taken more than a pop."

She sat up, folded her arms. "Go on."

He shook his head. "One day, maybe."

Another snort. "Saving it for your memoirs?"

He held her gaze. "At least I'll have something to write. You won't. Not if you go now."

She shrugged, drained the glass.

He leaned forward. "You're a good cop, Bev. Don't beat yourself up."

She bit back a line about beating up other people. It wasn't the only stick with which she'd hit herself. "I let him take me out, guv. How dumb was that? I must be the only cop in history to get wined and dined by a serial killer."

He turned his mouth down. "Jodie Foster? Hannibal Lecter?"

She rolled her eyes.

"Come on, Bev. Marlow, Collison, whatever you want to call him, was entirely plausible. He faked his own stabbing, for God's sake. He pulled the wool over everyone's eyes."

She sniffed. "Cashmere."

"There you go, then. If you hadn't stopped him, he might have got away with it. He had flights booked, cases packed. Him and his ladyfriend."

That was another thing. She hadn't even run a check on Grace Kane. The woman had lied through her teeth. She was no more into journalism than Bev was into anger management. It had been a ruse to try to get an inside track on the inquiry. Kane and Collison were lovers. Bev put her head in her hands. Talk about being wrong-footed. Christ. She should be walking with a limp.

"What I can't work out is how he got them to do his bidding." Byford swirled his glass. Tea-leaves would have been a better bet. "He had them all in the palm of his hand."

"Tell me about it." She shook her head. Charisma? Cash? Fear? He'd certainly given Davy Roberts the shits. With good reason. Jake had told him if he ever opened his mouth, Gert was dead meat. For the Shrek boys, Kevin Fraser and Robert Lewis, silence was golden. Jake had promised them megabucks to keep shtum.

He could afford to. He wouldn't have been around for the pay-off. He only existed when Collison adopted the persona. None of the lads had even heard of Collison, let alone Tom Marlow.

"Mind," she said, "they can't drop him in it fast enough now. They're still dishing the dirt."

Even Marty Skelton had come forward with a shovel. Soon as the story broke on the telly news, Marty offered a witness statement. He could identify the bloke he got the dog from – for a small fee. He eschewed payment after being threatened with a charge of withholding.

"And with the forensics," Byford said, "even if Collison changes his plea, he'll still get life."

"Damn sight more than his victims."

The 'lucky' ones had been damaged irrevocably. Even the indomitable Sadie jumped at every sound; she was scared staying in, hated going out. It could become a real problem when Bev moved to Baldwin Street next month. Sadie was already begging her not to go. An eight-week-old golden retriever wasn't much of a substitute for a kick-ass cop.

"There'll always be victims, Bev. All we do is keep the numbers down."

"We?" A vision of Byford lolling around on a beach flashed before her tired eyes. "Christ, guv, it's bad enough when you're here…" The Byford eyebrows were on alert. "You know what I mean. You're a good bloke, but the thought of working under Shields…"

Words petered out; she studied her nails again. She'd always imagined there'd be some short of showdown; pistols at noon, that sort of thing. The DI hadn't exchanged a word with Bev since Collison's arrest. It hadn't stopped her submitting a damning written report that would stay on file. Bev was under no illusion that her every step would be closely monitored for the foreseeable.

"You wouldn't be working under her," Byford said.

"What?" She reached for her drink but the glass was empty.

Months before hitting Highgate, he explained, Shields had been interviewed for a DI post in Devon. It had been close but no cigar. But now the candidate appointed had quit unexpectedly and Shields had been offered the job.

Bev punched the air under the table.

Byford shook his head. "Very mature." He poured a couple of refills and pushed her glass across the table. "Come on, Sergeant, you can't run out on us now."

There'd be an acting DI post up for grabs, she'd had two large Laphroaigs on an empty stomach and the guv was in a good mood. And she was a cop. What the hell else could she do?

"Tell you what, guv." She paused. "I'll stay if you will."

She held her breath as he rose, watched him pace the room, then perch on the edge of the desk. Could be the Leapfrogs or an oxygen shortage, but she felt dizzy.

"Tell you what, Bev." He winked, raised the glass and drained the last of the malt. "I'll think about it."


Bev was whistling an old Tears for Fears number as she strolled past the front desk. Vince Hanlon lifted his glance from the sports pages. "Can't argue with that, Bev."

"What's that, Vincie?"

"It's a mad world, right enough."

She laughed. "Sure is." Mind, it could be worse. It was Friday night. In a couple of hours, she'd be whooping it up at Frankie's gig in the Jug of Ale. Her hopes weren't high, but Oz hadn't ruled out dropping in for an hour or so.

There was serious sorting still to do but they had to start someplace. Either way her young friend, Jules, would be there. Bev had stopped off at the Texaco earlier in the week to invite her along. Apart from a promise to herself she'd keep in touch, Jules was a reminder that a cop's job was still worth doing. Sometimes.

She swung her bag over her shoulder. "I'm off, Vince. Catch you Monday."

"You haven't heard, have you?"

There was something in his voice that made her look back and reluctantly return.

"Heard what?"

"What do you want first? The good news or the bad?"

She folded her arms, tapped a foot.

Vince glanced in both directions than leaned forward conspiratorially. "The guv's not going anywhere."

She frowned. That was quick. It was less than an hour since she'd left him cogitating in his office.

"Just between you and me, right?" Vince paused for a nod of agreement. "He let it slip the other night in the Prince. He's knocked the retirement idea on the head."

"That definite, is it?" Bev was picturing Byford, perched on the desk promising, a tad patronisingly as she recalled, to give it some thought.

"Horse's mouth." He tapped the side of his nose. "You know what the guv's like when his mind's made up."

She certainly did. "I'll have my tenner back, then."

"Tenner?"

"The collection." She held out a hand.

"Please yourself." So why was he looking put out? "I thought it was a nice gesture, considering."

"Gesture?"

"Yeah. It was the old man's idea. A whip-round for

Danny Shields. She's only been here five minutes but the guv thought we should get her some flowers or something. She's off next Friday."

She pursed her lips. "Tell me, Vince. Do I look gullible?"

A wavering hand suggested a close call. She gave a wry smile. What the hell? The guv was staying. As news went, it didn't get much better. Vince could keep the cash – as long as he put it towards a bunch of daffs.

They both glanced round when the main doors shot back. Oz saw Bev at the desk, headed over like a man on a mission.

"Have you heard?"

She was about to mention echoes and déjà vu. Oz couldn't wait to share.

"DI Powell's in the clear. He's back. Monday week."

Vince opened his mouth but Bev lifted a hand. "Don't tell me," she said. "That so has to be the bad news."

# Epilogue

Faint light flickered from a corner of the room as Bev parked the MG and walked towards the house. Through the window, she could see Maude Taylor watching television. Must be a good programme; the old woman was rapt.

Bev raised the knocker then stilled it, loath to butt in, but she'd been spotted. Maude was reaching for her stick and struggling to her feet.

"Sorry to disturb you. I just wanted to return this." She proffered Sophia's journal. Maude took it, returned Bev's smile. "Thanks for letting me see it, Maude. Your friend must have been quite a woman. I wish I'd known her."

Maude opened the door and stood to one side. "Come in, dear. I'd like to show you something."

A half-packed suitcase and several boxes littered the hall floor. "When are you off?"

"Tomorrow. First thing. Do go through."

Maude hadn't been watching television. Bev's heart sank when she saw the screen and the projector. Holiday slides or home movies she could live without.

"I know what you're thinking, but humour me."

She hid a grin. The old woman never had missed much.

There were several metal canisters on the table but Maude rewound the film already in the machine.

"The others I've seen lots of times, but I didn't even know this existed."

Bev perched on the arm of a chair, waited patiently while Maude cued the old footage. The colours had faded to soft pastels over the years. Bev watched as the camera panned across extensive lawns, decorated with the palest of daffodils, before steadying and focusing on two figures on a bench.

"I think I can guess who took it," Maude said. "Only one other person in the world knew about the baby then."

"The father?" Bev asked

Maude nodded.

"And you've no idea who he was?"

"None."

Bev wasn't sure she believed her. "Where was it filmed?" Why am I whispering?

"In the grounds of the nursing home." Maude pointed with her stick. "Look, you can just see the edge of the building."

Bev was more interested in the woman and the tiny baby. Both were warmly wrapped against what was presumably a chill in the air. The child was swamped in a thick ivory shawl, her pale face and dark hair just discernible under a pink bonnet.

Bev felt an unutterable sadness as she imagined how often Sophia had watched this film, lingering over every frame, savouring every precious second of the motherhood she'd felt forced to sacrifice. Christ. The past wasn't a foreign country; it was an alien universe. Bev knew fourteen-year-olds around these parts with three kids by three different blokes.

Sophia was gently stroking her daughter's cheek.

"Did she want to keep her baby, Maude?"

"More than you can ever imagine, my dear."

Both women watched as Sophia Carrington lifted her glance to the lens. A gust of wind snatched at the blue beret. Maybe the cold was stinging her eyes, but it could just as easily have been a tear on the young doctor's cheek as she smiled for the camera.

# More action-packed crime novels
## from Crème de la Crime

**If It Bleeds**                                        Bernie Crosthwaite

ISBN: 0-9547634-3-2

There's only one rule in the callous world of newspapers: violence excites, death sells – so if it bleeds, it leads.

When hardened press photographer Jude Baxendale is despatched to snap a young woman's bloody body discovered in a local park she reckons it's a grisly but routine job – but she's horrifyingly, perilously wrong. For the murdered girl is her own son's girlfriend, and in a single chilling moment she realises nothing in her life is ever going to be the same again.

Why was Lara killed? Who stabbed and mutilated her? Who hated her enough to dump her body in full public gaze? Jude has to find out. Teaming up with reporter Matt Dryden, she begins to unravel the layers of the girl's complex past. But she soon learns that nothing about Lara was as it seemed…

Soon finding the truth will risk Jude's job, her health, her sanity – and place her squarely in the sights of a killer with a fanatical mission. And some deadly truths are best left uncovered. **Publication date April 2005.**

**Also available:**

**Working Girls**                                        Maureen Carter

ISBN: 0-9547634-0-8

**No Peace for the Wicked**                              Adrian Magson

ISBN: 0-9547634-2-4

**A Kind of Puritan**                                    Penny Deacon

ISBN: 0-9547634-1-6

# More gripping titles available later this year from Crème de la Crime

---

## No Help for the Dying
Adrian Magson

ISBN: 0-9547634-7-5

Runaway kids are dying on the streets of London. Investigative reporter Riley Gavin and ex military cop Frank Palmer want to know why.

They uncover a sub-culture involving a shadowy church, a grieving father and a brutal framework for blackmail, reaching not only into the highest echelons of society, but also into Riley's own past.

The second fast-moving adventure in Magson's popular Gavin/Palmer series.

**Available September 05**

---

## A Thankless Child
Penny Deacon

ISBN: 0-9547634-8-3

Life gets more dangerous for loner Humility. Her boat is damaged, her niece has run away from the commune, and the man who blames her for his brother's death wants her to investigate a suicide. She's faced with corporate intrigue and girl gangs, and most terrifying of all, she's expected to enjoy the festivities to celebrate the opening of the upmarket new Midway marina complex.

Things can only get worse.

A follow-up to *A Kind of Puritan*, Deacon's acclaimed first genre-busting future crime novel.

**Available September 05**